"*No More Empty Spaces* is an excellent debut—straight-forward and yet deceptively complex as it situates its multi-layered narratives between the competing forces of nature, both human and geological, over time. Green's depictions of the rugged and earthquake-prone Anatolian Mountain region of Turkey evoke a dangerously shifting landscape every bit as unstable and unpredictable as the broken American family that seeks to heal itself there."

—JAMES ANDERSON, author of *The Never-Open Desert Diner* and *Lullaby Road*

"American geologist, Will Ross, has landed the job of a lifetime, one that will take him from Philadelphia to a remote region of Turkey along the Euphrates River. At the eleventh hour, when he's packed and ready to fly, the divorced father of three discovers his ex—passed out and naked—on the family's living room couch. Will has to decide what to do. Without hesitating, he does the hard, risky, *right* thing. Turns out, it's a habit with him, one that impressed the hell out of this reader. *No More Empty Spaces* is a rich and rewarding read, a novel to savor, like a steaming cup of Turkish coffee."

—SHARON OARD WARNER, author of *Writing the Novella*

"D. J. Green is that rare writer who takes us inside worlds we may never be able to experience firsthand."

—WILL MACKIN, author of *Bring Out the Dog*

". . . a wonderful read, with some of the best prose I've seen regarding the intractable forces of nature. This struggling blended family faces every kind of overwhelming challenge, from love to liquor to the great dam at Kayakale in Turkey. The book made me want to go there and see this extraordinary landscape for myself!"

—A. R. TAYLOR, author of *Jenna Takes the Fall* and *Call Me When You're Dead*

"D. J. Green skillfully intertwines a story of what lies below: the Earth with its complex geology and a man's emotions, also buried deeply, each affected by history and environment. In *No More Empty Spaces*, Green takes us to the world of Turkey where Will, an engineering geologist, moves his family while he seeks to investigate a problematic dam structure, along with unexpected challenges to his beliefs about family and integrity. Green's debut is both masterful and engaging."

—SHARON BIPPUS, author of *This Blue Earth*

NO MORE EMPTY SPACES

NO MORE EMPTY SPACES

A NOVEL

D.J. GREEN

SHE WRITES PRESS

Published 2024
Printed in the United States of America

Print ISBN: 978-1-64742-616-3
E-ISBN: 978-1-64742-617-0
Library of Congress Control Number: 2023915532

For information, address:
She Writes Press
1569 Solano Ave #546
Berkeley, CA 94707

Interior design and typeset by Katherine Lloyd, The DESK

She Writes Press is a division of SparkPoint Studio, LLC.

For NRT

PART I

ONE

Will needed perspective, and flying afforded an outlook that walking-around life could not. He hustled across the Flying W Airfield, sweat soaking through the back of his shirt. It was a busy Saturday afternoon, but today he didn't stop to talk with the other pilots he passed.

When he got to the plane, Will flung his flight bag onto the tarmac and slammed his hand into the door. That stopped him. His palm throbbed. He lowered his hand, shook it out. It still stung reaching into his pocket for the keys. He unlocked the plane, flicked the light switches on, and began his preflight checks.

A 1953 Cessna 180, the plane didn't show her age. It was twenty years since she'd rolled off the assembly line, but freshly polished, she looked sleek. His hand skimmed the fuselage, almost a caress now. He checked the lights, the tires for wear, and the brakes for drips of hydraulic fluid. He loved the ritual of preflight, but today, running his eyes and fingers over the leading edges of her wings and prop didn't fill him with the usual mix of focus and excitement; instead he seethed in the summer sun.

Will unhooked the tie-downs and climbed into the cockpit. He donned his headset and adjusted the microphone close to his lips. Then he slid his aviator sunglasses on. He had never worn sunglasses before this summer—didn't care to have his views of the world altered. But he was compelled to try them back in June when the kids had pooled funds and given them to him for Father's Day. At the time, he'd been surprised they could agree on anything, but this morning Will saw that his children could cooperate in ways he wouldn't have imagined. Talk about altering his views.

Master switch on. Fuel mixture full rich. Throttle in. Brakes engaged. Will leaned out and yelled, "Clear prop!"

The plane shuddered to a start as if she'd been asleep since their last time up and was shaking off the nap. He taxied the short distance to the runway, turned ninety degrees to the left, and braked. His hands moved over the controls as his eyes scanned the gauges. He made his final checks quickly, wanting to get up and out of the heat. He looked for planes on downwind and base legs, and final approach. He found none, turned the plane the remaining ninety degrees onto the runway, and peered at the cornfield at the end of the airstrip through the blur of the whirling prop.

"Cessna one eight zero, two zero Mike Foxtrot, taking off, runway zero one, Flying W, over."

The engine's power vibrated from the soles of his feet up through his body. When no other air traffic responded, he eased his feet off the brakes and gave her full throttle. Sensing the velocity, he glanced down at the airspeed indicator—spot on at sixty miles per hour. He pulled back evenly on the yoke.

Airborne—the moment of lift. There was nothing like the feeling of gravity loosening its grip on you.

His plane was a partner he could trust. If he took care of her, she'd take care of him. He reveled in her grace in the dance of flight, and his lead. He was in control of everything except the wind and the weather, and it was his job to read them, understand them, and adjust to the ride. You studied and learned these things, and they all made sense. But you could spend your whole life studying people and not make sense of them. How do you adjust to a ride like that?

"Philadelphia Control, this is Cessna one eight zero, two zero Mike Foxtrot, heading three five five degrees to Stillwater V-O-R Sierra Tango Whiskey. Climbing to sixty-five hundred feet."

He'd go higher than usual today, get the wider view.

"Roger, two zero Mike Foxtrot. Squawk zero four one one," the tower answered.

Will regarded the landscape below and asked himself again how he'd ended up in New Jersey. He turned toward the Pennsylvania hills, what people here called mountains. *The Poconos'll be pretty today*, he thought. *Pretty can't hurt.*

Will had a weak spot for pretty girls. Pretty could cast a spell, like the day he'd met his ex some sixteen years ago. Her smile had drawn him across the barroom like iron to a magnet. When he slid his arm around her slim waist the first time they danced, she moved like a feline against him, and Kat had gotten her nickname that night.

A pretty scene could take him in, too. Like June 3, the day in 1968 he'd interviewed for the Philadelphia Port Expansion job. It had been perfect—warm but not hot, bright and clear, breezy but not blustery. The Delaware River Valley was all the things that Arizona, where he'd just finished his master's degree in engineering geology, wasn't. Spring in the Southwest was a hot, gritty, brown blast of a season, and Will had been ready for a change.

The folks from the Port Authority had flown him over the project area in a helicopter, then continued the tour of the wide verdant valley. To Will, the rich greens below were like luxuriant carpets unfurled to welcome him. The pretty had worked its magic, and when an offer came on the mid-June day with the mercury hitting 115 degrees Fahrenheit in Tempe, he'd accepted without a second thought.

Since then, Will had lived into a healthy mistrust of pretty. What took you in on June 3 rarely looked so good come winter.

With altitude, the temperature dropped. Will twisted the vents to get more air flowing, cooling him down. The vice-grip headache constricting his temples eased for the first time since that morning, when he'd followed the kids into what had been their family home before the divorce last year. But he couldn't erase the image of Kat from his mind. Passed out. Face down on the couch. Naked. An empty bottle of Johnnie Walker Red on the floor.

He knew she'd been drinking more the last couple of years. He'd seen the signs. He knew them all too well from his own drinking days. But he had no idea she'd gone so far down that road to nowhere.

Good thing she'd left the car, its fender crushed, out on the front lawn last night, or Will might never have known, united as the kids seemed in keeping her secret. Kevin, his fifteen-year-old, had shouted at Will to leave—actually pushed him out the door. Shocked, Will had stumbled down the porch steps backward, and stared at the door his son had slammed.

Will leveled the plane at sixty-five hundred feet, backed off the throttle, adjusted the pitch of the prop, and fine-tuned the fuel mix. Almost set, he reached down and spun the trim tab until he felt the balance he was seeking, the perfect trim, in which the yoke took the lightest of touches for the plane to go where he wanted.

Now, it would take more than a light touch to get where he wanted to go. He'd mapped his course with such care over the past weeks. It had started with an article in the *Engineering News Record*, "Swiss Cheese Rock Slows Kayakale Dam." Another dam where insufficient geological studies had impacted construction. Will had decided he was finished with his paper-pushing job at the Philadelphia Port. Turkey would be his next stop.

But now there was a big hitch in his plan; he couldn't leave the kids with Kat. He'd have to get full custody in the next two weeks, along with wrapping up at the port, packing to move, and selling the plane and the car, and, and, and. . . .

Turbulence jolted the plane—and Will's attention—back to the cockpit. He gripped the yoke and rode through the bumps. Leaving the wide floodplain of the Delaware River, he steered toward the peaks of the Poconos, the landscape rising beneath him. When he got to the Susquehanna River, he followed its green ribbon west–southwest. Where the river split, the confluence of the north and west branches, he left it behind and headed for the heart of the Valley and Ridge physiographic province.

Ridges of resistant rocks, sandstones, conglomerates, and limestones yielded to valleys underlain by soft shales, then climbed again on the harder rocks of the next ridge. The rock units spanned the land surface in parallel bands, except where anticlines and synclines, geologic structures like the crests and troughs of ocean waves, angled into or out of the subsurface—there the units formed striking chevron patterns. To the geologist's eye, those patterns told the story of Earth's processes through the ages.

In Turkey, Will would read the story in the rocks. And in that story, he would find the answers they needed to make Kayakale Dam work.

He looped among the lofty cumulus clouds, leaning into turns and rolls, feeling the physics of flying in his muscles. His internal gyroscope engaged. Then he pulled into a stall. The stomach-dropping sensation of losing lift tested him. He stayed with it, fighting any hints of fear that rose in his throat. Satisfied he was under control, he pushed her nose down, gave her more throttle, and resumed his private air show by plummeting through another cloud break.

His neck relaxed, and his jaw unclenched as he moved with the forces acting on the plane—never against them. That's what you do, he decided. Move with the forces acting on you.

There'd be no more lawyers, no more court dates, and no more negotiating. He would take the job in Turkey and take the kids with him.

Will banked the plane hard left, turning back toward Flying W. There was even more to do now, and he'd best get to it. Coming out of the steep turn, he steered due east.

TWO

The revolving door spun Will out of the hotel lobby onto the busy streets of an Ankara Monday morning.

Turkey, Will thought. *Made it.*

There were days during the past two weeks he'd had his doubts, but here they were at their first stop, in Ankara. The kids were asleep in a spacious suite upstairs. Jet-lagged, they'd probably snooze until he got back. If not, Kevin would watch out for his brother and sister.

A bellhop approached. He looked like an organ grinder's monkey in his red brocade jacket. *"Taksi?"*

Will waved the boy off. He had plenty of time before his eight o'clock meeting. He'd woken early, excited to start his new job with Design Engineers and Constructors Company. He consulted his map and began walking, smiling with satisfaction. As of this morning, he was DECCO's chief foundation geologist for Kayakale Dam.

The sidewalks bustled with men and women in workday garb, mostly suits in somber tones. This could've been any city, but the scents that surrounded him told Will it wasn't. Yeasty goodness wafted from a bakery. The tang of roasted hot pepper and smoked paprika made him slow his pace. Tall spits turned in a window. Juices glistened on the meat's surface.

Will passed a grocer, a tanned wiry man with dark, thick hair and an equally heavy mustache dominating his thin face.

"Merhaba," Will said. Hello.

"*Merhaba*," the man replied and handed Will a small apricot from the basket of yellowish-pink fruit he was stacking onto a stand. "*Amerikalı?*"

"*Evet*," Will said. Yes. He reached into his pocket for change.

"*Hayır*," the grocer said, refusing any money. "*Türkiye'ye hoş geldiniz.*"

Will ambled on, then stopped to thumb through his pocket-size Turkish–English dictionary to see what the grocer had said: Welcome to Turkey.

He ate the sweet, juicy apricot in one bite and spit the pit out. It flew into the gutter in a satisfying arc.

At the next shop, another one with spits turning in the window, Will paused to savor the spicy aroma. The words Kebap Lokantasi were painted across the expanse of plate glass. Consulting his dictionary again, he confirmed that *lokantasi* meant restaurant. Fiery Adana kebabs would become Will's favorite Turkish dish.

As he tucked the dictionary back into his jacket pocket, he caught his reflection in the glass. His freshly pressed khakis, crisp white oxford shirt, and brass-buttoned navy blue sport coat, which he'd always considered business attire, looked colorful and casual compared to the uniformly dark-suited Turks. He owned only one dark suit. It was black, and he reserved it for funerals. He certainly hadn't brought it on this trip.

The air warmed as the sun climbed into the man-made canyon of blocky buildings. Will shed his jacket, folded it neatly across his arm, and walked on. The small shops and restaurants wedged among the offices added color and character to Ankara's streets, like garnets and micas sparkling in otherwise dull gray stones.

Will wasn't much for breakfast, but every whiff of fresh-baked bread made his stomach growl. He stepped into the next bakery. "*Merhaba*," he said.

A short, stout woman wearing a red-and-yellow paisley headscarf looked up. *"Günaydın,"* she said. A shy smile plumped her cheeks and crinkled the corners of her eyes.

"Do you speak English?" he asked.

Her dark eyebrows pulled together. *"İngilizce? Hayır."*

He shrugged, remembering how he'd gotten by in Pakistan before he learned much Urdu. He pointed at the golden flatbreads she'd been placing in a basket, held up one finger, pulled all the change from his pocket, and extended his hand to her. "Okay?" he asked.

"O-kay." She dipped her chin. *"Tamam, tamam."* She took the coins she needed. The bread she handed him was warm.

There was a bust on the counter. The face had high, pronounced cheekbones and a wide forehead. The eyes were intense under arched eyebrows that drew together into deep lines. The man appeared both severe and noble. Will had seen portraits of this same man everywhere he'd been in Ankara—in the airport when they'd arrived, over the hotel reception desk, in the restaurant last night, and in several shops he'd passed this morning.

"Atatürk?" he asked, referring to the father of modern Turkey, whom Will had read about in the little time he'd had for research. The leader of Turkey's revolution in the 1920s, Atatürk transformed the country from a sultanate to a republic. Among other sweeping reforms, he'd outlawed the fez, a symbol of the Ottoman Empire; had linguists invent modern Turkish using a modified Latin alphabet, replacing the Arabic; and given women the right to vote. Without Atatürk, Turkey would likely not be the country it was today, seeking its place in progressive Western culture. And the dam Will was here to help build would likely not be underway.

"Evet, evet, Atatürk!" The baker folded her hands over her heart.

This adoration of their deceased leader was yet another sign this wasn't just any city. At least, not any city in the States. Even in Philly, where so much US history resided, the forefathers' portraits were not ubiquitous. And as for Nixon, it looked like he might end up in jail, rather than the White House. So much for reverence. What a relief to be away from the Watergate scandal headlines screaming across the front pages of the papers back home.

"*Tesh-a-cure-edearim.*" Will struggled with the Turkish for "thank you."

"*Evet.*" She bobbed her head, another smile playing on her face. "*Çok teşekkür ederim.*"

He returned the smile and sank his teeth into the bread. Even the bread here tasted of adventure, unlike the packaged fluff on the supermarket shelves of Moorestown, the New Jersey suburb that had been home for the past five years.

❧

Will slid into his jacket at the entrance to DECCO's office. The company logo spanned the width of the door; drawn in bold block letters, it increased in size from left to right, ending with the *O* in the shape of a globe. Under DECCO, in smaller print, it read WE BUILD THE WORLD.

Some four hundred miles east-southeast, DECCO was building Kayakale Dam. It would rank among the ten largest dams in the world. It would double the electricity Turkey could generate. It would provide water for industry and irrigation for crops. It was progress.

Or it will be, he thought. *If we can get it built.*

Will straightened his tie, pulled his shoulders back, took a deep breath, and stepped in. He'd rehearsed "good morning" in Turkish for the last few blocks of the walk, *günaydın . . . günaydın*, but there was no one in the reception area to greet. Across the room were two office doors topped with panes of frosted glass, both closed. A shadow was visible through the pane of the door with the nameplate reading Gus Browning, the man Will was here to see. The other office appeared to be unoccupied, and Will didn't recognize the name on it from any of the DECCO reports he'd seen so far.

A utilitarian metal desk sat along the left wall. Four brown vinyl chairs lined the right. Framed photographs—ground views and an aerial shot—and plans, maps, and cross sections of the Kayakale site hung on the walls. Since he was early, Will began at the far left and scanned the displays, searching for a hint of the story they told. Interpreting landscapes was what Will did, and studying maps and photos, particularly aerial shots, was a good start to the process.

From the time he took Geology 101, Will had been translating what he observed, mapped, and drilled in the field into words and drawings. As a professional engineering geologist, he'd been doing that primarily for engineers designing dams and water supply systems, and, most recently, the new port structure in Philadelphia. Because he could draw what he saw in the field, he could reverse the exercise. By studying a drawing or photograph, he could conceive the third dimension in his mind.

He examined the one aerial photo, squinting as he projected what he saw in the picture underground. He pulled out the notepad and pen he kept handy in his shirt pocket, and made a crude sketch, noting areas to investigate in the field.

He checked his watch again, then knocked on Gus Browning's door.

"Yeah."

Will entered the office, reaching his right hand forward. "I'm Will Ross. I'm here to. . . ."

"I know who you are," Browning said, interrupting before Will could finish. His beefy hand covered the receiver of his phone. "It'll be a minute," Browning said, and jerked his head toward the door.

Will stepped back to the outer office and pulled the door shut. He scowled at his watch, then shoved his hands into his pockets. He'd been staring at a photograph as the seconds ticked away before he realized he wasn't seeing it. He shook his head, refocused. There were seven men in the photo, two he recognized. John Heatley, Will's new boss from DECCO's New York office, was front and center. He was shaking hands with a man Will presumed to be Heatley's counterpart with DSI, Turkey's Directorate of State Hydraulic Works and DECCO's client on the project. Browning was second from the right in the photo and towered over the others. He probably played football back in the day.

The group was posed in front of a huge 'dozer. They all smiled widely at the camera. Must've been the groundbreaking.

But now the ground is breaking the project, Will thought.

The door latch clicked. "Come in," Browning barked.

Will strode in, extending his right hand again.

"Sit," Browning commanded, ignoring Will's outstretched hand. He cocked his chin at a low chair.

Will saw his résumé on the desk. Browning balanced a pair of squared-off, black-rimmed reading glasses above a bump on his nose that looked like a remnant of the football days Will had imagined. He picked up the résumé and began reading. The thick muscles of his arms and shoulders strained the fabric of his starched white shirt. His brown hair was sprinkled with gray and was buzz cut, military-style. After several minutes, he laid the pages down, placed his hands flat on the desk on either side of them, and leaned forward.

"Willard Ross, Philadelphia Port builder. What the hell good you can do us at Kayakale is beyond me, but Heatley didn't check with me before he slapped you onto my bottom line. Your kids too."

"It's Will, if you don't mind, Gus."

"Call me Mr. Browning. And I mind plenty."

"You won't when I figure out where to pump the grout so it'll take," Will said, also leaning forward.

"Don't fuck with me, Ross. We're not idiots here."

"You're not geologists either," Will said. "And you need one to find out what's going on in the foundation."

"That might be someone's opinion." He pulled his glasses off and glared at Will. "Doesn't happen to be mine."

"It happens to be our boss's opinion. I can help you here."

"*My* boss. I'm *your* boss."

"That wasn't what I understood," Will said.

"Then you understood wrong." Browning tapped his glasses on the desk.

Will's right hand wandered up to his shirt pocket, the old habit of looking for a cigarette, though he hadn't smoked in years. He was stalling, figuring out what to say. A younger, rasher Will would've pushed the point, and he had, too many times. He'd learned that sometimes saying what you think doesn't get you what you want. He took a measured breath.

"Well, your boss hired me, so you're probably stuck with me. And I know I can help with your problem," Will said.

Browning slammed his meaty hands on his desk. "You're my problem, Ross. This is my damn project, and I don't know who those assholes in New York think they are, going around me."

No stalling this time, Will pushed forward in his chair and said, "If I'm your only problem, Mr. Browning, that 'Swiss Cheese Rock' article we all read in the *Engineering News Record* must be the first fiction they've ever published."

Browning's face flushed, and a vein in his forehead pulsed. The sound of a door opening and closing broke the charged silence. Both men turned toward the adjacent office.

"Look, you're here, and I'll be in Kayakale. Out of your way.

Give me a chance to figure out what's going on. Six months. If I haven't got answers by then, I'll leave."

"You won't be leaving on your own if you don't have answers in six months."

"Where do I pick up my vehicle, and who do I check in with at the site? I'll be on the road to Kayakale before dawn tomorrow. I have a meeting this afternoon with Mehmet Alkumru."

"*What?*" Browning roared, standing and slamming his hands on the desk again.

"John, I mean Mr. Heatley, wanted me to meet him before I left Ankara. He had Belinda make the appointment."

"No fucking way, Ross," he yelled. "*I'm* DECCO's point man with DSI, *period.*"

"Okay, okay." Will raised his hands in a gesture of surrender. He'd let Browning win this one. "Like I said, Mr. Heatley set it up, not me. Look, you saw my résumé. I've worked overseas, and I get it. Headquarters doesn't really know what's going on in-country. Could you just call and tell the DSI folks you're sending me directly to the site?"

Browning stood a moment longer before sinking back into his chair. He picked up his glasses, working the hinges open and closed. Then he tossed the glasses onto the desk, yanked a drawer open, and fumbled around in it. He flung a set of keys at Will, a little out of easy reach.

Will half rose to catch them. "Thank you."

"It's parked around back. The Land Cruiser. Report to Erdem Borkan on-site."

"Right."

"Check in next door. Accounting. There're papers to sign."

Will nodded, stood, and turned. Only then did he allow himself a hint of a smile as he left Browning's office at a deliberate pace.

THREE

K evin glanced at his watch when the call to morning prayer echoed through the streets from every direction, louder than the rattling of the Land Cruiser over the uneven pavement. Twenty till six. He remembered learning to tell time by those calls when he was a kid in Pakistan. He looked up to find sunrise tracing a line of light along the horizon. Low-angle light was best for shooting, and Kevin tried to capture the dawning day on film. Clouds feathered across the sky like they were painted on a glowing orange backdrop.

"High winds aloft," Dad said.

Kevin was more entranced with the shapes than what made them. When the sun burst over the clouds and flooded the car with light, Kevin lowered his camera and rolled up his window to quiet the wind.

Rob and Didi were asleep in the back seat, and Kevin could hear his brother's soft snores. He fidgeted in the seat, uncomfortable, both on the cushion that felt like its springs would pop out and having seen all the stuff in the back of the Land Cruiser when they'd loaded up. He could quiet the wind but not his mind. It looked like way too much. He wanted to ask, but he knew when his father had a plan, that was *the* plan, so why bother asking.

He studied the familiar and intense features of Dad's face like he'd studied the clouds moments before. His nose was long and straight, its tip angled back to his nostrils like an arrowhead.

His chin and jaw were also chiseled. There the sharp symmetry ended. Though he couldn't see it, Kevin knew Dad's left eyebrow tilted lower than the right and the right side of his mouth drooped subtly. Kevin remembered being a kid, watching Dad shave, how he navigated the razor around the uneven lines of his lips. Kevin smelled his Old Spice aftershave. His father's hair was trimmed short and parted on the right side like always, but until just now Kevin hadn't realized how gray it was. Silvery strands shone in the sun. He added twenty-three to fifteen. Thirty-eight. Pretty old. Almost forty.

Squinting at him, trying to get him in better focus, Kevin couldn't believe Dad hadn't told him before Saturday that they were going all the way to Turkey. The man with the plan had to have known, at least a few days ahead. His father used to tell him things, important things, like about the divorce last year. He'd talked to Kevin before they all sat down for their family meeting. Kevin hated family meetings.

It was true that he used to tell Dad stuff too—about school and track and his dream of being a *National Geographic* photographer. But since the day he saw Alfred Stieglitz's photographs of his wife, Georgia O'Keeffe, which led Kevin to her paintings on a school trip to the Philadelphia Art Museum, he'd kept it to himself that he might want to be an artist instead. And that art was his favorite subject now, not science or math, like his father thought. Of course, he hadn't told Dad about Mom's drinking either. Or her boyfriends.

Kevin couldn't see Dad's sometimes-luminous, sometimes-piercing eyes, so he couldn't gauge his mood. But he seemed excited about everything here—the project, the food, learning Turkish words, everything. Life could be fun when his father was excited, like when they flew in his plane, or when he and Rob and Dad went fishing. Even the quiet hours developing film together in their darkroom had their magic.

Kevin lifted his camera and framed his father's face in the viewfinder. He liked how the landscape made a blurred background for the shot. Dad's beloved landscape. Kevin slid the focus ring in, then out a little. He clicked the shutter.

"What is it?" his father asked, turning to look at Kevin looking at him.

"Nuthin'."

"Don't mumble," Dad said.

Asshole, Kevin thought.

∽

Will floored the accelerator to pass an overloaded semi on the narrow two-lane highway. He checked the rearview mirror, then glanced over his right shoulder before pulling back into his lane. With that small sweep of his head, he caught a glimpse of each of his sleeping children. Kevin was in the passenger seat beside him. The boy was thin and rangy, having sprouted three or four inches in the past year. He stayed impossibly skinny no matter how many Rossano's pepperoni pizzas he devoured— his favorite. Last night, Kev ordered the Turkish equivalent for dinner, a long oval flatbread topped with spiced ground lamb—*lahmacun*, pronounced la-ma-joon. They all had a piece and agreed it was delicious. Will figured they could learn to make it. It'd be fun.

Kevin's sandy-brown bangs hung over his forehead and eyes as his head bounced with the vibration of the old Land Cruiser. The Nikkormat FTn camera, which Will had given him three years ago for his twelfth birthday, was about to slide off his lap. Will reached over and tucked the camera next to Kevin's narrow hip. He patted his son's knee ever so lightly, while moving his hand back to the armrest between them. Kevin stirred, but didn't wake.

The sun was high overhead. The Kızılırmak River valley was off to the right, and the city of Sivas lay ahead.

Will allowed himself another look at Rob and Didi in the rearview mirror. He could just see the outline of Didi's little figure curled up beside her twelve-year-old brother. Rob's sun-bleached hair, so like his mother's, ruffled in the wind from Will's half-open window.

The last time he'd seen Kat's hair flashed through his mind; the tangled mess had hidden her face. He shook his head to dispel that morning's image. What happened to the pretty girl he'd loved? That girl got giggly after one drink, the lipstick smudges on the side of her glass matching the Pink Lady cocktails she favored when they met.

He checked his watch and subtracted eight hours to calculate the time in New Jersey. Three in the morning by the kids' body clocks; no wonder they were tired. But Will felt fully awake. In all his years of international travel, right from the first when he'd landed in Korea in the fifties as a newly trained combat medic, Will's internal clock adjusted to wherever he was in the world. Both mornings in Ankara, he woke before his alarm, excited to launch into the unknown. That's what made life the adventure it was meant to be, a conclusion he'd reached at sixteen when he'd enlisted, not much older than Kevin was now.

He remembered that long-ago afternoon, strutting into the house in Payson, Arizona, announcing to his mother, "School's boring. I joined the Marines."

She'd looked up from the onions she was chopping and smiled at him.

He'd been surprised. He'd expected a fight, like usual.

"But I'm too young. You'll have to sign that it's okay, Mom." Will placed the page down on the table, pointed to the line on the form, and held out a pen.

She'd wiped her hands on her apron, taken the pen, and signed in her jerky, sprawling hand, not bothering to read the form.

"There ya go," she'd said. "You be proud to serve your country, sonny. You know, I served. Built them Victory ships in World War II. They called us Rosies. Rosie the Riveter."

Make that one ship, he'd thought. She'd hated the drippy Northern California weather and quit the shipyard after a couple of months, found her third husband, and hauled Will to the next town and his fourth school that year. But that had been seven years and two husbands before Will enlisted, and by that time, he'd gotten over expecting stability from his mother, or his life—or even wanting it.

Two sets of railroad tracks, one from the north and one from the southwest, merged just west of Sivas and paralleled the road into the city. When they passed a petrol station, Will checked the gas gauge and the kids. A third of a tank remained, and they were all soundly asleep. Their faces were so peaceful. What a contrast from three days earlier when Will told them they were leaving the States that very afternoon. Gathered around him on the Toll House Lane lawn, he could read their feelings on their faces—worry on Kevin, anger on Rob, and delight on Didi.

"No!" Rob had yelled. "I have a game today. I'm not going!"

"Sorry, son, you are. It'll give the benchwarmers a chance to play."

"But, Dad . . . ." Rob's chin had quivered.

"No buts. We'll call Coach Mazza from the station."

"You can't make me go!" Rob's voice had cracked. He'd pulled his mitt off and flung it onto the ground, hurled his backpack across the yard, and run. "I won't go!" he'd hollered and disappeared around the house.

"Rob, get back here." Will had started after him.

"Dad! Don't! I know where he'll go. You won't find it," Kevin had said. "I can get him."

And Kevin had. He'd known where to find his brother and how to coax him out of the woods and into the car.

Sitting behind Will as they sped to the Trenton Transit Center that day, Rob had wiped his nose with the back of his hand, his eyes puffy and red-rimmed. But the boy hadn't cried in front of, or rather in back of, Will. And Will was proud of him for that, though he'd have been prouder if Rob hadn't cried at all.

It was true that Rob was probably leaving the Moorestown Little League MVP award behind. He was the league's star shortstop, gliding over the infield with a grace that defied his short, sturdy build. Good hitter too.

Will pushed against the steering wheel, flexing his arms and shoulders. He stretched his neck from side to side, then settled back into the Land Cruiser's lumpy seat. He took a long breath of the hot, dry air.

Just a few more hours and they'd be in Kayakale—their new home. Tonight, Will would tell the kids this was more than a vacation. They would be happy here. Rob would settle down. Kevin would help with that. And Didi would be easy. He remembered how she'd skipped across the grass when he told them they were going. "A 'benture! Turkey! Gobble, gobble, gobble!"

The miles rolled by as they traversed this landscape where explorers had scouted, traders had bartered, conquerors advanced, and the vanquished retreated—the crossroads between the East and West for millennia.

Will looked ahead at the mountains to the southeast. He pulled the map from the dashboard and scanned it—Engel Dağlari, the first range they would cross when they turned off the highway for the last leg of the trip.

"A 'benture!" he whispered.

༄

Kevin felt the hours dragging on through too many towns (some colorful, some drab), too many missed shots ('cause Dad wouldn't let him take pictures of people until they found out what was okay in Turkey, despite Kevin pointing out that none of the subjects would know), two gas stops, one lunch (kebabs and pita bread), and way too much bullshit from the back seat.

His father pulled over when one of them was swatting the other, both of them yelling.

"Get out!" Dad ordered. "Rob, give me twenty. Didi, give me five."

Push-ups—one of his standard punishments. Kevin rolled down the window and leaned out to watch.

"How come she only gets five?" Rob said. He and Dad faced off, hands on their hips, while Didi was already in position, pigtails hanging down in front of her face, skinny arms shaking with each half push-up she managed.

"Because she's little. And a girl."

"That's not fair."

"Whoever said life was fair? Now, drop and give me twenty."

Coming to a stand, her five done, Didi said, "You'll see, when I'm twelve, I'll do twenty."

She stuck her tongue out, and Rob grabbed for her, but she dashed out of reach and around the car.

"Good idea, Dee. After Rob's finished, wind sprints. For all of you. C'mon, Kev, you too."

He paced off fifty yards and made the boys run out and back five times, twice for Didi. Running was another one of his standard punishments.

Then there was more driving through huge tracts of land (that Dad made too many geologic comments about), another gas stop, and way too many rounds of twenty questions and I spy.

"Almost there," Dad said, as they drove into a village with narrow winding streets lined with small stone houses. "This is Kayakale. The dam's just a few miles farther."

Fuckin' A, Kevin thought. *About time.*

"Almost here!" Didi said, kicking the back of Dad's seat.

"Shut up, squirt," Rob said, giving her a good shove.

"Didi, sit still. Rob, be quiet," his father snapped.

Kevin rolled his eyes. He pulled his camera from his pack, checked the light meter, and took a few shots of the old stone buildings. When Dad braked to let a truck maneuver around a tight corner, Kevin snuck a shot of two old men. They teetered on rickety chairs with a small table between them. They each held a curved glass with honey-brown liquid. The glasses looked too delicate for the men's gnarled hands. Their caps were pulled low over their weathered faces, but beneath them Kevin thought he saw their eyes following the Land Cruiser.

Leaving the village, the road paralleled a river.

"That's the Euphrates," his father said.

They crossed the river, and the road climbed up the other side of the valley.

"Bridge looks new. I bet the dam project paid for it."

The hills blazed gold in the late afternoon sun. Then buildings, big ones and lots of them, appeared on the hillside to their left. Weird to see them out in the country like this. They looked like apartment houses.

"Those must be dormitories for all the dam workers," his father continued to narrate the drive.

"All the *damn* workers," said Rob.

Kevin gave him a look.

"What?" Rob asked, laughing.

They pulled up to a wide metal gate with a guardhouse beside it, both painted puke green. A metal sign arched over the gate.

"Kayakale Barajı," his father read. "*Barajı* means 'dam.'"

Kevin raised his camera.

"Not now," Dad said, for about the hundredth time that day. But something in his voice signaled to Kevin not to push it this time. He zipped the camera into his backpack.

"And you two, be good," Dad said over his shoulder.

A uniformed man came out of the booth. He had small dark

eyes and a black mustache that was so long it hung down to his chin on either side of his mouth.

"*İyi günler,*" the man said, his mustache waggling when he spoke.

"*Merhaba, ismim* Will Ross. *Bir* DECCO *çalışıyorum.*"

He must've practiced that, Kevin thought.

Dad and the guard half-talked and half-motioned to each other. His father flipped through his little dictionary. The guard studied their passports, looking up and down between their faces and the documents. He handed Dad a form. The guard's eyes narrowed, inspecting the signature. Then he opened the gate, hopped onto a motorbike, and waved his arm, indicating they should follow.

"Here we go!" Dad said.

"Here we go!" Didi echoed.

Kevin tried to count the dormitories as they drove below them on the long entrance road. Fourteen that he could see, leaning forward to look past his father. Closer, the hills were a mix of white and tan and gray, and the concrete buildings blended in with the dirt and rocks around them. Past the buildings, the road was planted on either side with tall, thin trees, the first they'd seen for miles.

"Must be getting to the high-rent district," Dad said.

"What kind of trees are they?" Kevin asked.

"Poplars. They grow fast. They're probably just a few years old."

The road widened into a square where a skimpy layer of grass struggled to be a lawn. It was surrounded by small squat houses.

"Wow, look at that," his father said. "The Turks must've had one heckuva surplus of that paint." All the houses were painted the same gross green as the gate and guardhouse.

A tall, skinny lady in jeans and a red T-shirt talked to the guard. She had a short haircut that looked like a guy's. Her hair was a light brown that his mother would've called mousy. Her skin was tanned. She wore aviator sunglasses that looked too big for her face. She didn't look Turkish—at least not like the Turkish ladies they'd seen so far.

The guard pointed to the house they pulled up to and handed his father a key.

"*Teşekkür ederim,*" Dad said. Earlier, he'd told them that meant "thank you," and made them practice saying it.

The lady, who was nearly as tall as his father, walked up to him. "Mr. Ross," she said, shaking his hand. "*Merhaba. Kayakale hoş geldiniz.* Welcome y'all."

Kevin thought she was American, but she had an accent he didn't recognize. Definitely not New Jersey.

She turned to him and Rob and Didi, pushed the sunglasses up on her head, making her hair stick up in spikes. Her face wasn't mannish like her hair. She had big brown eyes with long light lashes. His mother would've called her nose "pert." Her light pink lips spread into a wide smile, showing neat rows of small white teeth.

"Hi! You must be the new kids. I'm Paula."

New kids? Kevin thought.

"Are you hungry?" she asked. "If we hurry, we can get dinner before the dining hall shuts down."

"We're starved," Dad said, speaking for all of them, like he always did, like he always knew what they were all thinking. "Lead the way," he said.

The lady matched his father step for step. Didi hiked up her baggy blue shorts and ran after them. Rob trudged behind. Kevin shoved his hands into his pockets and hung back, watching. And thinking.

"Hey, Rob," he said, trotting to catch up with his brother. "What do you think she meant by 'new kids'?"

"How would I know?" Rob said, pounding his right hand into his left, as if he was ready to field a line drive.

FOUR

Paula took long strides to keep up with Mr. Ross. Without slowing, he turned to her and said, "You know that 'new kids' thing? I'm going to tell them tonight that we're moving here. Right now, they think I'm staying, but they're only here for the first two weeks."

He glanced over his shoulder toward the children. "It's complicated," he went on, looking ahead again, not at her. "A thing with my ex. Could you let it go for now?" He ran his right hand through his hair.

His daughter scurried up to them just as he finished speaking. Speaking of speaking, Paula couldn't. She was struck dumb by what he'd said. Did he really fly his three children halfway around the world and not tell them what they were in for?

The family lined up behind her in the cafeteria line, from the youngest on back. The boys let their sister go first, jostling each other behind her.

Dinner service was nearly over, and even though they could still smell it, all the roasted meat was gone. Dishing up *mücver*, Paula explained that they were zucchini fritters, which got nose wrinkles from all three kids. She had to admit the fritters looked gray and soggy rather than golden brown and crispy like they were meant to. The *çoban salatası*, shepherd's salad, needed no explanation. It looked like they all liked it from the amounts they scooped onto their plates. Paula was impressed—kids who liked vegetables were rare in her experience.

Fortunately, there was plenty of dessert left—baklava, made with a mince of the slender, sweet pistachios from the Gaziantep region a few hours south. Though Paula had read that the city's name was derived from the Arabic, meaning "in praise of spring" or from the ancient Hittite language for "king's land," she always thought of the nuts grown there, because *antep* meant "pistachio" in Turkish. She'd eaten more than her fair share of the delicious nuts in the year she'd lived in Kayakale.

The dining hall was nearly empty, and they had their choice of tables. Paula chose one by a big window in the back of the hall. It looked out over the yard where the heavy construction equipment was parked. Not so scenic, but none of the views from the dining hall were, and they were shaded from the blinding glare of the early evening sun there.

Dishes and silverware rattled on the trays as they settled around the table in awkward silence. Given what he'd said on the walk over, Paula wasn't sure what they could talk about. She tried this: "What job will you be doing here, Mr. Ross?" He'd said the children knew he was staying. She hoped that was a safe subject.

"Will," he said. "Please, call me Will. I'm the chief foundation geologist. Yesterday was my first day with DECCO. I'm pretty excited to get to work."

"But there isn't much work going on now," Paula said. Everyone knew the construction was shut down.

"That's why they hired me. You've got to understand the foundation you're building on. I'm here to figure out the problems with it and get the construction going again. Do you know much about dams?"

Both boys rolled their eyes at their father's question, though he didn't seem to notice.

"I know the basics," she said.

"Well, obviously a dam is like a stopper stuck in the

bottleneck of a river system, and the reservoir fills behind that stopper. The most efficient way to do that is to find a narrow spot. Like here. The not-so-obvious difference between a river valley and a bottle is that earth materials aren't impermeable, so the geology of a topographically favorable dam site is critical. Most people don't know that all dams leak. Water seeps through the rocks in the foundation and abutments—that's the bottom and the sides. It's the job of good geologists and engineers to make sure dams don't leak too much. At best, too much leakage makes a dam inefficient. At worst, it makes it unsafe. With me so far?" he asked, taking a bite of fritter.

Paula nodded.

He swallowed and went on. "So, when we get the foundation ready for dam construction, holes are drilled and grout's injected. Grout is a runny sort of cement that can be pumped through long, thin pipes deep into the surrounding rocks to lessen leakage. And that's where the trouble is here. When they started injecting grout, they couldn't get it to take. That's the term we use. They pumped and pumped, and the foundation never stopped taking the grout. The pressures in the injection system never rose. That means there are big voids in the subsurface. So big, the grout couldn't fill them. It's my job to figure out where those empty spaces are, why they formed, and when we get them filled, how to keep them that way. Make sense?"

She nodded again. He did, indeed, seem excited about his new job. "I'm sure I'll have a question or two later on," she said.

"Dad would love that," the older boy said, smirking.

Relieved at the boy's interjection, Paula turned her attention to the children. She was used to talking with youngsters, not so much with adults, at least not adults who weren't asking about their children's history essays or math homework.

"So," she said, "I'm Paula. I'm twenty-seven, and I come

from West Virginia. From a tiny town named Dudley Gap. What are your names, and how old are you?"

The Ross kids offered up their information like the children ordered to by their captain-father in *The Sound of Music*.

"I'm Kevin. I'm fifteen."

"Rob. Twelve."

"My name is Didi. I'm four," she said, holding up four fingers. Then, with a proud smile, she added, "Almost five." She extended her thumb to display her upcoming advance in age.

"When's your birthday, Didi?" Paula asked.

"Halloween!"

"That's fun," Paula said. "And what do y'all like to do?"

"I'm a photographer," Kevin said.

"Baseball." That was Rob.

"I like to play," Didi said.

"Playing is fun," Paula said. "I bet you'll all have a good time here. There's great stuff to take pictures of. And a son of one of the Turkish engineers loves baseball too. He made a baseball diamond. I think kids from Kayakale village come up to play with him on it."

"Can we go see it?" Rob asked.

Paula looked over at Will, who nodded. "Sure. But finish up first." He licked honey from his lips after taking a bite of the sweet baklava.

∽

Kevin was surprised by the coolness of the air when he opened the dining hall door. Then he remembered it was like that when they lived in Pakistan, and Arizona too—how you could feel the temperature drop as the sun sank.

"It's drier here than home, isn't it?" he said.

"Right. It cools off faster. There's less humidity to buffer the air temperature," his father said, always ready to provide a science lesson.

As they gathered at the bottom of the dining hall steps, Paula asked, "Who wants to see the ball field?"

"I do," Rob said.

"Can I go, Daddy?" Didi asked.

Dad nodded, and Didi slipped her hand into Paula's. For some reason, Kevin's gut twisted, though he couldn't think why. Maybe the soggy fritters.

"I'm going back to the house," his father said.

"Me too," Kevin said.

They walked to the square and up to the house in silence. His father fit the key into the lock, with a look over his shoulder at Kevin. He pushed the door open.

The room was filled with boxes—moving boxes, labeled in Dad's handwriting. And then Kevin knew. The boxes. Too much stuff in the back of the Land Cruiser. A house. The "new kids."

They weren't here for just two weeks. They weren't even here for two months. Maybe two *years*.

Kevin braced his hands on the stack of boxes in front of him. He took a ragged breath. "You fucking lied!"

"I'm sorry, Kevin. I had to."

"You kidnapped us!"

"Not exactly."

"What the fuck do you call it?"

"Watch your language."

"Now what?"

"Now we live here."

"You can't do that."

"I can, Kev."

"But you and Mom share custody. It's illegal. They'll put you in jail."

"They're not here. I couldn't leave you with her. Not the way she is."

A tremor rolled through Kevin's body watching his father

standing there, hands on his hips, like that's that, done deal. Kevin's arms twitched with the desire to unwind and belt him.

"I shoulda let Rob run away. I shoulda gone with him. I bet you didn't even try to call her. Did you lie about that too? Not that she'd fucking care. How could you *lie* like that?"

"I'm sorry. I really am. But I had to take you with me. You know that."

"I don't know that. We were okay."

"Now who's lying?"

"Fuck you!" Kevin shouted and shoved the boxes as hard as he could. They crashed to the floor.

His father came toward him. "Son," he said.

Kevin threw a box down between them, and the sound of glass shattering filled the room.

His father stepped over the carton. Kevin shoved him back as hard as he could. "You son of a bitch!" he yelled and turned away, slamming out of the door and down the front steps.

Then he ran around the Land Cruiser and across the lawn facing the house. He stumbled on a clump of the dry, pathetic grass but regained his balance and accelerated. He crossed a footbridge. And kept running.

Approaching a fence, he looked wildly left and right. Wasn't there some way out of this fucking compound? He didn't see any. He shifted his forward momentum upward, jumped, and grabbed high up on the chain-link barrier. Metal ripped into the palm of his left hand, but Kevin hauled himself up, feet scrabbling on the thick wire mesh. He threw himself over the fence, his pack thumping hard against his back when he landed. Tightening the straps, he glanced back for a heartbeat, then he turned and ran for the hills.

His breath roared in his ears. His lungs burned.

When he had run himself out, Kevin bent double and vomited.

He trudged to the top of the rise before him and squinted into the sun, now low in the sky. He sank to his knees. Seeing blood on his pants, he remembered his hand. It didn't look too bad, and it didn't hurt. He flexed his fist in and out, and blood seeped from the cut. He dabbed it on a clean spot on his pant leg.

He tucked his shoulder and rolled onto his side, then shifted to his back. Stopped by the lump of his backpack, he twisted out of it. Sweat stung his eyes. He swiped at them, then his upper lip as he sat up and leaned back against a boulder. The ball-of-fire sun sank behind a mountain. Sweat dribbled down his temples, across the hollows of his cheeks, and onto his neck. He pulled his knees up to his chest and folded his arms over them. Watching the sunset's colors shift, red to pink to violet, he thought about his camera in his pack, just out of reach, but couldn't make himself move. The violet faded to blue then deeper blue. Stars began to flicker.

Kevin sat still, breathing, blinking, blank. He'd run his anger out, but disbelief clung to him like his sweat-soaked clothes. He was used to his mother's lies. He'd even learned to lie for her. At school. To his father. Even with Rob and Didi, who didn't need to know more than they already did. They wouldn't understand. Not that Kevin did either, but that's what he got for being oldest. Knowing more than he wanted to. More expectations to live up to. Having to be the grown-up at Toll House Lane that summer.

But he'd thought he could trust Dad. Despite the churning in his stomach when they left New Jersey on Saturday and Ankara that morning, he never imagined his father would look him in the eye and lie.

Kevin searched for a word for what had happened. He dropped his head onto his arms. *Betrayal*—that was the word.

∾

Swearing under his breath, Will extricated himself from the boxes he'd landed on and the boxes that had landed on him.

As he brushed himself off, moved the crushed cartons aside, and hoped he'd find a brush and dustpan to deal with the bits of glass sparkling on the floor, he was also thinking. *What now?*

It never occurred to him that Kevin wouldn't understand his position. He'd counted on it. Once they got to Turkey, he thought he'd be home free with the kids—key word, "home." They would all settle in and settle down. Kevin was supposed to lead his brother and sister to that conclusion. Just like he'd led Rob out of the woods, literally and figuratively, the day they left New Jersey. But what now?

Will walked through the house, opening doors and peering into the bedrooms and bath. Sheets were folded in neat piles on each bed, and towels hung in the bathroom. The hall dead-ended in the kitchen. He found a broom and dustpan in a tall corner cupboard.

While he swept up glass shards from the living room floor, he considered how to break it to the boys that they'd be sharing a room, something they hadn't done in five years. What would go over worse, staying in Turkey or the two of them having to bunk together?

When Rob and Didi still hadn't returned with the teacher, whose name he couldn't remember, Will decided to make the kids' beds. Try to settle in, and maybe the settling down would follow. No doubt Kevin would be tired when he got back.

He heard Didi's singsong, "Bye-bye, Paula," right before the screen door slammed. He'd just smoothed the last of the four hospital corners on the last of the three single beds.

"We met the kid with the ball field," Rob said, as Will came up the hall.

"He's nice," Didi said.

"That's great," Will said.

"Where's Kevin?" Rob said, looking around.

"He went out to walk awhile."

"Why?" Rob asked.

Will noticed his son's deep-blue eyes, which had glinted at the thought of baseball moments before, darken. He drew in a breath. "He was surprised by something and needed to think about it. He was surprised when I told him we're moving here. All of us."

Will swept his hand around the room. "I packed everything we'll need. It's all here. Some of the kitchen stuff got broken, but your stuff is fine."

Both children gaped at him.

"Huh?" Rob said, tilting his head. Then, lowering his eyes, he said, "I hate you." His voice was quiet and calm. He stepped around Will, paced down the hall, looked into each of the bedrooms in turn, figuring correctly his would be the room where both beds were made up, and shut the door behind him.

Will stared after his son, more disconcerted by that response than by shouting and shoving. Each of the boys' reactions seemed equally incongruous to him.

"I don't hate you, Daddy," Didi said.

Will turned and reached out to her, and she stepped forward, reaching her arms up to him. He swept his little girl into his arms and settled her on his left hip. She kissed his cheek, then nestled her head onto his shoulder. "I *love* you, Daddy."

"Me too you," he said, patting her back with his right hand.

"Is Mommy coming? For her two weeks?"

"No. It's going to be just me and you and the boys for a while."

"Oh," she said.

"But you'll talk with Mommy on the phone. Hey, Dee, let's find your books and read together, okay?" Any story aside from the drama unfolding in real time seemed like a good idea to Will.

He half listened for Kevin while reading to Didi. The boy still hadn't returned by the time Will tucked her in. Not a peep from the boys' bedroom, either. He looked in on Rob, who lay on his bed, back toward the door, and was either asleep or chose not to turn over and acknowledge Will.

Will settled onto the cool, hard concrete of the front steps and gazed into the night, hoping Kevin would appear. Could things get any worse? At least the boy was a Scout; he knew how to camp, and the elements weren't a problem this time of year. But this certainly was not the way he'd envisioned the family's first night in their new home. And he was supposed to start work in the morning.

Squinting into the dark, he imagined a flashlight beam where there was none. He sighed. Will should've known— things could always get worse.

FIVE

Kevin woke with a shriek. He swung his head around, scrambling to his feet. Were there bears or cougars here? Something wet and cold had nudged his hand. He was sure of it.

He strained his eyes in the flat light, seeking a tree to climb. There were no damn trees!

He grabbed his backpack and held it to his chest like a shield, while he felt around inside for the flashlight he hoped was there.

"Aaaagghh!" Another scream escaped him when he flicked the flashlight on. Two eyes glowed back at him, eerily green. They blinked. Then the creature woofed.

"Fucking shitballs." Kevin's body sagged to the ground. "You scared me."

"Boof, boof," the dog answered.

"Jeez." He exhaled, then making his voice as gentle and inviting as he could, he said, "Come on, boy." He lowered the light so it wouldn't shine in the dog's eyes, and the little green lamps went out.

Kevin noticed the sky brightening to the east and realized it was morning. He'd been out all night. Good thing there weren't bears or mountain lions around. Only a dog.

"Here, boy," Kevin coaxed. "You can do it."

The dog crept out of the shadows, advancing, retreating, and advancing a bit more until he was near enough for Kevin to reach for him with an outstretched arm. Palm up and open, he gave the dog a little scratch under the chin.

"Did you run away too?"

It was a puppy. Not a newborn, but a gangly legged, big-footed puppy with big brown eyes whose lenses must have caught the light and gleamed that alien green. He was so bony that his skin hung on him like a size-too-big suit, and his ribs and spine and hips stuck out.

By the time the sun was up, the puppy's head rested on Kevin's thigh. They'd each eaten a package of Lufthansa airlines peanuts. After wolfing his down, the puppy had rolled over, his legs waving in the air, and Kevin rubbed his belly.

"You're still hungry, aren't you?"

Kevin was hungry too. But he remembered from Boy Scouts that water was more important than food. He found his canteen at the bottom of his pack. He poured some water into his hand, and the pup lapped it up. Then Kevin drank.

The puppy was golden tan, the tips of his fur lighter than the darker gold shafts. His underside was lighter still, almost white. His eyes were outlined in black, like eyeliner, and the line curved up and back toward his ears, which were so velvety soft that Kevin couldn't stop rubbing them. His eyebrows, too, were black, and the puppy moved one up and the other down when Kevin spoke, as if inquiring further about what he had to say. The fur on the dog's snout was tipped in black rather than light tan, and the dark of his muzzle converged into a thin black line that ran between his eyes to the top of his head. Kevin traced the line over and over with his finger.

"How old are you? I don't think you're old enough to be out here by yourself, buddy."

The puppy swiped at Kevin with his paw.

"Buddy. You like that name?" He scratched the puppy's chest, then hugged him. Buddy licked his ear. His whiskers tickled, and Kevin laughed.

He leaned back against his rock, fondled the dog's ears, and looked around, finally seeing the stark beauty of the landscape he'd run through. The stony surfaces in shades of tan and gold reminded him of the hills surrounding their house near Lahore when he was little, or the Superstition Mountains in Arizona, where they camped on weekends when Dad was in graduate school.

Kevin stroked the puppy's flanks, and feeling the bones under Buddy's hide, he decided.

"We have to go back. You need food, and we don't have anything else to eat. Half our water's gone too. He'll probably come looking for us sometime; then we'd be in worse trouble than if we went back ourselves, dontcha think?"

What happened at the house the night before played like a movie through Kevin's mind. The boxes he'd smashed. His father stepping toward him, not threatening really. "Son" he'd said, like Dad was asking for *his* approval, *his* forgiveness.

ᘓ

Will jerked awake, his pulse racing, but he couldn't remember the dream. Fully clothed, he pushed himself to sitting on a bare mattress, linens tidily folded at the foot of the bed. Disoriented, he scanned the strange room with unadorned, whitewashed walls. The smell of fresh paint lingered. Then he remembered, this was his house, his family's new home, in Kayakale. Turkey. But was Kevin here?

He padded down the hall in stocking feet and opened the door of the boys' room. The sheets on the bed he'd made for Kevin were smooth, untouched. Rob was asleep in the other bed, as was Didi when he checked her room.

This development would make for a very different first day at Kayakale than Will had anticipated. Back in his bedroom, he dropped to the floor and did the morning push-ups he had done every day since he was in the Marines. After putting his shoes on, he hesitated at the bedroom door. Go left to the front door or right to the kitchen? He turned right. A quick cup of coffee would make whatever came next easier to handle, and it would give him a few minutes to wake up, gather his thoughts.

Last night's scene with Kevin replayed in his head. He wasn't pleased with Kevin's language, but he knew what he'd been like as a teen, so he didn't have much moral authority on that count. And he understood why Kevin was upset. Just weeks ago, Will would have confided in the boy about the move. But he couldn't take the chance of anyone, even Kevin, blowing the whistle on his plan. He would not leave the kids with Kat in her condition. There hadn't been time to develop a Plan B, so Plan A *had* to work. And it did.

He put the kettle on and spooned Nescafé into a cup. Distracted as he was, he still noticed that the kitchen was stocked with the basics, for which he was grateful.

He supposed he should be worried about Kevin, but he wasn't particularly. Might be good for the boy to push back at him. They were close, more like friends than father and son, but maybe that was hampering Kevin's growing into a man. Will had certainly pushed back at his mother, and it hadn't hurt him. In fact, it had helped him step into his own life. Maybe this was just what Kevin needed.

Though Will was sure that Kevin would come back if left to his own devices, he couldn't head off to work this morning like nothing had happened. He glanced at his watch. It was still too early to check in with Erdem Borkan at the office. Swallowing the last of his coffee and hoping she was a fellow early riser, Will decided to go talk with the American teacher. She'd been friendly. Maybe she could help him get a search party together.

SIX

Kevin stood and stretched, like before track practice. He swung his backpack on and tightened the straps, wincing when the canvas webbing brushed the cut on his hand. It was starting to throb.

"I'm not sure where we are," he said.

Buddy cocked his head.

All the mountains looked the same. He wasn't like his father, who read mountains like other people read books.

He thought he'd been running up a hill when he stopped yesterday. "That means we should start by going downhill. Right, Buddy?"

Buddy tilted his head the other way.

Kevin touched his rock for good luck. Then he marched off with Buddy trotting beside him. They descended, crossed a dry creek, and wound around boulders. Scrubby brush rustled as they pushed through it. They climbed a ridge, and Buddy slowed at the top. He raised his head, his nose twitching.

"What is it, boy?"

The dog sniffed the air. Kevin squinted in that direction. He didn't see anything but the dry, empty landscape.

Then they heard it, a woman's voice calling Kevin's name.

"Here! I'm over here!"

She answered, "Kevin! Kevin! Keep calling! I'm coming!"

It was Paula, the teacher they'd met yesterday. Her strides were long, and she covered the ground between them quickly.

Kevin scooped Buddy up in his arms. The puppy wiggled against his chest, barking.

She stopped short. "Whoa. You have a dog?"

"Yes. He's mine. I found him. Or he found me. I didn't steal him. He didn't have a collar or anything. He was lost."

A smile played on her lips. "I guess he wasn't the only one."

Kevin hesitated, even though she seemed nice enough. "I guess not," he said, holding tight to his squirming puppy. "He's hungry. Do you have anything to eat?"

"PB and J. But I brought them for you."

"We can share," he said.

"Are you okay?" she asked, pointing at his bloodstained pants.

"Yeah. I got a cut," he said. He put Buddy down and looked at his hand. "Is he mad?"

"More concerned than mad, I think."

Buddy scampered from Kevin to Paula and back.

"You don't know my dad very well."

"No," she said. "How could I? Y'all just got here."

Buddy pranced back to Paula, sniffed at her, then balanced on his hind legs and pawed at her bag.

"Can I have a sandwich for him? He's so hungry."

"Poor puppy," she said, sitting down cross-legged in one smooth movement. She pulled the bag slung across her shoulder into her lap and reached in. "What about you?"

Did she hear his stomach rumbling? "Yeah, me too."

"I've got a few. Like you said, you can share. I have water too. Aren't you thirsty?"

"We're okay. I have my canteen."

Buddy and Kevin each scarfed down a sandwich. Paula pulled two more out of her bag and handed one to Kevin, then asked, "Can I feed him? See if he'll cotton up to me?"

Kevin nodded and took a big bite out of his second sandwich, relieved Paula had found them, not Dad. It gave him a little more time. For what, he wasn't sure.

Buddy licked jelly from Paula's hand. She laughed and rubbed the puppy's skinny flank with her other hand. Then she poured some water into her cupped hand and Buddy lapped it up. Kevin watched her with his dog. Her laughter was musical. No one spoke.

He liked quiet like this. It was a patient kind of quiet. Different from the sullen silences after Mom's temper tantrums. He suddenly realized he was tired, really tired. Like he'd been carrying a heavy load for a long time and only just got to put it down.

Kevin licked some jelly off his fingers. Pulling his canteen from his pack, he sipped from it. He chewed at a hangnail. With a sigh, he dropped his hands into his lap. He flicked some dirt out from under his thumbnail. "Did he tell you he kidnapped us? All he told us was he got a new job, and he was going to Turkey, and we were going with him for his two weeks. He didn't say he was moving here, that we were all moving here."

"Oh," she said.

"What did he tell you?"

"Not a lot, actually. He said you two had a misunderstanding. And you got upset and ran out of the house. What do you mean 'his' two weeks?"

"We go back and forth between his place and our old house with my mom. Every two weeks. It sucks."

"So, what would you do now, if you could do whatever you wanted?"

"Not think about all this crap. I'd go work for *National Geographic*. Or be an artist."

"Would you go back to the States?"

"I don't think that'll work," he said, looking down again. "My mom wants some time"—he paused—"without us. My bedroom's next to hers; I hear her talking on the phone to her girlfriends. And to her boyfriend." He glanced up at Paula. "I'm not so mad about being here; I'm mad that Dad lied."

She nodded.

"How're Rob and Didi? Rob didn't even want to come for two weeks."

"I'm not sure."

"He didn't run away again?"

"Again?"

"He tried to run away before we left, when Dad said we were going that afternoon. I knew where he'd go. I told Rob I heard Mom talking about going away with Russell. And that he couldn't stay home by himself. Maybe I shoulda told Dad I couldn't find him, but I don't like to lie."

"That's a good thing."

He made a snorting sound, then asked, "Do you like it here?"

"Anatolia's an amazing place. The history's so deep. Sometimes I think I can feel the ancients beside me when I walk down the road to the village . . . that must sound crazy."

"No, it sounds neat."

"Kevin, we should go. If we stay out here much longer, one of the others could find us. They'd wonder why we're having a picnic instead of heading back. Your dad's worried about you."

He snorted again but didn't say anything. Knowing Dad, he probably thought being out here all night was a good, manly exercise.

"Okay. I don't want to get you in trouble too," he said.

Buddy romped around while they collected their things.

"This way," she said, leading them along the ridge.

Kevin followed, hoping the ancient people who walked with Paula would walk beside him too.

∾

Paula stopped to let Kevin and Buddy catch up just past the gate back into the Kayakale Dam complex. The closer they'd gotten, the farther behind her the two of them had lagged. Buddy was plastered to Kevin's left knee as if he'd been trained to do a proper heel, but she thought it more likely that the pup needed the comfort of his new master's touch. The leash they'd fashioned from a strap off Kevin's backpack hung loose between them.

When they reached her, Kevin shuffled to a halt. He pulled at the right sleeve of his shirt, yanked up on the belt loops of his dirty, sagging pants, fiddled with the leash. He glanced in the direction of the houses, then immediately looked away.

She wanted to hug him right then and there. Instead, she lightly rested her hand on his back. "It'll be okay," she said, hoping it would be. Then she propelled him forward, walking beside him and Buddy across the square.

"A doggie!" She heard Didi's voice and turned to see her tugging on Will's hand as they crossed the bridge toward the square.

"Lookee, Daddy, a dog!" Didi cried, jumping up and down, pulling on Will, trying to hurry him along. But Paula couldn't see Will's face with the sun in her eyes. Once they cleared the road, Will let go of Didi's hand and she catapulted across the parched grass. Kevin and Didi and Buddy merged into a tangle of arms and legs and paws and one wildly wagging tail, accompanied by the happy yelping of both Didi and the dog.

The commotion brought the neighbors out. The Kayakale compound was like most small towns, complete with nosy neighbors. Young, beautiful, and very pregnant Kadriye peeked out from behind her screen door. She and her husband, like the Rosses, were new here. Figen and Zeynep, both residents before Paula arrived, descended the front steps of their respective houses and stood together, staring at them, whispering to each other. Figen, also pregnant, though not as far along as Kadriye, wore her usual slate-blue headscarf, and Zeynep, holding little Elif on her hip, looked elegant as always in a purple-and-silver silk scarf, long-sleeved silver top, and sleek black slacks. Paula thought they must be hot in those clothes. She kept her shoulders covered, even in summer, as the culture dictated, but outside of school she lived in T-shirts and jeans, which she sometimes cut off to a modest pedal pushers length.

Paula waved at them, and they dipped their chins in her direction, as much acknowledgment as she ever got. They didn't like her. Or perhaps their husbands had directed them to steer clear of her. She never really knew.

The three American moms and their kids weren't there. The construction shutdown had offered a rare opportunity to visit the States along with their husbands. A treat for them, Paula imagined, since they usually had to manage traveling with their kids alone.

Kris and Kerry, also Americans, both worked on-site—she was the nurse, and he managed the maintenance team. They were taking advantage of the work stoppage to take a trip, but Paula couldn't remember where. They were adventurous, working here after a stint in the Peace Corps.

The residents of the last house on the square, a British couple, were both archaeologists. They'd be out at their dig in Kayakale Dam's future reservoir, but even if they had been home, they pretty much kept to themselves. They weren't lookie-loos.

The noise must have roused Rob's curiosity. The screen door whacked shut behind him, and he jogged toward his brother and sister. Buddy, his tongue hanging out, was happily being petted by four eager hands. Will had arrived in the square shortly after Didi, but he hung back from the kids, watching. Paula still couldn't see his face for the sun.

"Where'd you go?" Rob asked.

"Up that way," Kevin said, pointing, then resumed stroking Buddy's flank. "I found him out there."

"Can I pet him?"

"Sure."

Rob flopped to the ground with the others, reached out both hands, and scratched Buddy behind his ears. The puppy waggled every part of his body it was possible to wag.

After hanging back and observing them for several minutes, Will joined his children. He knelt down on one knee and extended a hand to pet Buddy.

"You mad?" Kevin asked.

Brave boy, Paula thought.

"No."

"'Course not," Rob said. "He never gets mad at you."

"Did you find what you needed out there?" Will asked.

"I found him. His name's Buddy."

"Buddy," Didi said, and pulled the wiggling puppy into a hug.

"Can we keep him?" Kevin asked.

"Have to make sure no one's missing him," Will said. "Since he's so skinny, I'm guessing not. He's a beauty, son."

"No, Daddy, he's our Buddy," said Didi.

Paula noticed it was noon. The rest of the searchers would be meeting up at the dining hall, so with one last look over her shoulder at the Rosses, she left to tell the others that Kevin was home.

PART II

SEVEN

Will shrugged his faded green canvas field pack into a comfortable position on his shoulder as he stood near the base of the rock formation that gave the dam its name, Kayakale—*kaya* meaning "rock," *kale* meaning "castle." Today, his second day at the site, he was finally getting to the field, to the work he'd come to do. Yesterday had been spent first in search of Kevin, then negotiating with Erdem Borkan, the third person to proclaim himself Will's boss at DECCO. The negotiation had been about Buddy. And Refik.

Will was determined that their family would keep the puppy. The kids loved him already, and Will was getting there too. But he'd been curtly informed that Turks don't keep pets, at least not Anatolian shepherds who grow large and fiercely protective of their flocks, whether the flocks were sheep or children. It was true that if Buddy grew into his paws, he would be one big dog, but even as a half-starved puppy, he'd caused consternation among the Rosses' Turkish neighbors.

The other matter was Borkan assigning a young geotechnical engineer, Refik Kaptanoğlu, as Will's field assistant. Will had no need, and certainly no desire, for an assistant. Under normal circumstances he would have refused outright, but these were not normal circumstances. And so a compromise had been reached—the Rosses would keep Buddy, and Will would keep Refik. Both Buddy and Refik would be on short leashes until they proved themselves well trained.

When he heard someone approaching the trailhead, he checked his watch. Seven sharp, as he'd instructed. Good start. He smiled a greeting at the young man; might as well make the best of this. "*Günaydın*," he said.

"*Günaydın, Bay Ross.*"

"You can call me Will." Pointing to himself, he repeated, "Will."

Refik dipped his chin. "*Günaydın. . . .*" He paused, looking down as if to study his shoes. "Will."

He followed Refik's gaze and saw that the boy was wearing loafers.

"Boots?" he asked, indicating his own well-worn hiking boots.

"*Botları*," Refik said. "*Hayır.*" No. He didn't have boots.

"Sneakers?"

Refik looked at him blankly. They were close to the same height and stood looking eye to eye. Close to the same build too—lean and long-limbed. There, the resemblance ended. Refik's eyes were dark brown; his hair was thick, black, and curly. His skin, though dark in complexion, was not weathered by the sun, like Will's.

Will typically didn't notice what people wore—he didn't care. But he cared about the work, and what he saw in his assistant was a man dressed for an office job, with pressed linen slacks, a neatly ironed button-down shirt, and those shiny loafers. He'd also arrived at the trailhead empty-handed.

Will pulled the dictionary, which had become standard equipment, from the pocket of his field vest and rifled through it, listing sneakers, backpack, canteen, and lunch as he found the words. The book didn't list hike, so Will chose walk.

"*Yürüyüş*," he said, sure he was mangling the pronunciation. He pointed down at the trail, then up to the gorge. "*Yürüyüş.* There." He patted his field pack on one shoulder, his canteen on the other.

"*Tamam*," Refik said, swiveled on the slick soles of those ridiculous shoes, and hurried away.

"A 'benture," Will reminded himself. He glanced over his shoulder toward the compound. Then he studied the notes he'd made in the Ankara office and squinted up the valley to where he wanted to be.

Will was tired of waiting—the minutes since Refik left, the days since they'd arrived in Turkey, the weeks since he'd accepted the job, and the years since he'd done his last real fieldwork in graduate school. The move to management at the Philadelphia Port had fed his ego and his bank account but not his intellect. Will was hungry.

As soon as he spied Refik in the distance, he started up the trail. The gravel gave a satisfying crunch underfoot.

The trail headed upstream and gained elevation, the dry channel of the Euphrates below. The river was diverted through tunnels so the dam could be constructed. From the research Will had done to land this job, then the maps he'd studied and reports he'd read from DECCO, he knew most of the rock here was marble, metamorphosed limestone and dolomite—carbonate deposits, marine in origin, that were recrystallized by intense heat and pressure.

Carbonates dissolve in the groundwater that flows through them more readily than rocks with silicate chemistry, rocks with more quartz. The reports noted some evidence of dissolution in the Kayakale marble, but only minor karstic features, small caves and sinks, reported to be limited to fractures and faults where groundwater percolated into and through the formation.

But what they'd found during construction proved those conclusions wrong. There were huge, unmapped voids beneath the dam's foundation. Learning their extent was imperative. So was finding their cause. Without understanding the geologic process that caused the cavities, he had no idea if it was ongoing,

or if it had ceased long ago in geologic time. When they managed to fill the empty spaces, would they stay filled?

His lungs burned. Out of shape from five years behind a
desk, the ascent left him winded. He neared the pillar of rock,
Kayakale. Seen from a distance the day before, when he and
Didi were searching for Kevin, he thought it looked like travertine. The closer he got, the more it looked that way. Travertine
wasn't shown on any of the maps of the dam site.

Will squatted to inspect a boulder on the trail. Gray and
rough and not distinctive to the untrained eye, the thin con-
voluted layers of the rock spoke of the heated waters that had
dropped their calcareous mineral loads. The only hydrothermal
deposits noted in the literature on the region were associated
with the mines several kilometers downstream, near Kayakale
village. None had been noted near the dam site, but there was
no doubt—this was travertine.

Refik huffed up the trail just as Will reached for the Est-
wing rock pick that hung on his belt. Its handle was smooth and
contoured to his hand, shaped over years of study and work. He
swung the hammer. Metal rang on stone. Rock dust drifted up,
and the smell of gunpowder stung Will's nostrils, as a thin film
of grit settled on his lips. He blew the dust off the specimen in
his hand.

"Travertine," Will said, holding the rock out to Refik. "Each
of these layers"—he pointed to them—"was precipitated when
hot, mineralized water surfaced and cooled. Cooler water can't
hold the mineral load in solution that hot water can, so when
the water daylights, minerals get deposited layer by layer by
layer." He traced them with his finger. "Like this," he said. "Do
you understand?"

"Little," Refik said. "*Daha yavaş, lütfen.* Hmmm. More
slowly, please."

"Okay. I mean, *tamam.*"

Refik smiled. "*Çok iyi.* Very good."

Will opened the leather pouch on the other side of his belt from the pick and pulled out the brown glass vial with dilute hydrochloric acid. He squeezed a few drops onto the rock and watched it fizz. The acid bubbled as it ran into the nooks and crannies.

"See? Definitely carbonate. Not that we didn't know that. But travertine, so close to the dam site, that wasn't reported. And it's a big deal. Hot water can dissolve a lot more carbonaceous rock than water at ambient temps. The implications of travertine so near the dam site are immense with respect to the foundation and abutments. More dissolution means more and bigger cavities. Exactly what shut construction down."

"*Yavaş, yavaş,*" Refik said, signaling with his hand to slow down, like you might to a driver who's coming toward you too fast.

"This deposit wasn't mapped. Did the geologist who signed the initial report only look at the footprint the dam would literally be built on? Didn't he hike up here? Didn't he even look up?"

"*Bilmiyorum, Bay Ross.* I do not know," Refik said.

"I know you don't. I'm just thinking out loud. You know, it seems like management is always willing to overrun construction costs, but never willing to spend a fraction of that on good geologic studies beforehand. I just don't get it. And call me Will, please. *Lütfen.*"

"Okay, Will."

"Let's go," Will said. "There's a lot more to do today."

He marched up the trail, shortening his steps to accommodate the steepening slope. It was rough going, more like a game trail than the well-worn track it should've been, had it been established for a proper dam-site investigation.

Jeez, I can't believe what they missed, he thought.

From the reconnaissance mapping where they hadn't noticed that Kayakale was travertine to the drilling program where they'd missed gaping voids, so much had been over-looked. Will was determined to find the missing puzzle pieces and put it all together.

He stopped and turned to Refik. "I want you to learn this now. There's no substitute for good, solid fieldwork, and lots of it."

Refik stared back at him. "Okay, Will," he said, as if he understood.

∞

Will crossed the square as the pinks and purples of sunset deepened to the blue-gray of dusk. A light shone from the front window of his family's little cinder block box. It silhouetted a figure on the stairs leading up to the stoop.

As he got closer, Will distinguished two figures on the front steps: Didi sat sideways on the teacher's lap, the gal who taught the American kids at the site, who had greeted them when they arrived Tuesday and escorted them to dinner that night. She hadn't hesitated to help in the search for Kevin, and she was, in fact, the one who'd found him, bringing him and Buddy home. But what was she doing at their house now? Surely Kevin hadn't run off again. Will trotted the rest of the way, his fatigue from the long day forgotten.

The teacher looked up when Will approached. "*İyi akşamlar, Bay Ross,*" she whispered.

He stepped closer. "What?" Will bent down until his face was less than a foot from hers.

"I said, good evening, Mr. Ross."

"Will. Call me Will," he said. "The boys?"

"Inside."

"They're okay?"

"I think so, but they're teenagers, so. . . ."

Will nodded. "Don't I know it."

"I came over to see if y'all wanted to join me for supper at the dining hall. I took them since you weren't here. You're pretty late."

He was too weary to bristle. Besides, she was right—he was late.

"Dinner's inside. Didi wanted to bring some home for you. Go ahead and eat. Then you can put her to bed."

"You don't mind waiting?"

"No," she said, laying her cheek on the crown of Didi's head.

He made his way down the hall to the kitchen.

"Boof." Buddy scrambled to his feet, his nails clicking on the concrete. "Boof, boof."

"It's okay." Kevin leaned over to pet him. "Sit, Buddy."

The puppy sat. Will was impressed. "Good dog," he said, bending to fondle Buddy's silky ears. "Nice start on the training."

Kevin sat at the table with his camera kit laid out like a nurse might arrange a surgeon's instruments. He didn't look up when Will spoke.

"Cleaning her up?"

"Yup." Kevin picked up a brush and carefully stroked the lens.

"Where's Rob?"

Kevin inclined his head toward the boys' bedroom, not meeting his father's eyes. Will observed his son at his task for a full minute. If Kevin felt Will's gaze, he didn't show it.

Will took the few steps over to the open bedroom door. Rob was sprawled on his bed, lying on his stomach, face toward the far wall, feet toward the door, a book propped open on his pillow. Again, Will stood silent, watching. Rob flipped a page and kept reading, either so engrossed he didn't sense Will's presence or pointedly ignoring it.

When Will returned to the kitchen, Kevin was packing up his equipment. The boy glanced at him, then turned his eyes away. He stood, scraping the chair across the floor, and left the room. Buddy followed, wide puppy grin on his face, tail wagging. Will heard the bedroom door latch and his sons' low voices, though he couldn't distinguish their words.

He sank into the chair where a plate covered with tinfoil was set beside a napkin folded into a pocket with a fork tucked inside—Didi's touch. *At least one of my kids still likes me*, he thought.

He unwrapped his dinner, a casserole of some sort, gone cold and mushy. He crushed the foil into a tight, hard ball and hurled it at the garbage. He missed, and it bounced across the floor with a hollow patter.

EIGHT

Paula jumped at the knock on her door. Who could it be at that time of night? She never had company, except for her students. School hadn't started yet, and those kids were mostly back in the States. Besides, they wouldn't come at night.

She flicked the light on over the door and moved the curtain aside. It was Will Ross.

Odd, she thought. *I just left there. What could he want?*

She opened the door. "Hi, Will."

"Hi. . . ."

"Paula," she said.

"Sorry. I'm not good with names."

She didn't know then how Will categorized people—what she came to think of as the Good, the Bad, and the Invisible.

They stood in the doorway, looking at each other. His eyes were an astonishing shade of blue, like the sky on the clearest of days. She wondered how old he was, because those eyes had a youthful mischief in them, but there were deep creases at their corners.

She smiled awkwardly and noticed her lips were quivering. Had she forgotten how to talk with anyone over the age of ten in the year she'd been here? She was pretty much left alone. It wasn't that folks were unfriendly, they just weren't friends. She tried not to think about it, but she was lonely.

"What brings you here?" she asked.

"The kids are settled for the night," he said. "I thought I'd come by and thank you for taking care of them today." Will ran his hand up and back through his hair, a gesture she'd seen in both him and Kevin. "And to ask a favor."

She couldn't place his accent and wondered where he'd grown up. Not New Jersey, where they'd just moved from.

"Where are my manners? Please, come in. Would you like something to drink?" She squeezed against the wall to open the door wide enough for him to get by. "I don't drink alone, and I never have company. I still have the little bottle of brandy I came with. Only had sips when I was down with a cold." Why was she babbling?

"No, thanks. Don't touch the stuff anymore," he said, looking from Paula to the book she'd dropped in her dash to the door. "You're sure you don't mind the intrusion?"

"Not at all," she said, following his gaze. She brushed past him, retrieved the book, and set it on the arm of her easy chair. "I know. How about some Turkish coffee? They say you can read your fortune in the grounds."

"I'm not sure I want to know ahead of time," Will said. "But the coffee sounds good."

Retracing the eight steps from the living room to the kitchen, she grabbed one of the folding chairs she used at her tiny table, hurried back to the living room, and shoved a potted plant into the corner so the two chairs would fit.

"Wow," he laughed. "Your house is even smaller than ours. But more colorful."

"I love color," she said. "I grew up in my granny's damp, gray house. I painted this place first thing."

Paula pointed to the easy chair, and Will settled into it while she fussed in the kitchen.

"Maybe it's so small because they don't want their spinster schoolmarm keeping any company," she said, and he laughed again.

She measured the water, then carefully spooned the fine, dark grounds and sugar into the hammered copper coffee pot she'd treated herself to on her first trip to Istanbul. "But what really happened was Mrs. Browning, the teacher before me, moved to Ankara when her husband got a promotion. None of the other wives had the qualifications to teach the English-speaking kids, so they contracted me through the Calvert School, which is the curriculum we use here. Then they built my apartment onto the back of the schoolhouse right before I got here."

"Is Mrs. Browning Gus Browning's wife?" Will asked, wondering what kind of person could live with that asshole.

"One and the same."

"I didn't realize he'd worked at the site."

"They were here at least two years before they moved to Ankara. Their twin boys finished high school here. Their daughter was in college when they came over, and she stayed in the States. She must be a senior now or maybe even have graduated."

Paula leaned back from the counter. Will sat with his elbows on his knees, her book in his hand, flipping pages. "*Angle of Repose*? You're reading an engineering book?"

"It's a novel. By Wallace Stegner. Tough read, but beautiful."

"That's an engineering term."

"I know. It's a metaphor."

He shook his head and set the book down. "Do you know what job Gus had here?"

She poured the coffee, pleased with the thickness and burnished gold of its foam. She let the grounds settle.

"The one Mr. Borkan has," she answered.

"I see." Will's forehead creased into a frown.

The cups rattled on their saucers as she carried them into the living room. She handed one to him, then perched on the edge of her chair and took a sip. He followed suit. Their eyes met over the rims of their cups, then flickered away.

"What brought you to Kayakale?" he asked.

"Have you ever been to West Virginia?" she quipped.

"Can't say I have."

"Then so much for that joke. Anyway, my little town put me through college with the agreement that I'd come back and teach. Which I did. At the end of those four years, it was time to go."

"This is a long way to go, especially for a young single gal."

"Woman," she corrected. "And I'm twenty-seven, not so young."

"Not so old either. Pretty gutsy."

"I'll take that as a compliment," she said and blushed. "I like an adventure."

"I'll drink to that," he said, hoisting his cup. "And you found what you were looking for here?"

"Yes and no."

He raised his eyebrows.

"Yes, it's an adventure to be halfway around the world immersed in a different culture, learning a new language, having this landscape and all sorts of history to explore. And no, it doesn't feel good to be part of something I was trying to get away from."

"What were you trying to get away from, if that's not too personal?"

"It's very personal, but not how you mean. I joke about it, but I love West Virginia. It's wild and lovely. And the mining and chemical companies, they're . . . there's no nice way to say this . . . they're raping the land. I had no idea building a dam would do the same thing. I suppose that was naive on my part."

"'Raping the land'? That's pretty harsh."

"Have you looked into the excavation? *That's* harsh. Plus, I don't know why it never occurred to me before I came here—there are towns and the people in them, and farmland

and wildlife habitat, and the wildlife that lives there and even archaeological sites that are going to be drowned once the dam's done."

"Come on, isn't that a bit overdramatic? We don't drown people."

"You haven't seen those villages. They've been here longer than our country's been in existence. You're right, though— the dam won't drown the people, it'll just uproot them. Some of those villagers have lived eighty or ninety years in that one place. And the term is 'inundate,' right? I guess they're going to feel pretty darned inundated, don't you?"

"There's a price you pay for progress," Will said. "People have to move for big public works projects, but when they do, they have electricity and clean water and flood control and irrigation for their crops. And infrastructure they've never had before to develop industry, and that helps the economy. They have to adjust, but it's clear, the gains are greater than the losses. It's a foundation to build on—better and stronger."

"Really? What price are you paying? You're getting paid. Me too. Do you really think one of those villagers is going to end up a rich industrialist? I think that villager's going to end up slaving away for the industrialist who lives in a fancy penthouse in Istanbul. Or New York. Who gets to say what progress is?"

He picked up his cup and took a few sips. "This is really good, thank you."

"Glad you like it," she said, disappointed and a little irked that he'd signaled the end of the conversation with the nicety.

Paula missed the give-and-take of a talk that stretched her mind. Her world was bigger than her classroom, and she'd been alone in those parts of it for a long time. She didn't quite fit in the Kayakale Dam community. She worked but didn't fit with the technical staff, because she wasn't an engineer or, more importantly, a man. She was a woman, but she didn't fit with the wives because she worked and, more importantly, wasn't a wife and mother. The only other foreign working women at the site, Kris the nurse and Margaret the archaeologist, didn't seem to have the time or inclination to mix much. Paula had tried— they both seemed so interesting, and she would have liked to know them better. It would've been nice to have a friend, but it seemed their husbands were all they needed. If she were at Kayakale with a husband, it might've been the same for her.

Paula finished her coffee and gazed down at the grounds. She felt Will's eyes on her and looked up.

"You're very sensitive," he said.

"I am. And I like it that way."

"I didn't mean it as an insult, just an observation," he said. "In my opinion, building a dam is progress. And progress is a good thing. I'm here to get this dam built. You don't have to agree with me, but you should."

What? she thought. *Did he really say that?*

"That's pretty black and white. I think there are shades of gray with respect to how we define progress," she said.

"Is that another metaphor?" He shrugged and patted the book, which was sitting on his lap. "After you get to the angle of repose, things fall down. That's pretty black and white. I suppose I don't do metaphors. Or shades of gray, either."

"Maybe 'layers of complexity' would be more apt."

It looked like Paula would need to up her game with Will, but she was, admittedly, out of shape in that department.

"You came to ask a favor?" she asked.

"Yes. Look, I know it's a lot, and I'll pay you for your time . . . I need to work long hours, to figure out what I'm dealing with here, technically. Would you mind staying with the kids for a few hours a day, for maybe a week or so? Till they get more settled. If you think they're okay, you can leave Kevin in charge. He's old enough. I'm just not so sure of them these days, with the running off and all. They've had a lot to deal with lately. Two weeks ago, when I dropped them off at the house, Kat— that's their mother—was passed out, naked, in the middle of the living room. She'd thrown up all over the place. Damn drunk. Oh," he said, "sorry."

She shook her head. "Don't worry about it. But I'm sorry to hear about your ex-wife."

"The boys are so angry at me for bringing them here. But I did what I had to do."

Black and white. Not always right, but never in doubt. She wondered what it was like to feel that self-assured.

"I tried to call Kat and tell her I was keeping the kids for a while, but I couldn't reach her," he said.

"Kevin said she was going away," Paula said. "With her boyfriend. That was how he got Rob to go with you after he ran off."

"What?"

"He told me yesterday, when I found him and Buddy."

He smacked the book, then leaned forward in the chair. "What *else* did he tell you that I should know?"

"Whoa," she said, raising her hands. "I don't know. He's a teenager. It's always easier for them to talk to anyone besides their parents. Don't you remember?"

Will snorted at that, like Kevin had when she found him and Buddy. "Yes, I remember. It's just that Kevin and I have always been close."

Again, she thought, *Not always right, but never in doubt.*

"Of course I'll stay with them," she said. "No need to pay me. I'll do it until school starts, and then they'll be stuck with me anyway. What time tomorrow?"

"We left for the field at seven this morning. We'll keep that schedule."

"Okay."

"I can't thank you enough." He stood up. "It's late. I should go." They walked single file to the door.

"Thank you again," he said, turning to her, holding out his hand to shake.

It felt hot and dry and rough against hers, and its warmth lingered after he let go. So did the mingled scents of earth and sweat and coffee.

Paula pushed the curtain aside after closing the door and watched Will walk away until he disappeared into the dark.

∾

Paula was restless that night, thinking of the Ross children. Will was so certain he'd done the right thing, not leaving them with a mother drowning in alcohol. But it couldn't seem that simple to those kids. She knew that from her own childhood. She couldn't help thinking of that little girl in West Virginia, also taken from her mother by a father sure he was doing the right thing. With Paula's mother, it hadn't been booze—it was nerve pills. And her father tried, she supposed, to keep their family together. But once he'd made his decisions, first to put her mama away and second to hand her over to Granny, his own mama, to finish her growing up, Paula never saw her mother again. And she never could get her father to talk about it—not whining at him as a child, not screaming at him as a teenager, and not asking him calmly, but urgently, as an adult.

Her old boyfriend, Curtis, would hold forth on the subject. He was a psychology professor, and sure, from Paula's descriptions, that her mother was manic-depressive and could have been treated. But, like Curtis, that conversation was academic. What could've or should've happened was of no consequence by the time Paula knew him. Mama was gone.

Paula only held snatches of memories of her. Mahogany hair, so long it hung down to her waist—she remembered watching her braid it every morning. Draped over her right shoulder, her fingers whipping through the silky locks at lightning speed.

Paula remembered waddling around in her favorite red snowsuit, while Mama bundled into a coat, hat, and mittens herself. Together they would wade through the deep snow in the backyard, find the perfect pristine place, then fall backward side by side, waving their arms up and down, making snow angels. Then all day long, Paula would press her nose to the kitchen window to see the angels flying low along the winter white carpet, which she imagined the surface of clouds might be like.

But there were also the memories of the closed door to her parents' bedroom, the sound of Mama's moans the only human contact she might have all day. Or the nights when she heard yelling from behind that door, her father demanding, "You pull yourself together, or else." Her mother either snarling or whimpering in reply, the words muffled. The threats so frequent, with nothing changing, that Paula had been stunned when the "or else" finally happened.

Tears trickled down the sides of her face and into her ears. She felt for the handkerchief she kept under her pillow. Two-thirty glowed on the radium-green dial of her Baby Ben alarm clock. She knew she should try to sleep. She needed to be at Will's by seven.

She hoped Kevin and Rob and Didi were remembering good things, if they were dreaming of their own mother tonight, not the picture Will had painted. Surely there were some good memories.

She fluffed her pillow and settled her head into its softness. Closing her eyes, Paula beckoned a happy memory of her own. Chasing Chance, a puppy then, round and round till she and Mama fell in a happy heap, spent and dizzy, on the soft spring grass.

NINE

Walking home from the field the next day, Will caught a whiff of dinner before he opened the screen door, and the spicy aroma grew stronger as he made his way to the kitchen. He hung back in the hallway and took in the scene. Kevin and Rob stood beside each other, trimming the ends off green beans. Didi stood on a chair, stirring something in a big pot with a big spoon. The teacher was bent over looking in the oven. She closed the oven door and straightened up, gliding behind each of the kids in turn, checking over their shoulders. She moved with a fluid grace that surprised Will, given how tall she was.

"Oh!" she said.

Was she blushing?

"How long have you been there?" she asked.

"Just got here."

"You're early. It's still light out."

Didi jumped off the chair, ran across the room, and threw her arms around his waist. "Hi, Daddy," she said, her voice muffled in his shirt.

He patted her head. "Hi, guys," he said.

The boys barely looked his way.

"What smells so good?"

"Roast chicken. And mashed potatoes with lots of butter, right, Didi? The boys're working on the beans. We'll steam them," she said. "You're back earlier than we expected. Dinner won't be ready for a while. How'd it go today?"

"Starting to see some patterns," he said. "Spent the day up on the abutments. We'll get into the excavation next week. I wish I had my plane. Nothing like a bird's-eye view to get the whole picture."

"You have a plane? Wow!"

"Paula, can you help me get the lumps out?" Didi asked, climbing back up on the chair.

Over dinner, Will announced he was going to take the weekend off, a change in plans. "What should we do, kids?" He bit into a juicy piece of chicken. "Mmmm. What spices?"

He glanced around the table at his children, but only Didi met his eyes. She shrugged. "Whatever you want, Daddy."

"Cumin, paprika, salt, pepper, and a little sumac," Paula said. "If you make a thick paste, it keeps the chicken moist."

"Don't know sumac. It's good. What's your favorite day trip?" he asked.

"I don't know if it's my favorite, I've never been, but I've always wanted to go to Nemrut Dağı," she said.

"What's that?"

"It's a temple and tumulus on top of a mountain about eighty miles south of here. It was built by Antiochus the First, a Commagene king. He did it to honor the gods and himself. I haven't gone because I'm not sure my car can make it up the road to the summit. But you have a Land Cruiser."

"We do. What do you guys think?"

Before they could answer, Paula continued, "From what I've read, it sounds amazing. The temples are like open-air altars with colossal statues on them, and they're famous for their huge heads, which are scattered all over because they fell off the bodies during earthquakes."

She tripped over her words like an excited kid. She had Will's attention, and even Kevin raised his head a bit, though Will still couldn't see his eyes.

"I've always wanted to go," she repeated.

"It's only eighty miles away?"

"I think so. But some of them are rugged miles."

"Like you said, we've got the Land Cruiser."

"We should leave early," Paula said. "It'll be a full day."

"What time?"

"Six thirty?" she asked.

"Done," Will said.

"I'll bring muffins for breakfast. I have some in my freezer. And I'll make sandwiches for lunch."

"Can't pass that up," Will said.

"I can," Rob said, finally looking up. "Can I stay home?"

"Why?" Will frowned.

"I'm hanging out with Timur tomorrow."

"Who?"

"The Borkans' son," Paula answered. "Those two have really hit it off. They had a plan to play baseball tomorrow."

"His cousins are coming from the village, so we'll have enough for teams."

Will took his time slicing off a bite of chicken. "You really don't want to go? It sounds pretty great, don't you think?"

"No, I don't care about some old king."

Will noticed that Rob had called Kayakale home. Maybe that was enough progress for one day. He chewed and swallowed, thinking it over. "Okay," he said. "You don't have to go."

"Thanks, Dad," Rob said.

"What about Buddy?" Kevin asked. The puppy was under his chair, and Kevin leaned down to fondle his ears. "Can he come?"

"I don't see why not."

"Thanks." Kevin nodded at Will, and a smile flitted across his face.

That was progress too.

Will and Rob left the others washing dishes and headed for the Borkans' house to ask if Rob could stay the entire next day with them. Will wanted to get things squared away and hurried to the task. He waited at the bottom of the stairs to the Borkans' house. Why was Rob lollygagging? Wasn't this for him? When he shuffled up, Will placed his hand on the boy's back and fairly shoved him up the steps.

Borkan answered the door in his office attire looking as crisply pressed as if he'd just dressed, which reminded Will he was still in field gear, dusty and sweat-stained.

"Mr. Ross," Borkan said, "to what do we owe this pleasure?"

Will cleared his throat. "I understand our boys have become friends. Our family's decided to go on an outing tomorrow, but Rob would prefer to stay here and play. Word is they have a ball game planned. I know it's an imposition, but would you and your wife be willing to watch him for the day?"

Borkan smiled under his well-trimmed mustache. "We are pleased the boys are acquainted and would be happy to have your son be our guest tomorrow."

Will spied Rob's friend peeking out from the archway to the living room. Borkan must have seen Will's gaze shift and looked over his shoulder. "Timur." He beckoned to his son.

"We'll be leaving early. I hope that won't be a problem," Will said.

"Where are you going, if I may ask?"

"Nemrut Dağı."

"It is beautiful and most impressive but quite a long trip for one day. The road is rough."

"So I understand. We have the Land Cruiser, and I'm experienced with backcountry driving."

"Very well," Borkan said with raised eyebrows. "You will, indeed, need to leave early. Perhaps your son should stay here tonight."

The boy grinned at his father's suggestion. And when Will turned to check, he saw the first smile on Rob's face since— well, he wasn't sure. Since his last Little League game back in New Jersey?

"You're sure that won't be too much trouble?" Will asked.

"Quite sure."

"Come on, Timur, let's go get my stuff," Rob called, sprinting down the steps and across the square, his friend on his heels.

"That's the happiest I've seen Rob in a while," Will said. "I can't thank you enough."

"Exactly," Borkan said. "I do not think I had the luxury of such. . . ."

"Angst?" Will ventured.

"Quite right. Angst. I did not have that luxury as a boy."

"Me neither," Will said. "Well, I'll get going then. *Çok teşekkür ederim.*" Thank you very much.

Borkan smiled at Will's attempt at Turkish. "*Birşey değil,*" he said. You're welcome.

TEN

Will got his still-sleepy crew loaded up, and they rolled out of the dam site compound at 0635. The trek began with the drive down to Malatya. Down, because Kayakale sat below the Mercan Mountains, and because in most of the directions you could drive, you drove down. Only the north road climbed farther up, into the mountains, a road to explore another day.

The topography eased from Kayakale's crags, to hillocks, to the gentle slope of the Malatya plain.

"What's that orange stuff on the ground?" Kevin asked.

"Apricots," Paula said. "See all the orchards? Malatya's the capitol of apricot growing here, and they're harvesting now."

"Why are they all on the ground?" Didi asked.

The fruit blanketed the landscape from the shoulders on both sides of the road to as far as they could see.

"To dry in the sun," Paula said. "Did you know that Turkey's famous all over the world for its dried apricots?"

"Are they good?"

"Delicious. Did you like the fresh ones we had for breakfast?" Everyone nodded.

"Well, the dried ones are even sweeter."

"That's a whole lot of apricots," Will said.

"Must be millions," Kevin said.

Malatya, the only sizable town they would pass through, was nearly sixty miles from Kayakale. They filled the Land Cruiser's tank and piled back in after walking Buddy. As an afterthought,

Will trotted back to the station and lucked into finding a larger-scale road map than the one he had. He wanted to see more detail and spread the map out on the hood to study it. At sixty miles from home, they should be three-quarters of the way to Nemrut Dağı, if Paula's estimate was right. According to the map, it was at least forty miles farther to the mountaintop with that name. But it was only 0800, and Will was undeterred.

They headed east on the last blacktop they'd see until their return. As soon as they turned off the main road, they began climbing. The level of the plain rose, but orchards still fanned out on either side of the road. They traversed rolling hills, then not-so-rolling hills. Slopes steepened, angles sharpened, and they left the apricot-covered hills behind. The miles wore on, the road got rougher, the going slower. They were an hour and a half past Malatya when the climb was steep enough that the Land Cruiser labored.

Will downshifted. "So much for eighty miles south of Kayakale," he said.

"Maybe they were 'as the crow flies' miles?" Paula said.

But they weren't crows, the Land Cruiser didn't fly, and the roads in central Anatolia didn't go straight.

"It's beautiful," Paula said.

"It is, and getting more spectacular by the minute," Will said, taking a quick look down the precipice that dropped from the driver's side. He concentrated on the road as it narrowed. Dropping a tire off the edge would be disastrous, but he wasn't complaining—you take what you get when you head into new territory.

The track leveled and followed a contour, side-hilling, with steep drop-offs to the left and soaring cliffs to the right. Then came switchbacks, the views shifting with each tight turn. They crossed the tree line, such as it was—not many trees here.

"Nice folds," Will said, commenting on a particularly contorted kink in the rock layers.

"Sure, Dad," Kevin said, lowering his camera.

"Could you explain the rocks when you're not driving?" Paula asked.

Kevin groaned.

Will laughed. "My kids'll love that. Right, Kev?"

"Yeah, right."

"Well, I want to hear it," Paula said.

"Turkey's an amazing place geologically. Last night you mentioned that the heads tumbled off the statues from earthquake shaking, right?"

"That's what I read."

"It makes sense; the tectonic framework of this country is really something. There are two plate-bounding strike-slip faults, called the North Anatolian Fault and the East Anatolian Fault. Do you know what the San Andreas Fault is?"

"I know where it is in general, if that's what you mean. And that it's sliding part of California up the coastline, right?"

"That works. So it's a strike-slip fault too, and what that means is the two sides of the fault move sideways relative to each other, not so much up and down."

"Okay," she said.

"The North Anatolian Fault is just like the San Andreas; it moves the same way, and it's about the same size. And the East Anatolian Fault moves in the opposite direction. I'll sketch it later to show you where they are and what I mean. But, basically, the Anatolian tectonic plate is being shoved west, kind of like toothpaste out of tube, because the Arabian Plate is moving north, pushing it against the Eurasian Plate, so the Anatolian Plate is sliding sideways out of the way. That's a simplified way of putting it, of course. It'll make more sense when you see a picture."

"A picture's worth a thousand words," Paula said. "You really get excited about geology, don't you? Maybe you can help me do a lesson plan on it?"

"Sure, we can do that some evening," Will said.

"Yup, he sure does get excited about it," Kevin said.

Will glanced at Kevin. "Do I detect a note of sarcasm?"

"Nooooo."

After the next switchback, a mountain with a perfectly conical peak rose before them.

"That doesn't look natural," Will said.

"That must be the tumulus," Paula said.

"He reconstructed the top of the mountain?" Will asked.

"Added to it, from what I've read. It's about fifty meters higher than the natural peak."

The track turned from dirt and gravel to carved paving stones, and the Land Cruiser rumbled over them. They rattled upward for several more minutes, and then the track widened into the first flat open space they'd seen in miles. Will parked beside the trailhead, and they piled out of the car, grabbing for sweatshirts when they felt the chill of the high-altitude air.

"I guess my information was a little off," Paula said. "It's almost lunchtime."

"A little?" Will said.

"Well, I'm not sorry we came," she said, sweeping her hand around at the view. "You don't have to agree with me, but you should. Let's picnic at the top." She shouldered the backpack with their lunch.

"Let me carry that," he said, reaching for the pack.

"I've got it," she said and strode up the trail.

As she walked away, Will noticed the elegant lines of her calves below the hem of her denim pedal pushers. They curved down to what might have been pretty ankles, but he couldn't see them under the thick socks she'd folded over the top of her hiking boots.

"Come on, she's getting away," Will said to Kevin and Didi and hurried after her.

∽

Will and the crew never did catch her. Paula waited for them at the top, not even breathing hard. Of course, she'd been living at this altitude longer and was a runner too, but Will didn't like the idea of a gal beating him to the top of a mountain. Clearly, he needed more exercise than the everyday push-ups he did. Good thing he was back to fieldwork now.

"This is the north side," Paula said, "and the temples are on the east and west, so either way we go, we'll get to one of them. Let's go around the whole thing."

She headed east with Kevin, Didi, and Buddy following her.

Will stayed behind. The summit views were impressive, surrounded by jagged peaks of steeply dipping sedimentary rocks—coarse-grained, dark gray sandstones, and massive, cream-colored limestones, the rocks they just scrambled over to get here.

He turned to the tumulus, built from fist-sized angular pieces of the limestone. This had been constructed more than two thousand years ago by hand-chipping stones from outcrops, hauling them to the top of the mountain, and stacking them just shy of the angle of repose.

"Not the metaphorical angle of repose," he said, smiling to himself.

The word "grueling" would hardly begin to convey work like that. It was an awesome accomplishment, but Will was baffled that any man, even a king, would presume that he could improve on what nature had provided.

He advanced around the slope of the tumulus. He saw one, then a second of the deities' bodies, then the entire temple— and his family in it. Kevin looked pensive, standing beside the head of a goddess, while Didi and Buddy sprinted around the scattered blocks and body parts as if the temple were their playground. And why not? Will liked to think of the world as his playground, something he hadn't felt for some time. That's why he loved flying, and skiing, surfing, and scuba diving. Or moving around the world to take a job overseas—the challenge of the problem, the move, the moment, the setting, or the speed. You rode waves of adrenaline. You *knew* you were alive, every cell in your body singing. He wanted that feeling back.

The deities' heads lay jumbled, some on their ears, some on their necks, having settled that way or been righted after their falls. There were animal heads as well—two eagles and a lion. The lion's visage struck Will as strong and noble.

He approached Kevin.

"Too bright for really good shots," Kevin said, squinting at his light meter. "This would be really great at sunrise. It's neat, though."

"Who is she?" he asked, pointing his chin at the head beside them.

"Paula said Tyche. She's the Greek goddess of fortune or chance."

"Lady Luck?" Will said.

Kevin rolled his eyes. He leaned closer to the goddess's weathered stone cheek. "Mom would say she had a bad case of acne as a kid. And she's having a bad hair day too. That's the kind of stuff she notices. I think she'd like this, though."

Will just nodded. He didn't think he could talk about Kat without saying something he didn't want to say, not to his kids anyway. "Do you think Rob would like it?" he asked.

"Probably. How could you not think this was neat?"

"Maybe we'll come back. We could do an overnight. Camp down where we parked. Hike up for the sunset, and the sunrise the next morning. It'd be great."

"Really?" Kevin asked.

"Sure. That's part of why I wanted to come here. It's not

just the job. There's always so much to learn in a new place. Remember Pakistan?"

"A little," Kevin said. "I remember being happy there."

Will nodded again. He was uncomfortable with where the conversation might go, but they *had* been happy in Pakistan. All of them. Together. Long before the divorce and everything that went with it.

"What f-stop're you going with? You loaded one hundred speed film?" Will asked.

"Well, yeeaaahh."

"You shooting black and white, or color?"

"Black and white. I want to print them myself. Can we get a darkroom set up?"

"Sure," Will said, grateful for the request—an invitation for a project to do together, and maybe a sign that Kevin was settling in.

Kevin turned from Will back to the goddess. He held up his light meter and studied it, made some adjustments to his camera, then framed his shot.

It was quiet. Kevin was engrossed in composing his shots, and Will couldn't see the others, but he heard Paula's twangy voice coming from across the temple, behind the lion's head. He sat on the top step of the altar facing the gods. Much like he surveyed a landscape and visualized the geologic framework that lay beneath the surface, he imagined the temple as it had been, reconstructing the massive limestone statues, rebuilding their bodies, replacing their heads in his mind's eye. They would have risen to heights of more than thirty feet. He re-erected the sandstone tablets with figures sculpted in profile—holding mighty staffs, corralling the moon and stars, grasping the hands of the gods. The tablets had peg-like extensions from their bases, which fit the evenly spaced openings on the row of gray sandstone slabs that capped the temple platform. It would have been majestic.

He blinked, and the temple lay in ruins again.

Will made his way around the tumulus, pausing on the south side to observe the expanse of land below, where the landforms sloped away, downdip. Tan, gray, and brown rocks outcropped on the descending slopes, with green swaths of vegetation where streams flowed through the valleys.

They picnicked on a blanket Paula spread on the altar of the West Temple. She handed out sandwiches and tiny cans of apricot nectar.

"You must be the goddess of plenty," Will said to Paula, at which Kevin rolled his eyes again.

After wolfing his sandwich, Kevin lay down and appeared to be scanning the sky, his hand shading his eyes. He rolled onto his side, facing away from the rest of them, then reached behind him, his hand feeling around on the blanket. Will bent down and put his camera in his hand.

The boy seemed to be snapping pictures in a half dream. He tipped his head back to look at the camera's settings, his bangs ruffled on his forehead in the light breeze. He flicked a knob, slid the focus in and out, squinted into the viewfinder, pressed the shutter. *Click, click, click.* Will followed the lens of Kevin's camera to see where his son was aiming, but all he saw were puffy white clouds gathering in the distance.

Paula stood and stretched. She reached her hand out to Didi, and the girls wandered off to explore the fallen heads of this temple. Will lingered, watching Kevin and listening to him murmur to Buddy, who'd snuggled up to his master's chest. Though they were close in proximity, he felt so far, so detached from him. He hoped Kevin would forgive him, that he'd come to understand that Will had done the only thing he could have.

He looked north and west, again following Kevin's lens, and

found the puffy white clouds were building into thunderheads. The wind had picked up.

"Time to go," Will called out. "Storms build fast in the mountains." Thunder sounded, as if to punctuate his statement. "I don't want to take that road in a downpour."

Cold, fat drops began to fall as they scrambled down the boulder field just before the last part of the trail.

"These rocks'll get slippery. Didi, climb on," Will said, stooping to pick her up piggyback. "Come on, you guys," he said, looking back to check on the others. Kevin picked Buddy up and leapt from one rock to the next. Paula moved fast, nimble and steady, using both her feet and hands.

They were soaked through and chilled in the few minutes it took to get to the Land Cruiser. Didi shivered against him. But Will was more concerned with the condition of the road than their own condition. He'd turn the heat on to dry out and warm up on the way down.

"Load up! Fast," he shouted over the building wind.

He had the wipers on their highest speed and still could barely see the road. Wind gusts slammed sheets of rain into the windshield. He caught a glimpse of the track with each swipe of the blades, but he was feeling his way more than seeing it. The sky darkened to steel gray. Though it didn't seem possible, the rain got harder. Will eased to a stop.

"Maybe it'll lighten up in a few minutes," he said. "It blew in fast. It could blow out fast."

The rain pounded on the roof, and the wipers beat back and forth. Kevin held Buddy against him, and Paula held Didi. No one spoke. Will turned the defroster up a notch.

The sound of the rain changed.

Hail? Will thought.

There were *plinks* and *tinks* against the metal of the roof. He strained to see out the windshield but didn't see any hailstones.

Then something crashed onto the hood.

"What the. . . ?" Kevin started.

"Shit!" Will jerked the Cruiser into gear. "We can't wait. That's dirt and rocks raveling off the cliff."

He drove ahead as fast as he dared, occasionally scraping the side view mirror on the cliff face. Better that than losing a tire off the drop-off he couldn't see but he knew was there on the right.

"Shit," he muttered. "Shit, shit, shit."

Then came a sound like a train approaching. Will pressed harder on the accelerator. He knew it could only mean one thing here where there were no trains—a rockfall. He hoped like hell it was behind them, not ahead, or worse, right above. The Land Cruiser curved around a bend and thumped over a rock Will couldn't see in the track.

It got louder. Will gripped the wheel and leaned forward, though that didn't improve his vision in the least. He pushed harder on the gas. Another crash. The air roared.

And then it was just the rain drumming and the wipers thrashing.

∾

Off the mountain, at the intersection with the road to Malatya, Will pulled the Land Cruiser over and cut the engine. He exhaled long and loud. He was proud of his crew. Though their eyes were wide, they'd all hung tough during the storm and the rockfall. Even Buddy hadn't so much as whimpered. He reached over and tousled the puppy's ears.

As luck would have it, the rockfall had been behind them. No telling how far, but not very. Hadn't Will been musing about feeling truly alive a few hours ago? The physical manifestations of fear and excitement were not so easy to tell apart, and on the trip down the mountain, his cells were singing in high C.

෬

When Will pulled up to the house, he left Kevin and Buddy asleep in the passenger seat, climbed out of the Land Cruiser, and opened the door behind him. He and Paula did a slow-motion dance as she maneuvered out of the car holding his little girl. He slid his left hand under Didi's dangling legs and reached his right around her back. His hand swept up the side of Paula's body as he did, his fingers briefly noting each bone of her rib cage. Without thinking, he leaned down, and his lips brushed hers. Her eyes widened, then she closed them, raised her chin, and returned his kiss. Her lips felt warm against his, and he let it linger. He began to explore her mouth with his tongue, her teeth small and smooth, her taste sweet.

Didi shifted, and the kiss ended. Will scooped his daughter out of Paula's arms and stepped back.

"I should get her to bed," he said.

"Yes," she said. "Quite a day. We were lucky."

"Very. A 'benture, Didi would say."

"What would you say?" Paula asked.

"I'd say I feel very lucky right now." He leaned forward over his sleeping daughter and kissed Paula again.

ELEVEN

August 4, 1973

Dear Mom,

Merhaba! That means "hello" in Turkish. How are you? I'm fine. Dad said you guys just talked, and you were away the whole two weeks we've been gone. I hope you had a good time.

It's pretty neat here. We're in the mountains again. I hadn't realized how much I missed them. It's sort of like where we lived in Pakistan, hilly and almost like a desert. Our house isn't as nice as it was there, and we don't have any servants. We cook or go to the dining hall to eat. Dinners are better when we cook, but there are no dishes to wash when we go to the dining hall.

The best thing about being here is Buddy. He's our puppy! Poor little guy was all by himself outside, and after we checked with the villagers and no one said they'd lost him, Dad said we could keep him. He's the best dog ever. He's an Anatolian shepherd and they can get really big, but Dad thinks maybe he won't, because he was malnourished. He's eating and growing like crazy now. I take him on a hike every day. We'll do that until school starts on August 20. Seems kind of early for school to me. It's almost a month earlier than the Turkish kids in the village start. We'll be going to a school for all the American kids here at the dam.

Rob and Didi are fine. Rob made friends with a Turkish kid named Timur. He loves baseball too, only he's a Mets fan. His uncle in New York sent him a Mets jersey. Rob's pretty jealous, so maybe we can get a Phillies jersey for him for Christmas. Timur has his own baseball diamond, and he and Rob hang out there all the time. Some days, Timur's cousins come up from the village and they make teams and get a real game going. I played a couple of times, but I'm bigger than they are, so it isn't really fair.

Didi loves Buddy. Sometimes she pesters him, though. When I tell her to quit, she goes and works on her cartwheels. She's learning to do handstands too.

We're all learning some Turkish words. The teacher says we'll learn even more when school starts. I guess that's all that's going on here. Miss you, Mom.

Love, Kevin

P.S. I'll send some pictures after we get the darkroom set up.

Kevin reread the letter. It wasn't exactly "all that's going on here," but he didn't think his mother would appreciate hearing about how he really found Buddy, or the rockfall that nearly trapped them on Nemrut Dağı, or Paula. Especially Paula—whom they saw every day, who taught them the Turkish words they knew, who helped Didi with handstands, who baked the dog treats he used in Buddy's training, and who he thought might be Dad's girlfriend.

He folded the loose-leaf pages into the envelope Paula had given him. She'd offered him the stamps he needed, but he asked Dad if he could walk to Kayakale village on Monday to buy some at the *postane*, which meant "post office" in Turkish.

Since the week before, they all had chores—Kevin mopped

the floors, Rob cleaned the kitchen, and Didi helped Paula with the laundry. When his father assigned their tasks, he took cleaning the "head," which was what he always called the bathroom. Kevin thought he got the hardest task, but Dad took the worst one, so he didn't say anything.

They got their allowances that day, so Kevin had some "walking-around money," as his father called it. He'd buy the stamps and mail all their letters to Mom (which Paula said they should write). He'd check out the film in the village store too (even though he had enough for a while longer). Maybe he'd even get some *dondurma*, which meant "ice cream" in Turkish. Not that he'd admit it to anyone, but this was an adventure, and he was kind of enjoying it.

TWELVE

Will leaned over the drafting table in his office. He had two maps in front of him. One showed the boreholes from the site investigation, and the other showed the foundation grouting plan. He studied one, then the other, then he clicked some lead out of the tip of his mechanical pencil. Correcting for the maps' differing scales, he marked the borehole locations on the grouting plan. Next, he slid the stack of borehole logs down from the corner of the table. One by one, he compared the logs against the records of the failed grouting operation.

It took hours. A niggling feeling that there was a problem started with the first few logs and grew as the hours passed. Something was wrong. What he thought might be a mistakenly located borehole or two was instead a disturbing pattern. Log after log noted long runs of Kayakale marble with only minor fracture zones, if any. But those boreholes were colocated with grout holes that had never stopped taking grout, indicating huge voids in the subsurface. One of the data sets was very wrong.

Will knew the grout hole locations were correct. The pipes, abandoned when the grouting program floundered, were still in the field to be measured. And he and Refik had done that—twice. The survey locations on the plan were correct.

He set his pencil down and massaged his temples with his fingertips, while staring at the maps and logs spread out before him. Could he trust *any* of the data gathered prior to his arrival? As he had every day in the field, he wished he'd found a way to bring his plane over. He was sure a view from above would give him clues that the ground work and this so-called data couldn't. He ran his hands up and back through his hair. He considered what to do next. Measure the grout holes one more time? Or go talk to Borkan now? He drummed his fingers on the desk.

The metal chair scraped on the concrete floor when Will shoved back from the table. After one more glance at the bogus borehole logs, he left his office, crossed the open room where the junior engineers' desks were lined up, and knocked on Borkan's door. He stepped into his colleague's office and closed the door behind him. "Something's wrong."

"Good afternoon, Mr. Ross," Borkan said, looking up from a pile of papers, pen in hand. "We are aware of that. I believe that is why you are here. No?"

In spite of himself and the problem at hand, Will smiled at Borkan's formality.

"I don't just mean with the foundation," Will said, serious again. "I mean with the entire data set from the site investigation."

"Perhaps you could be more specific," Borkan said.

Will explained what he'd been doing since morning and concluded, "So either the drillers didn't know what they were doing, or the borehole loggers didn't, or the surveyors who put those locations on a map didn't. Or some combination of the above. Or maybe those logs were fabricated. Maybe they didn't do any drilling at all. They might as well not have, for the good it did."

The two men looked at each other for a long moment.

"How can I use *any* of the data from the site investigation?" Will asked. "I can't." He answered his own question.

Borkan peered across the desk at him. "You are certain?"

"Absolutely," he said. "Who was responsible for that study?"

"I assume it was my predecessor here," Borkan said.

"I figured," Will said, sliding his hands into his pockets and leaning against the back of the door.

"You know, Erdem . . . may I call you Erdem?" Will paused. Borkan dipped his chin in assent.

"Browning told me he didn't want me here. Maybe that's because he knew I'd figure this . . . this"—Will waved his hands in front of him—"*mess* out. Is he trying to cover it up?"

"Perhaps he didn't know of the errors. Assuming you are correct."

"I am," Will said.

"We can resurvey the grout holes. I will have that done." Borkan made a notation on a pad. "We cannot go back and resurvey the boreholes, of course. The surface has been disturbed. I agree that if we cannot be sure of the data, we cannot use it."

"So what's next? Don't we need to tell someone?"

"I do not see what good that would do." Borkan tapped his pen on the notepad.

Again, the men looked at each other, silent for a moment. Then Borkan sighed. He picked up the pile of papers in front of him and tapped them to straighten their already-straight edges. He replaced them on the desk and glanced up at Will. "We must define the foundation conditions properly. I have been authorized to spend what is needed in order to do that. Please write the specifications for the field program you need, Will. May I call you Will?"

Will nodded.

"How soon can you have them done?" Borkan asked.

"Two days?"

"Please proceed then. We will go over them first thing Thursday morning."

"I'm on it," Will said over his shoulder as he strode out of Borkan's office.

But when he got to his office door, Will decided not to go in. He'd been buried in the logs all day. His eyes felt bleary. He needed a break. He trotted down the office steps to go outside, get some air. With his hands on his hips, he stood and squinted up toward the sun. The hot, dry breeze of the August afternoon ruffled his shirt.

He remembered it was the kids' first day of school, so he headed for the schoolhouse, thinking he'd have a quick look. The boys still seemed at loose ends to him, and he was hoping school would tie up some of the frayed bits of their lives, like work was doing for him. He climbed the schoolhouse stairs. There were windowpanes in the top half of the door, and Will stepped up and to the side, where he wouldn't be visible from the classroom.

Paula stood at the front of the room. She wore a silvery gray skirt, straight and slim and down to just below her knees. He supposed it was meant to be conservative, but instead it accentuated her sleek figure. Her button-down shirt was bright white and neatly pressed. The sleeves were what Kat used to call three-quarter length, when she went on and on about her shopping excursions. They showed off Paula's thin wrists and graceful hands, which fluttered a bit as she talked. She looked professional. Also lively. And pretty, from her head to her toes. These were not qualities that Will generally expected in one package.

He heard her lilting voice through the open windows but could only catch a word or two. From where he stood, all three of his children seemed as intent on Paula as she was on her students. Satisfied, he backed down the schoolhouse stairs. Better not to be seen, interrupt the lesson, and embarrass his kids. An ironic smile twisted his lips when he thought about how mortified he'd have been if his mother had ever barged into one of his classes.

The truth was his mother had never shown up at any school event, not even parent–teacher conferences. Will had always made excuses for her—at school, if not in life. She'd made it clear he was an inconvenience at best. Leaving him with distant cousins or accommodating friends for months at a time when he was a boy, she'd happily let him sign up as a Marine at sixteen. But when he finished college (which she'd repeatedly declared a waste of time while he attended) and landed his first professional job, then she crowed long and loud about all she'd done to make her son a success. As he walked across the compound, a short, sharp snort escaped him at the memories.

Before mounting the office stairs, Will looked back at the little schoolhouse and congratulated himself on how different a parent he was for his kids.

∽

Kevin thanked his father for taking the day off, and he glanced over from the driver's seat and smiled.

"Getting the darkroom set up'll make this more like home. Besides, it's the weekend, and I'm waiting to hear back on a big piece of work, so there's really nothing for me to do. When was my last day off, anyway?"

Kevin thought a minute. "The day after we went to Nemrut Dağı."

He recognized that his father just told him he was only doing this because it wasn't interfering with something more important. It would be nice if, every now and then, their family was the something more important.

"You're right. Wow, that's something like a month ago. I'm due," his father said, rubbing his whiskered chin.

"You're growing a beard," Kevin observed.

"I guess so. It's just something I've done ever since field camp in college. If I'm working in the field, I don't shave. There wasn't a good option back then; we were camping. But I could shave now. I just haven't. What do you think?"

"It's okay," Kevin said, but he noticed that Dad's beard was even more silvery than his hair.

Then they rode in silence again. It was quiet, like the hours they used to spend developing film on weekend afternoons. And now, they would have a darkroom here. They'd measured out the space in his father's bedroom to partition off, and they were on the way to Elazığ to get the materials to build it. His father was handy that way. He'd finished the whole basement at Toll House Lane himself. Kevin and Rob had helped some with that, and Kevin was actually excited to do the darkroom together now. He wouldn't admit it to Dad, but it was getting a little harder to keep being mad at him for taking them here, though that was less a function of his father and more a function of *here*.

Kevin pushed his bangs out of his eyes as he gazed out the window at the dry grassy hills, golden in the morning sun. Without thinking, he started to hum the Turkish alphabet song.

"What?" Dad asked.

"Nuthin'."

"Come on, Kev. What were you saying?" his father pressed.

"It's stupid," he said with a sheepish smile. "I didn't realize I was doing it until you said something. It's the alphabet song. Only in Turkish. It's babyish, but it helps me remember the letters and how to pronounce them."

"Refik's teaching me. Let's see . . . the letters we don't have are the *c* that sounds like *ch*, the silent *g*, and the *s* that sounds like *sh*. And three vowels, right?"

Kevin nodded. "Yup, the *i* without a dot, the *o* with two dots, and the *u* with two dots. The song's helping me remember how to say the letters, so I can sound things out. I like learning a language where I can use it, not like home, where it's just a class you have to take."

"You did great with Urdu as a little guy, but you probably don't remember much of it."

"Not anymore," Kevin said.

"Well, I'm glad you're liking school. Is Paula a good teacher? You've got her all day. That's pretty different from Moorestown High."

"It's better than MHS. I know I was only a freshman, and Mom went on and on about how great high school was, but I didn't fit in there. Except maybe for track. What's the big deal about going from class to class? Paula gets us started on stuff, and we learn on our own. I like that."

"Like an old one-room schoolhouse, like my first school, before your grandmother and I left Kansas. I remember Miss Wilson, my teacher there," Dad said, chuckling. "I was a little in love with her, even if I was only in second grade. Come to think of it, Paula kind of reminds me of Miss Wilson."

"So you're in love with Paula?"

Dad laughed. "That wasn't exactly what I meant. But maybe a little." He paused a moment, then said, "Hey, Kev, teach me the alphabet song!"

∾

Paula's days with the Ross children continued but in the schoolhouse once classes started. She wasn't surprised to find they were smart and curious students.

She showed Kevin new drawing techniques, and his pencil work was lovely. He seemed to be a natural artist, with his trained photographer's eye for composition.

She noted that Rob was great in math, but lukewarm on science. She took that more as rebellion against his father than real disinterest. Seemed to be where Rob was—if his father liked it, he didn't. He couldn't be bothered with history or art. She created math problems with baseball stats, since she knew he'd be into them, and assigned Jackie Robinson's *My Own Story* for his reading, which snuck some history in.

Paula found that Didi bubbled with enthusiasm for learning and was more than eager to please—almost too much so. Paula worried that she'd spend her life pleasing other people and never herself, but Didi was young, and Paula admitted to herself she was probably projecting some of her own emotions onto the little girl. In any case, Didi was the kind of pupil any teacher hoped for, even as a kindergartner.

After the first weekend when they went to Nemrut Dağı, Will pretty much worked seven days a week and often late. Most days, Paula had dinner with the Ross family, cooking at their house or going to the dining hall. If Will worked really late, she slept in the extra bed in Didi's room. She knew the kids would've been fine, but she liked being with them. They seemed to like it too. Paula saw the looks on the neighbors' faces and imagined the whispering among them, but no one said anything to her directly. Or to Will, as far as she knew. And they weren't sleeping together.

She kept going back to a passage in *Angle of Repose*, the novel she'd been reading when she first met Will. The narrator was delving into the relationship between his grandparents. His grandfather was a mining engineer pioneering in the American West, and his grandmother was an artist and writer enamored with New York literati. He stated, "What I find myself held by, in imagination, is their tentativeness, their half-awkward half-willingness to admit their understanding, as they faced each other in the doorway by the light of the lamp she carried. That too is like one of her drawings—narrative, side-lighted, suffused with possibility." In Paula's interpretation, the grandparents' unspoken understanding was that, although they barely knew each other, they would spend their lives together.

Though she and Will had become friends, she was tentative about anything more. The children's almost constant presence when the two were together helped in keeping some distance, but it certainly felt "suffused with possibility" to Paula. Would she find a metaphorical angle of repose with Will, like the characters in the book? Would it feel solid, the way she thought the best relationships would? Or would it always be on the edge of tumbling? She didn't know.

She found herself thinking of his stunning blue eyes when she looked at the sky on sunny days. She'd seen that blue deepen in intensity when he talked about earth processes and spark with creativity when he spoke of his work. He was handsome and fit, but his curiosity and confidence were just as attractive to her.

They had only shared three kisses that one night, but they'd shared many conversations—about home, about flying, about what they read and why, and about the way they saw the world—his views as a scientist, a pilot, and a photographer, and hers as a teacher, an athlete, and an artist.

Since Curtis, and the embarrassment and shame that had come, and the trust and dignity that had gone with that relationship, Paula had forgotten how attractive intelligence was to her. She'd sorely missed the exchange of ideas and opinions. Even if Will seemed to think his opinions were facts, smart was sexy. But his "girls" and "gals" and "I'm rights" and "blacks and whites" gave her pause. *Was he safe?* she wondered. Not in the physical sense, but to her hard-earned, and still fragile, sense of self-respect.

Not that she had much of his time or attention. Will was, first and foremost, in love with his work. Paula reminded him that his kids needed him in the little time he could spare. There was no rush. Paula was hesitant for a reason, and although she pondered the possibility, she was content to let the reality reveal itself slowly. Apparently Will was too.

In stark contrast, she fell in love with the kids fast and hard. Buddy too. How could she not love them?

Evenings around the kitchen table felt cozy—the kids did their homework, and Paula graded papers while Will worked on maps and cross sections, which he explained were like vertical maps that he drew using the data on the logs from drilling.

Paula watched as the Ross family settled into life in Kayakale, each in their own way: Will immersed in his work; Kevin taking and developing pictures and training Buddy; Rob and Timur forging a bond—they were inseparable to the extent they could be, given they attended different schools. Paula spent more time with Didi than the others since Dee didn't have a Buddy or a Timur of her own. Paula asked if she missed her mother, and the little girl got quiet, then shook her head. She said, "Mommy makes me wear dresses. I don't like dresses." That was all she'd say. Paula asked the boys too and got grunts and shrugs for answers.

None of them seemed willing to engage much with the topic, so Paula mostly let it go. She only pushed on one thing— having the kids write weekly letters to their mother.

Being part of their "crew," as Will called them, was filling the empty spaces in her days. And in her life. She was the happiest she'd been since coming to Kayakale.

∽

Kevin crumpled the bright pink page and threw it across the room. It ricocheted off the bedroom wall, bounced twice, and rolled to a stop by Buddy's nose. The dog raised his expressive eyebrows, then chomped it.

For a moment, Kevin felt inclined to let him chew the whole damn thing up. That's what he thought of his mother's letter.

Then he commanded Buddy to drop it. He guessed he'd read it one more time. He smoothed the page out on his pant leg. Buddy sat up and placed his snout on Kevin's other knee, gazing hopefully at his master. He had to laugh; Buddy made everything better. "I'll get you a biscuit in a minute."

No letter would be coming for either Rob or Didi. At the end of Kevin's, his mother said she'd planned on writing each of them, but it took longer than she thought it would and Russell was coming soon. Fucking Russell. And Mom.

He'd tell his brother and sister about the letter, but he would not show it to them. Not with all the bullshit in it. About why she didn't bother to get on a plane to get them back. Why she needed this time to be wild and free—Kevin nearly gagged at that line. How she never had the time to be young and careless—Kevin figured she meant carefree, as she was plenty careless, if you asked him. Having them so young—like whose fault was that? Like that magically happened? *You were careless all right*, he thought. He snorted. Now he knew why he'd felt like the adult during their stints with Mom last summer . . . *he was*.

He scrunched the letter back into a ball and tossed it to Buddy, who made a graceful leap to catch it, then settled in for some serious chewing. The dog ate it, a clichéd excuse Kevin had never used before, but there was a first time for everything.

Like finally understanding that your mother was selfish and immature. Thinking about it, Kevin realized she'd always been that way. He wondered why he'd never recognized it in quite those terms before. Lots of reasons: first, in Pakistan, they had all those servants. Mom could be with the kids pretty much when she good and felt like it. After that, back in Arizona, when Dad was in graduate school, she'd just drop them at Gran's house. Seemed reasonable enough at the time. Once they got to New Jersey, and then the divorce, Kevin had slipped into being the grown-up degree by degree, like the proverbial frog in a pot.

THIRTEEN

Will's technical specs were approved, and the field program was underway. He'd proposed comprehensive investigation practices—surface mapping (in undisturbed areas, where they still could), drilling boreholes (both vertical and angled), driving adits, and geophysical logging. He'd also asked for a fly-over of the site, the one budget item Borkan turned down.

Weeks went by, then months. Drillers mobilized. New cores were collected and logged. The geology, though not simple to deal with as a dam foundation, was not so hard to understand. Engineers were correct in thinking that most problems could be engineered around, but only if those problems were fully understood. That was Will's aim: intimate knowledge of Kaya-kale Dam's foundation.

All large-scale projects—dams, bridges, tunnels, power plants, even skyscrapers, projects with big footprints and deep foundations—were like huge puzzles. Piecing together a complete picture of the subsurface of the dam's foundation, an area of more than half a square mile and hundreds of feet deep, was no small task. It engaged Will fully, and some days it consumed him.

Most evenings, Paula asked how his day went. A frequent presence at the Ross home, Will was surprised that he didn't consider her an intrusion but rather liked it. She was certainly good for the kids. And maybe him too, though he didn't think much about it, aside from the occasions his hand brushed hers, and when Kevin asked about it on their way to Elazığ.

If he was tired, he might give her a one-word response; other times, excited about the work, he'd launch into a long technical explanation of what they'd done and what they'd learned.

"More mapping today," he said one night a few weeks in. "There are a lot more faults crisscrossing the dam site than were mapped before. We're naming them after you gals."

"Faults? Like the ones you told us about pushing Anatolia west like toothpaste out of a tube?"

"No. Those are plate-bounding faults. They're regional in scale. But any fracture or joint, where one side's moved relative to the other, is a fault. There are lots of sizes and orientations and senses of movement on faults. Some are still active, but more of them aren't, meaning they moved long ago in the geologic past. When faults move, it crushes rock up. We call those areas brecciated zones. Faulting, fracturing, and jointing make the rock weaker than it would be without it, and the rock strength properties are important to the dam design. That's why we're mapping all the faults in detail."

"And you're naming them after women?" Her voice went up with the question.

"And girls," he said. "We're naming them in *honor* of the gals in our lives. You two each have a fault now."

"That seems like more of an insult than an honor to me," Paula said.

"You're so sensitive. I forget that. I picked a vertical fault for you—straight up, like you are."

Paula pursed her lips but didn't say anything else.

∼

Just as Paula asked about his work, Will quizzed her on what she knew about Gus Browning's tenure at the dam site. Not much—she'd never met him, only his wife, who had stayed in Kayakale long enough to help Paula take over the schooling of the English-speaking children.

According to his wife, through Paula, Browning was ambitious and had been more than eager to climb up the management ladder and "stop getting his hands dirty" at the site. Will wondered how dirty those hands were, metaphorically, as Paula would say. If the investigation had been behind schedule or over budget or both, would Browning have faked records to look like the success he hoped it would be?

It might have worked at a site with a more forgiving foundation than Kayakale's. Since the initial study concluded (wrongly) that the geology was more uniform than it actually was, Browning must have thought (wrongly) he could get away with it.

All of this was supposition on Will's part, but it was a plausible explanation for what he'd observed in the data he inherited and why Browning was so damned defensive.

For the most part, Will was too busy getting his work done, completely and correctly, to spend much time thinking about it, but nagging thoughts about Browning surfaced now and again.

∽

As the autumn days cooled and shortened, Will rushed his team to finish drilling the new boreholes throughout the footprint of the dam. Many nights, he spread the borehole logs from that day out on the table after dinner and drew cross sections.

"What are you doing?" Paula asked one of those evenings, looking up from grading papers.

"Taking the data from each borehole, which are recorded on these logs, and correlating them from one to the next. Try this," he said. "Put your hands up in front of your eyes, palms out, close together, about an inch apart, and look through the narrow space between them, then turn and look again, and again, and again. Then from those four narrow views, describe what the whole room looks like. That's what doing a subsurface investigation is like. Those narrow snapshots are like the boreholes we drill, but sometimes we don't get a complete sample from every hole. The cross sections I'm working on are like the description of the room."

She did what he said, and one of her bright hazel eyes peeked through the space between her hands as she turned to get the different views of the room.

"That seems hard—getting the whole picture from just that," she said.

"It isn't easy, but it's always interesting. We locate the boreholes based on our best understanding of the geology at the surface, from the mapping," he continued, "which you didn't get from that exercise. Still, it's a big puzzle we put together, piece by piece by piece."

As more boreholes were completed, Will drafted cross section after cross section, both parallel and perpendicular to the dam's alignment. He extrapolated what he couldn't see from what he could, reading the story in the rocks and reading between the lines of the story into the voids of those same rocks.

And there were voids. Will knew that, of course. That's what shut construction down in the first place, but each time he thought he had a three-dimensional picture of the foundation, he found more, bigger, and deeper cavities. With each discovery came more questions, and he went back to Borkan for funds several times. The investigation needed to go to the next level, literally. The allocations always came, because every day the construction stood still cost more than the studies did.

The hydrothermal deposits revealed themselves as part of a vast network. Will presumed it started with the syenite porphyry intruded during the Miocene. The intrusion, and the subsequent hydrothermal activity, had formed the lead deposits that were mined several kilometers downstream of the dam site, near Kayakale village. The pinnacle of that hydrothermal network was the towering rock of Kayakale that he and Refik had hiked to on Will's first day in the field. The faults and fractures that cut across the site provided the pathways where the heated waters had flowed, dissolving the marble and sculpting the spaces that honeycombed the foundation.

He mapped and strength-tested the walls of the adits, then proposed additional drilling from the adits themselves, to explore deeper into the foundation. Will planned to have a winter's worth of data to compile, correlate, and interpret by the time snow fell.

FOURTEEN

Kevin settled into his seat on the Turkish Airlines DC-3, a plane he now knew all about, because Dad filled them in on its aviation history while they waited for the flight to be called. His father could talk about planes almost as much as he could talk about rocks.

They'd just boarded for the flight to Istanbul. Istanbul! Kevin had been reading about it. At one time, the city was called the Paris of the East, and the famous train, the Orient Express, connected it to the real Paris. The Ottoman sultans had ruled their empires from palaces all over the city. One of them, Topkapı Palace, was just steps away from where they were going to stay.

Before it was Istanbul, it was Constantinople, the capital of the Roman Empire for a thousand years. A thousand years! Before that, it was Byzantium. And before that—well, before that, it was just a fishing village. But people had been living on its shores since 1000 BC. Almost three thousand years ago!

Istanbul was where Europe and Asia met. Imagine a city that's on two continents. Paula said they would take a boat ride up the Bosphorus Strait, which connected the Sea of Marmara to the Black Sea and separated that narrow tip of Europe from Asia Minor. The famous Golden Horn was the long, curved, and therefore well-protected harbor on the west side of the Bosphorus. It was the port that made the city a center of trade and travel.

Kevin unzipped his backpack under the seat, checking again

that he had his camera. Paula sat across the aisle, twisted sideways trying to get his squirming sister belted into the window seat beside her. After she got Didi contained, she leaned forward and asked Rob and Timur to settle down. Kevin smiled at that. Paula had told Kevin about teaching her old dog the command "settle," and he'd been working with Buddy on it. It was what it sounded like, and from the looks of it, Buddy had a better handle on it than Rob and Timur did. They were busy being Rob and Timur, and the seat in front of Paula was bouncing against her knees. Kevin was happy for his single seat on the opposite side of the plane from them.

Paula looked over and grinned at him. "Excited?" she asked.

He nodded.

"Me too."

"Dad says you must be a little crazy. That you must like herding cats," Kevin said.

"He's right. I am a little crazy." Pointing to the book in his lap with the colorful Turkish carpet design on its cover, she said, "You have the guidebook."

"I'm trying to figure out what I want to see most. There's a lot."

"We'll be busy. It'll be. . . ."

Whatever she was saying got drowned out in a flood of sound filling the cabin when the engines started up.

Paula looked over Didi's shoulder out their window, and they both waved. Dad was still there, outside the chain-link fence around the Elazığ airport where they'd waved to him as they got on the plane. This seemed uncharacteristically sentimental of him, and Kevin thought it was nice. Dad did have his moments. And he was letting them all go to Istanbul for their school break. Kevin hoped he wouldn't be too busy at work to take care of Buddy, like he'd promised. He'd left his father with detailed instructions.

When the engines' tone deepened and the plane began to roll forward, Kevin watched out his window as they taxied toward the runway. They'd be in Istanbul in a few hours. Istanbul!

∿

Aromas washed over Kevin like a wave when he pushed one of the heavy wooden doors—twice his height, spanned with iron bands, and studded with nails the size of his fist—and entered Istanbul's spice bazaar. Its name, Mısır Çarşısı, pronounced *ma-sar char-sha-sa*, didn't exactly roll off the tongue, and he mentally stumbled over the words as he stepped into the hazy golden light. Inside, his senses were inundated with smells and colors and sounds, and he felt like he could taste the air swirling around him as the massive door closed behind him.

Nuts and beans rattled into bins. Cans and jars clinked against each other as they were stacked higher than Kevin would dare. Bakers placed cookies artfully, like edible mosaics. Candy sellers carefully built structures of their rolls of freshly made sweets that reminded Kevin of the Lincoln Logs he'd played with as a kid. The merchants seemed so casual, shaping their powders and pods into steep pyramids, and Kevin wondered how it didn't all cascade over the rims of the bins and boxes. Red, ocher, black, green, and even deep purple spices filled stall after stall. Some were labeled with just the price. Others, more helpful to Kevin, named the spices on small placards, like curry, sumac, paprika, and chile (or chili or chilly—the spelling varied from stall to stall). Some had the names displayed in Turkish and English, so now he knew that cumin was *kimyon*, oregano was *kekik*, anise was *anason*, and cinnamon was *tarçin*.

He never knew there were so many colors of pepper—white, green, red, and black. Mild, medium, and hot too. Then there was "Mother-In-Law Chilly," which the vendor said was extra hot, for unhappy brides to mix into their husband's mother's dinner.

Kevin wondered if his mother ever did that to Gran. Gran would tell Mom her pie crusts were tough, her fried chicken soggy, and her cookies burnt. If there was an American version of Mother-In-Law Chilly, Gran probably deserved a helping of it, even if her fried chicken was way better than Mom's.

Kevin wandered up and down the narrow aisles, the burnished ceiling arching high overhead. He ducked under braided strands of garlic bulbs and clusters of gold and red and burgundy peppers. Shoppers trickled into the market, and Kevin tested his Turkish trying to understand their transactions, but they all talked so fast, he could barely catch more than a word or two.

There were teas and more teas. Fruit teas, like apple and orange. Flowery teas, like lavender, rose, and jasmine. And teas with a purpose, like relax tea, slimming tea, and love tea. There was Turkish coffee, and he thought he should get some for Paula, a little gift for taking them all to Istanbul and for letting him go out on his own this morning.

He passed stalls of dried fruits of every kind. Apricots, of course, and strawberries, apples, dates, and figs. And exotic ones, like papaya and mango, in colorful, leathery slices. Even a fruit he'd never heard of, called pomelo, its slices a bright light green. There were bins of nuts of all kinds, shelled and not, and barrels of beans in shapes and sizes he'd never seen.

Kevin glanced at his watch and realized he'd lost track of time. He'd promised Paula he would be back by ten o'clock, and it was twenty after nine. The market was only a few minutes' walk from their hotel, but he wanted to buy a treat for the crew before he left.

He hurried up the aisles on his way toward the doors, which were now propped open with people streaming in. He was watching the time, while trying to decide what the crew would like, when he nearly passed a Turkish delight vendor. Everyone liked Turkish delight. He stopped short and considered the display with every color and shape of the candy there could be, from small cubes coated with powdered sugar to bricks with nuts embedded within the sweet chewiness. The sign read 20 TL (which he knew meant Turkish lira) for a kilo. Kevin had shopped a bit in Kayakale village, and he knew a kilo was a lot of candy. But a half kilo would be about right, and he could afford ten lira.

He approached the booth. "*Günaydın*," he said.

The merchant was the first plump Turk Kevin recalled seeing in the months since they'd arrived. The buttons on the man's blue-and-white striped shirt strained against their buttonholes. He had ruddy cheeks and a friendly smile beneath a thick mane of salt-and-pepper hair.

"*Merhaba! Bunu dene*," he said, picking up a piece of light pink candy and holding it out to Kevin. Try this.

Kevin popped it into his mouth and chewed. It was sweet and kind of flowery, tasting like roses smell, and he couldn't help wrinkling his nose. "*Bu ne?*" he asked. What is it?

"*Gül suyu*," the vendor said. Rosewater.

"*Afedersiniz, sevmiyorum*," Kevin said. I'm sorry, I don't like it.

"*Tamam*," the man replied. Okay. He swept his hand around the display, asking Kevin to choose.

He took a minute. "*Çilek severim*." I like strawberry.

"*Çok iyi*." Very good. He gave Kevin a brighter pink piece of the confection.

"*Lezzetli!*" Kevin said. Delicious!

The man smiled.

It *was* delicious, plus Kevin was pleased with himself because he'd only learned that word a few days before.

He bought 125 grams each of *çilek, antep fıstık, tarçin*, and *kahve* (strawberry, pistachio, cinnamon, and coffee) candies. The *kahve* was meant especially for Paula.

After he made his selections, while the man measured out his purchases, Kevin asked if he could take a picture of his stall, and him.

"*Evet, evet*," the vendor said and smiled wide for the camera.

By the time Kevin paid, he really needed to hurry.

I'm coming back tomorrow, he thought. *With color film.*

∼

Kevin liked the Bosphorus Family Hotel in Istanbul's old city. True to its name, they were in a suite with enough beds for the whole lot of them. Kevin found it old-fashioned, but with more personality than the fancy new hotel where they had stayed in Ankara back in July.

From the hotel, they could walk to the rambling and ornate Topkapı Palace, the Blue Mosque, Aya Sofya, the archaeology museum, the Grand Bazaar, the Süleymaniye Mosque overlooking the Golden Horn, and the spice bazaar that Kevin discovered on his first morning walk.

Istanbul's architecture was full of curves and layers, its scents swarmed from those of the salty Bosphorus to the overwhelming mix of the spice bazaar's, and its silhouettes transported Kevin's imagination to the time when the Ottomans ruled lands from the northern Adriatic Sea to the southern tip of the Red Sea.

Back from his walk on their second morning in the city, he opened the suite door to find Paula in the sitting room drinking Nescafé. None of the others were up and around.

"Where's Didi?" Kevin asked. She was usually awake and bothering everyone, first thing.

"I think we wore her out yesterday. I let her stay up with you guys last night, way later than her usual bedtime. Do you drink coffee?" she asked, holding up her cup.

"No, but I like the smell of it. I made it for Mom every morning when we stayed at the house."

"Want to try some?"

Kevin nodded.

"There's enough water." Paula pointed at the electric kettle on the counter. "Just plug it back in. Put a heaping spoonful of Nescafé in the cup. That was nice that you made coffee for your mom."

"Dad got a Mr. Coffee as soon as they came out. They both thought it was so neat. Mom kept it in the divorce. Dad had to get another one for his place."

"Mr. Coffee didn't go back and forth every two weeks?" Paula said, grinning.

"Ha ha." Kevin smirked.

"Divorce is hard on kids," Paula said.

"So is living with parents who fight all the time."

"Good point. What happened with them? Do you know? Or did they always fight like that?"

"I guess they really didn't fight so much. Mom did, and Dad didn't, and that made her even madder. But I remember them being happy when I was little. I'd sneak onto the stairs and watch their parties in Pakistan. They were always laughing and dancing together."

"I've heard you and your dad mention it before. Why were you in Pakistan?"

"Dad was working on the Indus Basin Project. It was really a bunch of projects—dams and big water well fields, stuff like that. I don't remember going over; I was two when we got there."

"So your first memories are from there?"

Kevin nodded. "We lived there six years. Then at Christmas, when I was eight, Dad told us we were moving back home, not coming back after the holidays. He quit his job to go to graduate school. I think that's when things got bad between them."

"Do you know why?"

"Mom loved the house in Lahore. We all did. Dad says that

she got too used to being treated like a princess, having servants and a cook, and an ayah for us. He said that in Pakistan she was a lady who lunched, and she didn't like it when she had to make lunches and clean up after them again. I remember her asking him, 'How many degrees does one person need?' Mom always talked about how much she loved high school. She was all excited for me to go last year. But the way she talked about it, it wasn't because of *school*, it was because of being a cheerleader and her boyfriend and being popular—stuff like that. I don't think she got why Dad wanted to go back to school again, after he'd been to college and had a job. And then when we moved to New Jersey, Dad said she should go to college. And she *really* got mad about that."

Kevin unplugged the kettle and poured the boiling water into his cup. He stirred it and swirled the spoon to make little designs in the gold foam on the coffee's surface. When he turned around with his cup in his hand, Paula was looking at him intently.

"It doesn't make sense to me, but Mom said that Dad thought she was stupid," he continued. "That she needed to go to college to get smart. But I think he thought she was smart enough to go to college. I guess he thought she liked doing what he did . . . like school. But I don't think they really liked to do *any* of the same things. Not by then, anyway."

Kevin sat on the edge of the chair across from Paula, who was leaning back on the couch, her legs crossed, her top foot bouncing up and down. He blew into the cup, then took a sip. He made a face. Coffee didn't taste as good as it smelled. He glanced up and saw Paula smiling at him.

"Bitter? The sugar bowl's on the counter," she said. "And there's milk in the little fridge. I bet you'll like it better if you add some of each. Then tell me all about where you went this morning."

His story finished, their cups drained, Kevin rose and took them to the sink.

As he reached for Paula's cup, she said, "*Bir kahvenin kırk yıl hatırı vardır.*"

He thought about that while rinsing the cups. "A cup of coffee will be remembered for forty years?" he asked over his shoulder. "Do you mean I'll always remember my first cup of coffee?"

"That's the literal translation, but it's a proverb. To share a cup of coffee—and they really mean Turkish coffee, not Nescafé, but we'll do that another day—means we'll share a forty-year friendship."

That was a long time, longer than Kevin could really imagine, but he hoped they would.

∾

Paula was surprised by each of the children in some way in Istanbul. Out of the shadow of their father's considerable expectations, they each shone in a different light than she'd seen them before—especially Rob.

She hardly recognized the sweet boy with the beaming smile who showed up on the trip. He and Timur were inseparable, seemingly delighted in everything they did, from fishing off the Galata Bridge, to making faces back at the masks in the archaeology museum, to pitching pistachios into each other's mouths. Each night, the whispering and laughing from their corner of the suite would wake her. She felt like the chaperone at a week-long pajama party.

One day, she remarked on how much fun they had together. Timur, who was also more animated than she'd seen before, smiled wide and his dark eyes glowed when he said, "Rob is like the brother I did not have."

"Timur too," Rob said, draping his arm across his friend's shoulder.

"You *have* a brother, goofball," Timur said, pointing at Kevin and laughing. "That's a good name for you. Thank you for teaching it to me."

"Oh, yeah," Rob said. "Sorry, Kev."

Kevin played along. "Timur's probably like the brother Rob *really* wanted."

They quipped back and forth like that all week. They even included Didi sometimes, which Paula thought was unusual, and nice, for boys their age.

As for Dee, who at home was always glancing at Will for attention and approval, she was downright mischievous in Istanbul. "Mischievous" was putting it mildly since her impromptu game of hide-and-seek left the rest of them scrambling to find her in the Kapalı Çarşı.

The Grand Bazaar spanned something like fifty city blocks in area and had *thousands* of shops, selling everything from clothes to carpets, foodstuffs to shoes, and linens, and toys, and curios galore. The place was overwhelming. One minute, Paula was measuring a pretty little embroidered vest against Didi's narrow shoulders, and the next, Didi was gone. All Paula did was turn to ask the vendor how much it was, and poof—it was like the child vanished into thin air.

They did find her. Well, Kevin did. Paula had seen him do this before—catch his sister from falling just as she tripped on the top step of their porch or grab her foot when it slipped off a boulder she was climbing on. That day, it seemed he had a sixth sense of the path she had taken through the sprawling market. He found her tucked behind a counter, peering through a kaleidoscope, in a shop several twists and turns from where she had started. Paula knew she should have punished Didi for running off, but she was so relieved to see her little hand firmly in Kevin's that Paula just hugged her hard.

"Don't ever do that again," Paula said into Didi's hair.

"What?" Dee asked.

"Run off!" Paula said, holding the child at arm's length.

"I didn't run off. I don't like clothes; I just wanted to find something funner."

"More fun," Paula said.

"Okay." Didi smiled up at her. "More fun."

Then Didi's brows had pulled together. "Are you mad at me, Paula? I didn't mean to make you mad."

"I'm not mad, sweetie. I was scared that you were lost."

"I was right here; that's not lost."

"Will you promise to stay with me or Kevin or Rob or Timur the rest of the trip? It would make me feel better. Then I won't be scared."

Didi leaned in and hugged Paula. "I'm sorry I scared you."

How could Paula be angry? But she did keep a closer eye on Didi the rest of the time in the city.

And then there was Kevin—dear, sensitive Kevin. They shared coffee and conversation before the others woke each morning. In his quiet, thoughtful way, he revealed his story to her, his take on the Ross family's travels and troubles. His trust was a gift Paula did not take for granted.

She had to admit, she was exhausted when the week ended, but she was also grateful for the chance to see the amazing Jewel of Turkey through the children's eyes.

FIFTEEN

Though Paula felt closer than ever to the children after the trip to Istanbul, not much had changed with Will. The relationship was much more a possibility than a reality. Sure, they talked, and his hand occasionally skimmed hers. Sometimes they exchanged a smile over the rim of a cup of Turkish coffee.

Then, one chilly night in November—the thirteenth, Paula remembered—after tucking Didi in, she returned to the kitchen to find the boys and Buddy gone to their room. Will sat alone at the table bent over a map, his shoulders drawn up. He looked tense. She slipped behind his chair and began rubbing his neck.

"Mmmm," he said after a few minutes. "Nice."

He leaned into her hands as she massaged his neck and shoulders. She slid her hands down the length of his arms. He rolled his neck from one side to the other. "Mmmm," he said again as she kneaded the knots from his muscles.

She inhaled his scent, like earth and well-worn leather. Then she brushed her lips across the soft skin below his left ear, and with that, he pushed his chair back and pulled her onto his lap. He reached his arms around her, and she took his face in her hands, let her fingertips play in his beard. He smiled, and his eyes smiled too. He pulled her hard against his chest, and they kissed. And kissed. More than three times. No need to count; she'd have kissed him all night. Their breath mingled, both of them tasting of basil from dinner, but somehow sweet too. Her body reacted like it hadn't in a very long time—she wanted him.

"The children," she whispered. "They'll hear."

"I know," he said, but he took her face in his field-rough hands, ran his fingers through her hair, and kissed her more deeply. He slid one of his hands down to her breasts, cupped one then the other.

She thought about her short hair, how small her breasts were. She'd seen a picture of Kat, with her flowing hair and hourglass figure. And as if he'd read her mind and wanted to assure her, he whispered, "So pretty."

His lips moved down Paula's neck and lingered in its hollow. Then his hand was under her shirt, in her bra, and he rolled her nipple between his thumb and finger. She moaned. She felt his erection against her leg and was so wet she wondered if he could feel it.

He exhaled. "We better stop," he said, but his fingers stayed and played.

"I know," she said. If his children weren't those few steps away, that night would have ended differently. But they were. Paula moved to the chair beside his, letting her hand glide across his lap when she did. She straightened her shirt. He took her hand and entwined his fingers in hers.

She took a quavering breath. Then a steadier one. "The others are making their plans for Christmas. Are you taking the kids home? Are they going to see their mom?"

"This is home now," he said. "And, no, I've got all this data to interpret, the report to write, and the presentation to get ready for corporate and DSI in Ankara in January. Besides, she won't be there. Her boy toy's taking her to the Caribbean for the holidays."

"Do they know?"

"We haven't talked about it yet. They don't know that their

mother said I could keep them for as long as I want, just so long as I keep sending the alimony *and* child support. She's letting me buy them from her. And I will too." He paused. "Are you going home for the holidays?"

"No."

"Do you have plans?"

"I was kind of waiting to hear what you were doing."

"Maybe I should take a few days off," he said. "Let's go somewhere with the kids. Where should we go?"

"You haven't been to Istanbul yet, right? But you'd want more than a few days; there's so much to see."

"And the kids have been there. Somewhere new for them. And closer."

"Cappadocia?"

"Isn't that near Erciyes? Do you ski?"

She nodded to both questions.

"I hear it's great skiing," he said.

"And Cappadocia is beautiful. It's different from anyplace I'd ever been before. I loved it. And the rocks are what make it so different."

"Maybe I'll go ahead and take a week. I'd have taken more than that if we were going stateside. And no nosy neighbors. We'll figure something out with rooms," he said, and squeezed her hand.

∽

November 25, 1973

Dear Mom,

Hope you had a happy Thanksgiving. Did you get our card in time? Did you like the pictures? Our teacher made us all dress up for them. I got to shoot, develop, and print them. There's only nine of us, so it wasn't that many, but still it was fun. The darkroom is all set up, and I've been developing all the rolls I shot since we got here. I'm printing the good pictures, and I'll put some in this letter. Didi can hold a handstand long enough to get a picture of it now, and Buddy can hold a sit long enough too. Even Rob and Timur let me take a shot of them.

I guess that's all that's going on here. Miss you, Mom.

Love, Kevin

Again, it wasn't "all that's going on here," but Kevin didn't think his mother would want to know that the turkey they had roasted on Thanksgiving was better than any he could remember her making. And that they'd made pies instead of buying them.

Sometimes he wondered how Mom was, but not every day. Lately, he only thought about her when he wrote his weekly letter, which Paula made them all do. And he didn't really worry about her, which kind of worried him. Shouldn't he?

In his letters, he told her he missed her, because he thought she'd want him to. Truthfully, he was relieved to be away from the shitstorms that had raged at Toll House Lane since his parents' split. He did hope she was happy doing whatever she was doing with whoever she was doing it with. He was trying to get that way himself. It was getting a little easier all the time.

SIXTEEN

A rooster tail of snow sparkled in the morning sun when Kevin skidded to a stop, laughing out loud with no one but himself. He loved skiing. It was like gravity let go of you and you flew. Flying or gliding or dancing—or how he imagined dancing would be if he could, which he thought he'd like to one day. His cheeks flamed red from the chill air, and snowflakes settled around him. He blinked them out of his eyelashes and squinted back up the slope at the curves he'd carved in the newly fallen snow.

Erciyes Dağı was a beautiful mountain, its ridges arced up to the summit, which was more than twelve thousand feet high. His father called it a classic stratovolcano, which accounted for its distinctive cone shape, but Kevin preferred to imagine the eruptions that built it and the snow that carved it as sculptors shaping the mountain into its graceful and enduring form.

Last night he'd read that Sinan, the renowned Ottoman architect who was born nearby in Kayseri, designed the enormous Süleymaniye Mosque in Istanbul to emulate the mountain he'd grown up in the shadow of. Is that why the mosque's silhouette had captivated Kevin? It was like a man-made mountain towering over the Golden Horn.

The four days of skiing went by too fast. If it were up to Kevin, they would have skied the whole week, floating down the slopes all day, falling into bed exhausted and happy every night. But it wasn't up to him.

They pulled into Uçhisar late. After finding the *pansiyon*, which meant "guest house" in Turkish, where his father had rented the whole second floor, they all had to pile back into the Land Cruiser and wait for half an hour while Dad and the innkeeper argued about Buddy. Dad finally agreed to pay extra, and the family, Buddy included, unloaded and went straight to bed. The place was huge, and they each had their own room. Good thing, because everyone was tired from skiing and driving, and cold and cranky from the enforced interval in the car.

One door after the other closed, slammed or softly, depending on whose door it was. Buddy let out a boof at each one.

"Shh, Buddy, shhhhhh. Hup," Kevin said, patting the bed, and Buddy jumped up, made three tight circles, and settled in beside him. "Turks don't get you, you know? They just don't get *pet*." Rubbing the dog's tummy, he murmured, "They don't know what they're missing."

Their breathing found a rhythm and they fell asleep, Buddy's snout on Kevin's thigh, Kevin's hand on Buddy's head.

∽

Paula pulled the door to Didi's room closed, and the latch clicked. They'd read together, like they did every night, until Dee fell asleep. It hadn't taken long, then Paula had draped the extra blanket from the foot of the bed over her and kissed her cheek.

Out in the hall, Paula hesitated. Go to her room and wait? Wonder? Hope?

She padded past her room, down to the end of the hall, her steps cushioned and quiet in her ski socks. She peered back over her shoulder, listened for any sounds from the children's rooms. None. She grasped the doorknob of Will's room, turned it slowly, and pushed the door inward. It squeaked! She stopped and looked up the hall again, tilted her head, only hearing the sound of her own breathing, her own heart thumping.

She leaned against the back of Will's door while her eyes adjusted to the darkened room. Then she smiled, almost laughing out loud at herself. Will was asleep, his breathing deep and even. She didn't need to be nervous that night. Propriety would have dictated that she take herself out the door, up the hall, and into her own room. But she wouldn't have been there—in that room, with that family, in her job, in Turkey—if being proper was her main motivation in life.

She unzipped her ski pants, slipped them to the floor, and left them in a pile. Pulling her sweater over her head, she tiptoed to the bed, lifted the covers and slid in beside Will, still in her socks and long johns. Paula snuggled up against him, and without waking, he shifted and wrapped his right arm around her shoulders. She nestled her head onto his chest and listened to his heartbeat.

∾

She woke to the roar of Will's snores. It was *really* loud. Lying there, not sleeping, she recalled hearing him snoring on some of the nights she'd spent in Didi's room. It hadn't occurred to her then how loud it would have to be to hear it two rooms away. There was no way she was getting back to sleep.

"Will," Paula whispered. "You're snoring."

Nothing.

"Will. Roll over. You're snoring."

Still nothing.

She sighed, flopped over, and put the pillow over her head. She could have sworn it just got louder. The bed seemed to vibrate with his shudders and snorts. Surely that couldn't be good for a person.

She flipped back, facing him, and reached over and gently rubbed his arm.

"Will," she said, not whispering this time, hoping to rouse

him enough so he'd roll over. She slid her hand back and forth on his arm, squeezing his hand, trying to wake him tenderly, but he just kept snoring. Later, she would find the spot on his right rib cage where a well-aimed elbow would get him turned over and quiet, but that was their first night together, and she hadn't figured it out yet. Besides, she did like caressing him. Paula leaned in and kissed Will's shoulder. She ran her hand along his arm, feeling the definition in his muscles, the strength of his forearm, the smoothness of the skin on the inside of his wrist, and its contrast to the rough skin of his hand. She kissed his neck and nipped his earlobe. And then his other hand covered hers and pushed it down. And she wasn't rubbing his arm anymore.

In a sleepy dance, he pulled her long johns top over her head. She slid her hand into his boxers. And somehow they were off and so were her bottoms. She held him and felt him swell in her hand. She swung her leg over, glided on top of him, and guided him inside her. He moaned. But Paula gasped; it had been a long time and it hurt. With Will inside her, she held still, letting her internal muscles relax. As the tension eased, they found their rhythm. He moaned again. Paula leaned down and kissed him. He kissed her back, and they rocked together in the dark, in the warm tangle of the blankets. And after a while, when they were done, he whispered, "Thank you" in her ear. Then they fell back to sleep, as if they'd made love in a dream.

Will wasn't much of a romantic, but he always said "thank you" in a husky whisper whenever they made love. Always. That was romantic enough for Paula.

But they would forever remember that first night with laughter.

"Rub my arm?" he would ask.

She would answer, "It *was* your arm."

And then he'd wink, and they would laugh.

∾

When Kevin opened his eyes, Buddy's nose was inches from his. The dog's tongue hung out of his wide dog grin, and Kevin grinned back at him. He rubbed Buddy's head. They both yawned.

"You have dog breath," he said. "Imagine that."

Kevin hopped out of bed. Arms folded across his chest, he shivered, standing in bare feet by the one window in the room. It overlooked a deep, narrow valley.

It was quiet in the *pansiyon*, except for the click of Buddy's nails on the tiles. Kevin assumed the others were still asleep, and he decided he and Buddy should go exploring before anyone else could even think about tagging along. He dressed quickly, pulling his jacket, hat, and gloves on as they headed for the door. He was careful to close the door quietly, then snapped Buddy's leash to his collar.

Outside, he took the steep steps, carved into the rock of the valley wall, slowly. They were icy.

"Buddy, heel," he commanded. Still a puppy, Buddy pulled on the lead in his exuberance to get anywhere they were going, until he was reminded to mind.

At the bottom of the steps, Kevin stopped and gazed up at the cone shapes of the queer rock formations colored white, gray, pink, and yellowy gold in the soft morning light. He reached around his back for his camera, then realized in his hurry he'd forgotten it, something he hardly ever did. He viewed the tableau with his photographer's eye but could take only mental pictures.

A small smile crept across his face, thinking about how Paula had gone on and on about the Göreme Valley the evening before on the drive from the ski hill. He could hear her singsong voice reading from the guidebook, "This valley is the heart of the Cappadocia region, which is known for its fanciful landforms, *peribaca*, which means 'fairy chimneys.'" Then, of course, Dad had to explain that the so-called chimneys weren't really chimneys at all, but had eroded out of the volcanic tuff, rock formed from ash spewed into the air when Erciyes and other nearby volcanoes erupted. Since ash wasn't very hard, neither was tuff, as rocks go, so people could carve houses out of it and even whole underground cities. They were going to go see one of those, named Kaymakli, tomorrow.

Kevin crunched through patches of snow where the winter sun hadn't reached, pausing to marvel at the myriad shapes sculpted by nature over millions of years. Maybe he'd bring the others here later. Or maybe not. Maybe he'd just keep it for himself and Buddy.

They ambled up to the base of a tower of tuff where ocher striations crisscrossed pure white rock, as if a painter had stroked a brush across it. The light moved over it as the sun rose, making the lines dance on the rock's surface. Transfixed by the colors in the shifting light, Kevin could see why his father loved being a geologist; knowing how it all happened didn't make it any less beautiful but maybe more so.

Buddy veered off the main path, his nose to the ground. The side trail led to an ancient house carved into the steep valley wall. Buddy sniffed around what would have been the front yard, while Kevin ducked through the tiny doorway and stepped inside. *The people who lived here must've been shorter than people now*, Kevin thought. Then he remembered he was already taller than most of the Turks he'd met, and he was still growing.

Enough light filtered in through three small square holes cut into the outer wall to show the roughness of the walls and ceiling. He ran his hands over them, feeling the divots and grooves, tool marks from the implements used to chip these spaces out of the rock. Niches were carved into the walls. They were stained with soot from holding the candles or oil lamps that Kevin imagined were used for lighting. There were two rooms on the ground level. The inner space, stained black on one whole side by cooking fires, would have been the kitchen. In the bigger room, which Kevin thought was a living room, there was a shaft in the ceiling leading to a second floor.

Standing on tiptoes, he could just get his hands flat on the floor above. He hoisted himself up in a pull-up and twisted onto his butt, sitting on the edge of the opening. There must have been a ladder to reach the second story, and he pictured a hand-made one of gnarled wood with animal-hide lashing, the rungs polished from all the comings and goings.

There were two rooms upstairs, and Kevin stooped under the even-lower ceiling of that level. *Bedrooms*, he thought. *The bigger one for the parents and the smaller one for the kids.* He settled in a corner of the smaller nook, leaned back against the stone wall, pulled his knees up, and hugged them to his chest. He tried to imagine what it would be like to live here. Crowded.

"Talk about not having any space to yourself," he said out loud and laughed, the sound reverberating.

Buddy barked. Kevin looked down through the hole to the ground floor where his dog was jumping and barking for him. "Okay," he said. "I'm coming, Bud. Let's go back and get some breakfast. I'm hungry. Are you?"

∾

Paula woke to the feel of Will's hands and lips on her body. She surfaced into wakefulness, appreciating the lines of his torso in the dim light. Her finger traced the ridge of muscle over his right hip bone.

He looked up at her touch. "You're awake," he said and kissed her, hard and long.

They made love, with an urgency to it this time—a need to feel each other. The night before, they were barely awake. That morning, their eyes were wide open. The blue of his seemed darker than usual, more liquid, like the ocean abyss, beautiful and mysterious. Paula stared into them as she came. Her legs quivered, her internal muscles gripped him, and it was all she could do not to cry out. She wrapped her legs around him, pulling him deeper, her body still humming. He entwined his fingers in hers and pushed them back onto the bed, seeming to open her up to him even more. Then he made a noise in his throat she couldn't quite describe. It was visceral—but quiet.

They would always be quiet lovers, as if there were always children just down the hall, even long after the kids were grown and out on their own.

They held each other's gaze. Then he blinked and smiled at her. He leaned down, kissed her neck, and murmured, "Thank you."

Paula untangled her fingers from his, reached her arms around his back, and drew him down, onto her chest. She wanted to feel his whole body against hers. She unwrapped her legs from his hips and slid them beneath him, holding his body inside hers. They lay like that for a long time, his lips moving on her neck. Their breathing slowed and fell into the same rhythm.

His lips stilled, and just when she began to wonder if he'd fallen asleep, he rolled to the side and propped himself up on his arm. With his other hand, he ran his finger along her jawline.

"*Günaydin, güzelim,*" he said. Good morning, beautiful.

And she felt beautiful. She craned her neck and kissed him.

"*Kahve?*" he asked. Coffee?

"*Evet, lütfen,*" she said. Yes, please.

He swept his hand down her body, then climbed out of bed. Her eyes wandered over his body while he stretched. He turned to sort through his bag.

"Should I be worried?" he asked.

"Worried?"

"I've already got three kids," he said, taking a pair of sweatpants out of his duffel.

"Oh. No. I only plan to have kids if I *plan* to have kids. I'm on the pill."

He stood, regarding her. "I've never been with a gal who took care of things herself."

"Woman," she said. "Really? Did you miss the sixties? Civil rights! Free love! Women's liberation!"

"Sort of," he said. "We were in Pakistan, in a big house with a cook, a housekeeper, and an ayah. I worked, and Kat was a lady of leisure. She was liberated from housework, if that counts. Never forgave me for taking her away from all that to go to grad school. So I guess I did miss the sixties. But hey, I'll show you what a liberated guy I am. I'll go make your coffee, baby."

He pulled his sweatshirt over his head while he crossed the room back to the bed. He bent down to kiss her and lingered when she put her hand on his cheek. Again, he held her gaze. Paula loved that about him, even if he did have quite a way to go in the liberation department. Always looking her in the eye counted for a lot in her book.

Paula would savor that time, because that night, that morning, that week, was the most she'd get of him for quite a while. After that trip, for Will, it was work, work, and more work.

PART III

SEVENTEEN

Will stood at the back of the room, his hands jammed into the pockets of the dove gray suit Paula had given him the week before for this all-important meeting. His right foot tapped, and he fingered the knot of his new tie, also a gift from Paula. For the third time in as many minutes, he paced over to the slide projector to check that the carousel was seated properly. The evidence that he and Erdem Borkan were about to present for sweeping changes to Kayakale Dam filled the slides in the carefully loaded, checked, and rechecked carousel.

Will made another trip to the lectern, assured himself the clicker was secured there with its cord run along the far wall so as not to be tripped over and pulled out. A pointer was propped behind the podium, and an extra, the extendable metal kind about the size of pen, was in his suit jacket pocket, just in case.

Reaching inside the lapel of his jacket, his finger probed his shirt pocket, that old nervous habit of searching for a smoke. No pack of cigarettes was tucked there; instead, he felt the index cards outlining his part of the presentation. That was a comfort, though the likelihood Will would need those cues was slim. He knew the material inside and out, forward and back.

But where was everyone? Everyone important, that is—the young men milling around, talking in small groups, were not project managers from either Ankara or New York, and they certainly weren't the money guys. Will glanced at his watch.

Moments later, right on time at nine o'clock, the door

swung open and Borkan entered. Formal as always, he swept his hand, ushering those behind him in. "Gentlemen," he said.

Gus Browning stepped in, followed by Mehmet Alkumru from DSI, then three others who Will assumed were DSI engineers and managers. Next came John Heatley and Joe Gallimore from DECCO New York. The collective of financiers, as far as Will could tell from their slick suits and slicker hair, followed.

Will was the first technical speaker. He would lay the groundwork for the rest of the presentation since he was addressing the dam's foundation. He strode to the podium after the welcoming statements and intros from DSI and DECCO.

"Lights," he said and cleared his throat. "First slide, please."

Will's edginess eased as soon as the image flashed onto the screen. The waiting was over. Each photo and figure were cue cards for what needed to be said. He'd taken every shot and drawn every map, cross section, and schematic.

The picture of the foundation that Will drew was truer than they'd ever seen, and it wasn't pretty—riddled with voids, two of them massive (nicknamed Moby and Babe for the legendary behemoths and their respective shapes, though Will didn't mention that in the presentation, as befitted its formality), and crisscrossed by faults and fractures (named for the women in the lives of the site team, also not mentioned specifically). Some scored the near subsurface, and others plunged deep into the foundation. Many of them intersected the mapped voids, providing conduits for the groundwater that had dissolved the marble, creating the cavities.

Given the realities, finally clearly defined, building this dam would cost more than twice what had been estimated when the project was proposed. The foundation preparation would be deeper and more extensive, including excavation and over-excavation in brecciated zones, rock cleaning, emplacement of "dental" concrete, cutting and backfilling of now deeper cut-off trenches, and, of course, grouting. The dam's alignment would shift upstream to skirt the biggest part (the "body") of the Moby void that in the current alignment was directly under the dam's centerline where it keyed into the left abutment. In addition, the entire design would change from a rock-fill dam to a concrete gravity dam, making the structure's footprint smaller, limiting, to the extent possible, the huge problem the foundation treatment had become and the massive undertaking it remained. The boots on the ground—Will, Borkan, and their team of engineers at the site—agreed that these changes had to be instituted for Kayakale Dam to be safe and viable.

Returning to his seat after handing the presentation over to Borkan, Will saw that Heatley and Gallimore looked stoic, while Browning scowled. They'd been briefed beforehand, but this was new information for the others. They all wore expressions of concern, their brows furrowed, mouths tight-lipped or frowning. But how could it be a surprise to them that the dam was in trouble? Construction had been shut down for months. Pretty big clue.

At the end of Borkan's talk, the room fell silent. The only sound was the quiet crackling of the fluorescent lights flickering on. The interval seemed interminable, but it was probably on the order of a minute at most.

"Mr. Ross, please join me at the podium to take questions from our esteemed company," Borkan said.

Will advanced to the front of the room and took his place beside Borkan. He rested his left hand on the lectern and slid his right into his pants pocket, trying to appear more casual than he felt.

Questions were asked, but not many, and not the one that seemed most obvious to Will—why hadn't the foundation conditions been properly studied and understood before the start of construction? Perhaps the men in the room already knew the answer—they were the ones who hadn't allocated adequate funds to investigate the site thoroughly in the first place. The cliché that there was never enough money to do things right the first time, but always enough to do them over, rang true. Or was it never enough time? Both, maybe. Time was money. Yet another cliché.

He was relieved that no one pointed out the glaring inconsistencies between what was just presented and the previous site investigation reports. Perhaps Gus Browning was the only one in the room, besides Borkan and Will, who was well versed enough in those reports to know. And Browning certainly wouldn't be inclined to draw attention to his own incompetence. Will didn't believe it made a difference, not now, given the additional work they'd done, the questions they'd answered.

Over the months of Will's tenure at Kayakale, he and Borkan spent hours in intense discussion, starting just days after Will's arrival and up to the week before this presentation. During those exchanges, they had come to know and respect each other professionally and to like each other personally. Why else would Erdem have opened up about his deep roots in Kayakale? Upon meeting him, Will had assumed the dapper engineer was a city boy, based on how he dressed and spoke. So much for judging a book by its cover. Erdem and his wife, Lale, had grown up in the nearby village. Their mothers, both widows, still lived there. So did almost all their siblings and their many cousins.

He and Lale had missed Kayakale during their years away, and they'd jumped at the chance to come back. They were happy to be raising Timur in the valley, surrounded by loving family. In response to Erdem's confidences, Will had divulged some of his own background—why he'd longed to get away as a teen, sought adventures around the world as he grew up, and why he thought giving the same to his children was beneficial. The key difference in their stories lay in an adjective. Erdem could speak of his *loving* family. But their respective journeys had landed them in the same place, with the same mission—to build a monumental dam, well and safely, in the shadow of the beautiful rock tower, Kayakale.

After all their talks, both Will and Erdem stipulated that, although the mistakes made had hindered understanding of the dam site conditions, the level of exploration previously completed, correctly or not, simply wasn't sufficient. That was the real problem. Together, they decided not to blow the whistle about the errors, in order to get the project moving again and to keep DECCO, and admittedly themselves, on the job.

Will worried that he was complicit in the deception, if not the incompetence. But he and Borkan were in agreement that keeping silent was in the best interest of the dam and of the progress it would bring to Kayakale, and to Turkey in general. The necessary data had now been collected, the errors corrected. And no one said a word about it—not in the Q&A, not at the lunch that followed, and not as they were all taking their leave, back to New York, to Istanbul, some staying in Ankara, and Will and Borkan back to Kayakale.

Weeks passed. Will finished the final field investigation report and started drafting specs for continuing the geological study of the foundation and monitoring conditions during construction in anticipation of its resumption, though they hadn't gotten word when that would happen.

"What's taking so long?" Will asked. "Don't they want to get the construction going again? Why haven't they come back with questions if they aren't sure of things?"

"The report is with the panel of reviewers; that is all they tell me," Borkan said.

"Panel of reviewers," Will mumbled. He walked slowly back to his desk, as there was no rush, but Will hated the waiting.

EIGHTEEN

Kevin and Buddy were out on walkabout one Saturday morning in late February; between school and the short winter days, their wanderings were restricted to weekends. The family had come to expect that Kevin would finish breakfast, make sandwiches for himself and Buddy, and head out the door in anything short of a blinding blizzard. It all worked since his father was in the office most days, Rob and Timur did whatever it was Rob and Timur do, and Didi seemed happy tagging along with Paula, who seemed happy to have her tagging along. Kevin wasn't missed.

The day was cold and crisp, the first time the sun shone after several gray, gloomy days. Kevin smiled as he strode along, and Buddy pranced.

They took a break at Kevin's rock, the one where he'd spent his first night in Kayakale, where he'd found Buddy. Kevin couldn't count the number of pictures he'd taken of Buddy at that spot—sitting alert, curled up and snoozing, or even perched on the rock posed like Rin Tin Tin. Kevin was also dabbling in sketching portraits of his pup. He liked the fine pencil work, the sharp detail and contrasting softness.

But today was for stretching their legs and breathing in the clear, fresh air. As they trotted up hills and down valleys one after another, Kevin had a feeling wash over him that he had not felt in a long time, and it stopped him in his tracks. Buddy ran back to him, wagging his whole body.

"Are you happy, Bud?" he asked. "I am."

Kevin lifted his face and let himself soak in the sun and the feeling of contentment. Life didn't have to be exciting to be good. He wondered if his parents would ever get that. They both chased thrills, each in their own ways, but they never seemed satisfied.

He squatted and looked deep into Buddy's brown eyes. He stroked his beautiful dog's head. "You get it, don't you?"

A sloppy, wet kiss was the answer, and Kevin laughed out loud.

They went on.

At the top of a steep rise, Kevin stopped to catch his breath, scanning the valley below. Downslope, there was a flat spot with four tents arranged in a perfect square. He squinted to see it better. "I wonder what that is?" he said and started toward it.

On each side of the valley, there were two big steps in the slope, and he remembered that Paula called them terraces. People took what the natural landscape gave them, stream terraces in this case, and enhanced them. They built their villages on them and farmed them. Located above the streams, they were safe from flooding, but still close to the water they needed. Pretty smart.

"C'mon, Buddy," Kevin said. "Let's go check it out."

They weren't tents after all; they were four big canvas tarps. Pulled low and tight, stout ropes secured the tarps to stakes hammered into the ground. Kevin slid his camera strap across his shoulder and around his back, got down on his hands and knees, and peeked under the edge of a tarp.

"Neat," he said. "Ruins!"

He crawled around trying to get a better look. He could just see the outside of a wall, but it was out of reach when he extended his arm as far as he could. It looked like the remains of a wall, now two to three stone blocks high. The blocks themselves were roughly a foot square and nestled neatly into each other. Kevin wondered if they had taken natural rocks and fit them together like a puzzle or if they'd cut them that way and placed them artfully, like an oversized vertical mosaic. He scooched lower to see better.

What would it feel like to find an archaeological site? How cool would it be if he and Buddy crested a ridge and looked down at an undiscovered ruin? Or even to unearth a new treasure at a dig that was already in progress, like this one.

And then, without another thought, Kevin untied the knot in the rope and lifted the tarp.

∾

February 24, 1974

Dear Mom,

Buddy and I found a ruin when we were out hiking yesterday. It's partly excavated, so I guess some archaeologists started working on it already. There are a bunch of teams that come and go, but they're all away for their winter break now. They call this salvage archaeology, because after the dam's done, these sites will be flooded, which makes me kind of sad. But Dad says you can't stand in the way of progress. He says they wouldn't even be studying them if they weren't going to be inundated by the reservoir. That's what they call it. Inundation, not flooding. They make a big deal of it like there's a difference, but it seems like the same thing to me.

I think this ruin was a whole village, even if it is just four houses. It's a lot smaller than the dig we saw on a school field trip last fall. That was called Aşvan and it was a city in Altınvadi, which means "golden valley" in Turkish. The archaeologists think a lot of people lived in the valley from about 3000 to 2000 BC.

They figure out those dates two ways. One is doing something called quantitative age dating that uses radio-active elements to calculate how old something is. The second way is by analyzing the pottery they find. From one age to another, there are different pot shapes and colors, and they're decorated differently. Archaeologists can tell the age of a layer in a dig from the pots, or even really small shards.

I guess this is a longer letter than I usually write. I got kind of excited about finding that ruin. I think it's pretty neat. That's what's going on here. Hope every-thing is good there. We're all fine. Miss you.

Love, Kevin

NINETEEN

Will arrived at the office on a morning in early March to find the whole place buzzing with the news that the panel of reviewers had rendered their verdict, and DSI and the investors had adopted the panel's recommendations verbatim. Two of the three proposed design changes were accepted as presented by Will and Borkan—the expanded foundation treatment and the dam realignment. But the third, the change in the dam's overall design, was only partially approved. The change to a concrete gravity dam structure over the area of the Moby void was approved, but the remainder of the dam would be completed as the initially proposed rock-fill dam.

Erdem Borkan finished reading the letter to the site team, who had assembled in the main room of the engineering office. Uneasiness rippled like a wave over the men sitting at their desks, standing at their drafting tables, and leaning against the walls. Will could see it in the way they moved, or didn't, but only he spoke up. "Wait a minute. Am I understanding this correctly? It's going to be a rock-fill dam *and* a concrete gravity dam?"

"Yes," said Borkan. "That is what this says."

"There is a precedent for that," Will said. "Folsom Dam in California, for one. It was built in the fifties, but it's a whole lot smaller than Kayakale Dam's going to be."

Borkan looked around at the younger men in the room. "You're recently out of school; did any of you study examples of . . . hmm . . . what's the word?"

"Hybrid?" Will said.

"Yes, hybrid. Hybrid dams? Anyone?"

The engineers exchanged glances but remained silent.

"We have our work cut out for us," Borkan said. "I will call Ankara to find out when construction is to begin again. While we wait for that answer, we have research to do, no?"

Rapid-fire, Borkan made assignments. This was a quality Will had not observed in his colleague before. Erdem Borkan was nothing if not deliberate in his words and actions. But Will had come to trust him and respect his decisions over the months they'd worked together. Maybe Borkan had been considering who would do what going forward for some time. Hard to say. Despite their friendship, he wasn't the most forthcoming man. That was also a quality Will appreciated, as he could play a hand close to his chest as well.

Will and Refik, who was a geotechnical engineer, would continue to work together in the office and field to determine the subsurface issues, specifically for the tie-in of the cut-off trenches beneath the two sections of Kayakale's now-hybrid dam.

When he'd given everyone an assignment, Borkan swiveled on his heel, walked into his office, and closed the door behind him.

The men around Will were settling in to work. And he would too, but he needed to talk to Borkan first. He tapped on his colleague's office door. Borkan unbuttoned his suit jacket and sank into his desk chair as Will stepped in.

"Erdem," he said, "we've already got a foundation that leaks like a sieve, and now we're going to add a joint between two kinds of dams?"

Borkan looked up and sighed. "Yes, apparently we are."

Will placed his hands on the desk and leaned in to make his point. "We need to push back, make them reconsider the gravity dam. The whole thing."

"No, Will," he said. "What is it you say . . . we have to pick our battles? We won two of them. We'll make this work. We'll just have to make sure the joint doesn't leak. We're good engineers. And a good geologist," he added.

"You don't think they'd listen."

"No."

"To do it right, it might cost just as much as making the entire dam a gravity dam."

"It might, but they will pay, as that is what they ordered to be done."

"You think so?"

"Yes," Borkan said. "If they complain about the budget, be assured I will remind them that this was their choice. I want this dam to be safe more than anyone. Don't forget—my mother, most of my family, and Lale's family live in the village. I love this valley. And I will protect it."

Will looked at Borkan for a long moment. His colleague's gaze did not waver. Then Will straightened and backed up a step. "Okay," he said. "I don't like it, but I understand."

Closing Borkan's door behind him, he headed for his office.

"Refik," he called to his assistant, "come on, let's get to work."

∽

News of the start date for construction came two days later. They had a few short weeks to complete the new designs, develop round-the-clock construction schedules, and begin staffing up.

After making the announcement to the assembled staff, Borkan followed Will into his office and closed the door behind him.

"Is there something else?" Will asked.

"There is," Borkan said. He reached into the inner pocket of his suit jacket and drew out an envelope. "The letter of appreciation was written to all of us. Isn't there a saying, 'time is money'? It seems that is so. Corporate is very pleased that construction is resuming."

Borkan extended the envelope to Will.

Will read the letter, then his arm dropped to his side and his head snapped up. He stared at his colleague.

"You, me, *and* Browning? *Browning?*" he said. "For Chrissake, the VP of operations thinks Browning *helped?*"

"Yes. We succeeded in appearing as a united front, as we had hoped. The bonus is generous. Take a look."

Will did, shuffling the back page forward. Again, he looked up and stared.

"We made a choice for the good of the project," Borkan said.

"And Browning gets rewarded for our efforts."

"Yes. Along with us, he does."

"For Chrissake," Will said again, shaking his head.

Erdem gestured toward the check Will had set on the desk. "I hope you find some good in that." He turned to go.

"It's a chunk of change. I'll try," Will said. "Close the door, please. I think I need a minute."

Will sank into his desk chair and contemplated the check. After glaring at it a few more moments, a smile crept across his face. *That looks a lot like a plane to me*, he thought. He'd been grounded far too long.

TWENTY

Paula grew closer to Kevin and Didi through the winter. To Rob, not so much, since he spent all his free time with Timur.

If Will was home during daylight hours, it was only on the weekends. Kevin was never home during daylight hours on the weekends, as he and Buddy habitually wandered off on their own whenever Kevin wasn't in school or doing homework. Paula thought Kevin and Will might be getting on better, but she had to acknowledge that might be because they didn't share the same space much.

As far as getting on better, neither Will nor Rob made much pretense of it. Will, perhaps, didn't realize it, but if Paula could feel his indifference to his younger son, she was sure Rob could too.

Paula tried to encourage Rob not to please his father, necessarily, but to find what he loved to do himself—in school, that is. Not that baseball wasn't a worthy pursuit, but she also hoped for something more for him. Paula had seen too many boys in West Virginia think that sports would be their ticket—out of West Virginia, out of poverty, and into fortune and fame—only to find themselves down in the mines or doing shift work in the chemical plants when they woke up from their high school, or even college, dreams. Rob was bright enough, but she couldn't seem to find any subject that piqued his curiosity for long. He just got by in class, when she knew he could excel. But he and

Timur seemed happy enough with the spring training regimen they'd devised; there was no shortage of passion on that front.

Didi craved Will's time and attention, something he didn't notice and didn't seem to take much account of when Paula mentioned it. She got Paula instead and never complained. But Paula saw the look in the little girl's eyes gazing at her dad across the dinner table or up from her pillow on the rare nights Paula got him to read to her at bedtime.

Paula was surprised to find that she was not yearning for Will's attention herself. She had to admit she was in love, but she was also scared. The last time she'd been in love, it had not turned out well. Not for her, anyway. Will's lack of availability left her safely within her comfort zone. Paula got the affection she wanted without feeling pushed further than she wanted to go.

∾

Kevin spent every day he could at his dig, as he'd come to think of it. He didn't disturb it. He pulled the tarps back with care. He put Buddy in a down-stay, so the dog wouldn't romp into the ruin. He took pictures.

He loved the way the stones in the walls fit together perfectly. He sketched them, making abstract art of the architecture.

The blocks were cut from the same stone that had occupied so much of his father's attention the last six months. Medium gray, no fossils that Kevin could see, and not very distinguished in any particular way to his aesthetic, except that it seemed to attract several types of lichen. Patchy white, flakey black, freckles of burnt orange that favored tiny nooks weathered into the rock, and splashes of chartreuse, all akin to a Jackson Pollock painting.

Each time Kevin picked up an artifact, he scrupulously placed it back in the same position he'd found it. His fingers traced the curves of pot shards. He held a bit of handle, possibly from an amphora. He imagined the hands that dug and shaped the clay, and the grains or seeds or oils the vessels might have held. He wondered what life was like for a teenager like him in that village.

When shadows lengthened in the afternoons, and Buddy got antsy for his dinner, Kevin tightened the tarps down and retied the knots that secured them.

At dinner, he asked his father how all the work was going in and around the dam site. Were the digs going to be done before the reservoir started filling up? He inquired about when the archaeologists were coming back. He made it seem like casual conversation, but he really wanted to know how long the site would be his to explore.

∾

Kevin felt like Paula was reading his mind when she started a unit on the history of the cities in the Golden Valley.

"We got to see Aşvan last fall, but with the rush of the holidays, we never really got to talk about it, or the rise and fall of that culture. Plus, it'll give us a chance to go over the history of what's right here in our backyard with our new arrivals."

Paula smiled out at all of them, but her gaze rested a moment longer on each of the kids who had just gotten to Kayakale. Their fathers were new hires at the dam site, part of the gearing up for construction to restart. Last August, there were only nine students in the schoolhouse, including the Rosses. They hadn't even filled up the first two rows of desks. The new kids were all around Didi's age, and along with his sister, they now filled the entire first row.

His father mentioned that there might be even more soon. Four geologists were going to join his team, and they might have children. Kevin was the only one in high school, and he wondered if there would be any new kids his age. He was pretty happy with the way things were, but it might be nice to have a friend or two, aside from Buddy, who would always be his best friend.

Kevin's attention turned back to Paula as she explained that Aşvan was the central city in the Altınvadi region. It was surrounded by smaller towns and even smaller villages. The towns and villages were located to supply the population center of Aşvan with the food and raw materials it needed.

This was how she taught kids with such a wide range of ages. She presented an overview of the lesson at a level even the younger kids could understand. Then she gave separate assignments to each grade level. So the littles (as Kevin thought of them) might color in a picture of what she'd just talked about or spell out some of the words, while the older kids read more, then wrote an essay.

That day, she talked about how economies and cultures developed. Archaeologists knew that there was habitation in the region at various times—in the Stone and Chalcolithic Ages and then later, even up to the Ottoman Empire—but the area so near Kayakale, where not many people lived now, fairly bustled four to five thousand years ago.

Kevin raised his hand. "Why those years?" he asked.

"Good question," Paula said. "The people in the mountain villages were supplying ore for the metallurgic industry, which was really taking off. It was the Bronze Age, and bronze is an alloy made mostly of copper and some tin. And lots of wood was needed for the smelters, and it was also floated way downstream for building the castles of Sumer."

"Wood?" Kevin asked. "But there're hardly any trees."

"Precisely," she said. "This landscape was deforested in about a thousand years. It ended up with no wood to fire the smelters or to send to Sumer, and the massive cutting of trees made the soil less stable. With no roots to hold it in place, the soil sluiced away with the mountain meltwaters and heavy spring rains. The Euphrates was laden with silt. The economy struggled, and the culture, which was fueled by the economy, began to suffer, so this pocket of civilization died out."

One of the new little girls blurted out, "Everybody died?"

"Remember to raise your hand please, Terry. No, something dying out doesn't mean that everybody died. I'm sorry. I should've been more clear," Paula said.

She explained that *can* happen, like where a volcano erupts and buries a town in lava or ash, or a flood wipes out a settlement or even a whole valley. She said that was why people like their parents were so important—they would explain where hazards were, so populations and cities could be prepared and protected.

Did any of the other kids in the room make the connections Kevin did with what Paula said? A flood, like the one that was going to happen in the valley behind Kayakale Dam, could kill a way of life.

He also noticed that Paula said, "your parents," not just "fathers," and he smiled at that. It *was* their fathers, at least it was for all the kids in this room, but Paula was a women's libber (that's what Dad said), and Kevin thought that was cool. Why shouldn't Didi grow up to be whatever she wanted, just like he and Rob could?

Paula went on to say that the ancient people moved away when they didn't have work to do anymore. They'd have moved to where there was work. Farmers whose land wasn't washed away may have stayed if they were content with just feeding their own families. Others might have moved to where they could feed their families and also sell their surpluses to make more money. So they built an economy and culture somewhere else. There were settlements of all different ages all over Anatolia.

"Does that make sense?" she asked.

The little girl, Terry, nodded, along with most of the others. Then Terry raised her hand, and when Paula called on her, she said, "I'm glad they didn't all die."

∽

On a Friday afternoon at the end of March, Kevin felt a tap on his shoulder as everyone rushed out of the schoolhouse for the weekend. He turned to see Paula behind him.

"Wait a minute, Kev," she said. "I want to ask you something."

He hung back from the others.

"Seems like you're really interested in archaeology these days. The archaeology here especially."

Did she know? Was he going to get in trouble for hanging around his dig?

"Is that right?" she asked.

He yanked up on his pants, tried not to fidget, but didn't succeed. "I'm interested. Not, like, especially though."

"Oh, well, I was going to ask if you wanted to help out with one of the archaeological teams when they get back next week. I thought I'd ask if you could intern with them. But only if you're interested. We'd make it part of your schoolwork. You could write one paper on what you learn about archaeological practices and another on the site. There's enough time before school lets out, and I bet they could use the help. You're a quick study, plus you're strong. Those big sieves must get heavy, don't you think?"

"I guess so," he said. "I mean, yes, that would be really neat."

"Okay, then. I'll ask them when they get back."

"Thanks, Paula."

She patted his back and smiled. "You're welcome. Let's go," she said and headed for the door.

"You really care, don't you?" he asked. It just came out, without him thinking about it. He realized it must have sounded stupid and looked down at his shoes.

"I do. I care about you. I care about all my students."

"If I was a teacher, I'd want to be like you," he said.

She put her arm around his shoulder and squeezed. "Thank you, Kev. I really appreciate that."

They walked out of the schoolhouse together, and she even knew to let go of him before anyone saw the teacher hugging him.

TWENTY-ONE

W ill didn't want any surprises like those that had gotten him this job in the first place, so the specs he wrote for mapping and inspecting the foundation excavation were detailed. The ranks of engineers tripled and geologists quintupled. Of course, Will had been the only geologist before. He'd convinced at least some of the team members, ones with hiring authority, that geologists were necessary for the project to succeed.

Right on schedule, the equipment for rock cleaning and emplacement of the dental concrete, the curtain grouting, and cutting and constructing of the key trench lumbered down the road into Kayakale Dam's foundation excavation. Some of the work would be done with hand tools, some by behemoths, even by heavy-equipment standards.

Dormitories filled with laborers. The dining hall fed crews around the clock. One program would roll out, and they'd push to start another right behind it. They could barely train new staff before the next wave arrived.

Will and his team mapped joints, fractures, and faults, from less than a centimeter in width on up. They monitored the volume of grout that went down every hole. They recorded every pressure reading as the grout pumped. Where there was rock, they checked how tight it was. Where there were voids, they filled them. And where there were cavities or cracks infilled with clay, they cleaned them out, then filled them too. They did it from the surface down and outward from the network of tunnels beneath it. The frayed fabric of Kayakale Dam's foundation was being stitched up as tight as it could be.

The technical staff scrambled to stay ahead of the construction crews. A mix of Turks and Americans and Brits—old hands and young pups, engineers and geologists—were united by the enormity of their task. Shifts were twelve hours but always seemed to go longer by the time they'd handed work off to the next crew and caught up on record-keeping. Will took considerable pains to see that the team's field notes and data sheets were complete. That data would tell them if the foundation treatment was working. It would tell them if the dam would be safe and if it would perform up to the design specifications.

Work proceeded twenty-four seven. Will's team traded day and night shifts every other week, and he managed the schedule so that everyone had one day off a week. On his day off, Will most often worked on planning the next week's program. There was little time for anything else, though he did have some feelers out to find a plane. And Paula pushed him to glance at the kids' homework or look in on them in their beds as they slept, being the good mama bear that she was to his cubs. She also insisted he have dinner with the family at least once a week, and he made it work. He'd largely handed his children over to her to manage, and it didn't seem right to deny her that.

Busy, yes, but he loved it. Will felt sharp and focused, compared to the flatness he'd felt those last years at the Philadelphia Port. What he was doing mattered. As spring approached and the landscape around Kayakale began to bloom, Will felt like he too was coming back to life.

❧

Will squinted at the papers spread out across the kitchen table. He looked up, surprised to see it was dusk. Seemed like he'd just sat down to work, but that was right after lunch. It was his day off, so he'd decided to work at home.

Paula crossed the room and stole a quick kiss. "I need you to clear the table," she said. "Chicken and dumplings tonight. They're ready. I'm going to fetch the kids."

He stood and stretched and smiled at her. He walked to the one window in the room and closed the curtain, which she, of course, had made for it. He was aware at that moment of just how grateful he was for her. He pulled her into a hug.

"Chicken and dumplings, eh? The smell's been making my mouth water all afternoon."

"Felt like making something homey today," she said.

"You always make it homey around here." He slid his hands down to her waist and extended his arms. He studied her, and she held his gaze in return.

"You should move in," Will said.

Paula stared at him.

"You should move in," he repeated.

"I should?"

"Yes."

"And what would the neighbors say about that?"

"I don't know and I don't care."

"Shouldn't we? Care? Didn't you just close the curtains so they wouldn't see you hugging me?"

"I closed the curtains so we could hug in private, not because I care what they think," he said and kissed her neck.

"I don't want to lose my job. Or jeopardize yours."

"The neighbors didn't hire us. Besides, they need us too badly. How many more students do you have than when we got here?"

"Eighteen."

"They need those guys, and their children need a teacher. And they sure as hell need a chief foundation geologist right now. But that's not what we should be talking about."

"No?"

"No." He took a deep breath. "We should be talking about how you've changed my mind about family. And about women. See, I even know to call you a woman, not a 'gal.' How's that? We should be talking about how smart and good and kind you are. We should be talking about that I love you. And I want you here. With me and my children. Will you move in?" He reached up and stroked her cheek. "Please?"

Her eyelashes glistened with tears. He leaned in and kissed her.

"You're very sensitive," he said, as he always did when something moved her.

"I am. And I like it that way," she said, as she always responded.

She stepped forward and pressed into his chest. He drew her close.

"I love you too," she said, her voice muffled in his shirt.

The next day, Paula and the kids carted the contents of her quarters behind the schoolhouse to the Rosses' house.

Ostensibly, she moved into Didi's room. That's where her belongings resided, and when Will was on night shift, she slept there. But when he was on day shift, they spent those nights in Will's bed.

Will believed what he wanted to believe, so he thought his children didn't know about this arrangement. Then again, he also believed that growing up without his father hadn't affected him, notwithstanding the various sundry and sometimes violent stepfathers his mother had provided. Or that his mother's leaving him with friends or relatives for months on end hadn't shaped the man he'd become. Or that he wasn't still an alcoholic because he didn't drink anymore.

Hiding the evolving nature of their relationship was likely more important to Will, and Paula too, than to the Ross children. Long before Will and Paula got together, the kids had accepted their parents' divorce. Though Will didn't know until the previous summer, Kat had moved on from the marriage to a parade of boyfriends, whom the children witnessed marching through their home on Toll House Lane.

Whatever ruse was playing out in the little house in Kayakale was for Will and Paula, while they got over their hesitation about being a couple.

∽

In the midst of all the work and moving Paula in, Will found himself a plane. A sweet, sky blue '62 Cessna 150B. Will actually thought the paint job a bit precious, but the US Air Force colonel out of Incirlik Air Base who sold it to him said he'd chosen that color "because if God wasn't a Tar Heel, then why'd he go and make the sky Carolina blue?"

The colonel was North Carolina born and bred and was headed back there upon his retirement. He had twenty-five years in and was ready to get out, though he was not many years older than Will.

"I'm looking forward to settling down and staying home," he said. "Got myself a 150 Aerobat there to play with. Sure am happy to find this pretty girl a good home here," he said, patting her polished flank.

Funny, Will thought. He had hit his professional stride and couldn't imagine even thinking about retirement. As far as settling down and staying home went, well, why would he want to do that? Not that he even knew where he'd call home. There was no place that he felt like the colonel obviously did about the Tar Heel State. He'd gotten picked up and moved so many times as a kid and then done the same to himself and his family. The world at large was home, no settling needed.

Speaking of home, he found one for *Blue*, as he'd come to think of the plane, at the Elazığ airfield. Then he waited for a work and weather window.

∽

"A what?" Paula asked, the day he told her about *Blue*, which happened to be just three days before he planned to bring the plane home from Adana.

"A plane. I found myself a plane. She's a beauty too," Will said.

"When did you find time to look for a plane?"

"Where there's a will, there's a way."

Paula groaned.

"I know. I'm sorry." He smirked. "I couldn't resist."

Not to be deterred by the quip, Paula said, "You don't have enough time for your kids, but you have time for a plane?"

"A plane'll help with family time. Ask Kevin how much he likes flying with me."

"You have two other children."

"They like it too. And I recall you sounding pretty excited about flying when we met."

She didn't know what to say. He was right; she had been impressed with his being a pilot. But that didn't mean she expected him to go and buy a plane.

"Come on, babe," he said, giving her that mischievous smile of his, like the little boy he must have been. "Don't be like that."

"Okay, I won't be like that," she said. "But I can't drive all the way to Adana and back on Sunday. I have work to do, for one thing. And Kevin can't stay with Didi; he works out at the dig on weekends, remember? Plus, Rob's got a game with Timur and his cousins, and Didi and I promised to go watch."

"Fine. I'll figure out a Plan B. *Blue*'s coming home. You'll see, it'll be great," he said with a wink.

After that conversation, Paula both kicked herself *and* patted herself on the back. The kick because she didn't need to have reasons or make excuses not to haul back and forth to Adana on short notice—on any time frame, for that matter. And the pat on the back because, even if it didn't sound like it, saying no to the Bring *Blue* Home mission was a big deal for her, with or without reasons.

For a woman who took a fair measure of pride in how she'd constructed her life—finding a way to get an education in a family that didn't value it, supporting children in that same educational mission in her work, and realizing her dream of seeing the wider world than the one she'd grown up in—Paula still struggled with not ceding control to a man. She had done it with Curtis, giving herself away to be loved. After that, she'd come to believe that if she had to give herself away, then it wasn't really love at all. Paula was determined not to go there with Will. It didn't serve her, and she was sure it wouldn't serve him, or what they had together. At least, not in the long run. And by that point, she hoped they would have a good, long run.

Taking care of herself, along with the people she loved, was hard for her. At twenty-eight, Paula was just learning how.

∾

The forecast looked favorable that Sunday, so Will and Refik left Kayakale at 0500 for the seven-hour drive to Adana. In return for the favor of Refik driving the Land Cruiser back while he flew north in *Blue*, Will would wangle a few days off for his assistant, in addition to letting him borrow the Land Cruiser for a camping trip when Refik's brothers came east to visit in July.

Will asked Refik to wait while he did his preflight check. In case any problems came up, he didn't want to be stranded hours from home.

He grabbed his new flight bag from the back seat, thanked Refik again, and jogged across the tarmac. He reached into his pocket for the keys, unlocked the plane, leaned in, flicked the light switches on, and began his inspection. He'd be extra careful. The plane was new to him, and he'd only flown once since last summer, a few weeks before, when he took *Blue* for a test flight.

He circled her, inspecting the tires for inflation and tread wear, scanning for drips of hydraulic fluid around the brakes, and checking the lights. With his fuel-sampler cup, he drained a small measure from each tank. No water, no sediment. Around again, he moved her elevator, rudder, flaps, and ailerons. His fingers slid over the leading edges of her wings and prop, feeling for nicks or chips or dents. He squinted into the pitot tube to be sure it was clear. He opened the engine cowling, checked the oil, looked for drips and wear, then resecured the cowling fasteners. It looked like the colonel had cared for her with military precision.

He just wanted to start her up before he let Refik go. He climbed in and, without hesitating, pressed his feet onto the brakes. He flicked the master switch on; adjusted the fuel mix; pushed the throttle in; shouted, "Clear prop," though there was no one else around (it was a habit so ingrained by his first flight instructor, he always did it); and turned the key.

Blue barely shook as her engine turned over, and Will let himself enjoy its even hum for a moment. Then he checked and rechecked all the gauges. Everything looked good. He shut her back down and stood up in the plane's doorway, waving to Refik that he could be on his way. Will would be waiting for him at the airfield in Elazığ.

Minutes later, Will's heart thrummed along with the engine as he taxied her to the runway. He couldn't wait to get into the air. He *loved* to fly. He hadn't realized quite how much he'd missed it.

TWENTY-TWO

Will happened to be trotting down the office steps at the moment Timur shattered his leg jumping off the schoolhouse roof. The boy's screams could be heard throughout the Kayakale compound, and Will ran toward them.

Timur thrashed on the ground behind the schoolhouse, beside a bed that must have been meant to be his landing pad. Rob knelt beside his friend, trying to hold him. A jagged end of bone stuck out of Timur's bloody pant leg. His shrieks pierced what had been a still afternoon.

Will rushed to the boys. Borkan arrived right behind him and dropped to his knees, reaching out for his son. Timur's arms flailed, slapping his father away.

"*Hemşire çağır,*" Borkan barked at the men who were gathering around them. Call the nurse.

"Tell her to bring morphine," Will shouted. *"Acele!"* Hurry. Then to himself: *if she has any.*

Will took hold of Rob's shoulders and moved him aside, but his son twisted out of his grasp and crawled to the other side of his prostrate friend. At that point, Timur grabbed Rob's arm and dug his fingernails into it. Rob winced but didn't pull away.

"Talk to him, Erdem," Will said. "Tell him we're going to take care of him."

Borkan bent low, whispered into Timur's ear, stroked his forehead. The boy began to quiet. He kept holding Rob's arm with one hand and reached for his father with the other.

"*Acıyor, Baba,*" Timur said, his jaw clenched. It hurts, Papa.

Kris, the nurse, arrived, out of breath. She had a vial and syringe in hand.

"How much does he weigh?" Will asked.

"About forty kilos," Borkan said.

"Five milligrams?" Will asked.

Kris nodded and prepared the syringe. Borkan and Will each held one of Timur's shoulders.

"Timur, *kıpırdama,*" Borkan said. "*Bu yardımcı olacak.*" Hold still. This will help.

She injected the morphine into his arm.

"It'll take some time for full effect. At least fifteen minutes," Will said.

"It will," Kris agreed.

He searched the men crowded around them and spotted his assistant. "Refik, go with Kris. Bring scissors, saline solution, sterile bandages, and tape."

"A pressure bandage," she added. "And penicillin. We should get him started on that."

"Bring a clean sheet or blanket, okay?"

"Yes, and we have a stretcher. Anything else?" Kris asked.

Will thought a moment. "I don't think so."

"Let's go." She waved at Refik to follow her, and he pulled another young engineer along to help.

Timur moaned, and his eyelids fluttered.

"Erdem, this is going to need surgery. We'll get the leg stabilized, then I'll fly him to Ankara. I'll check, but I think it's in *Blue*'s range. If not, we'll stop to refuel—it'll still be faster than driving. It's the best bet for a good outcome."

"How do you know this?" Borkan asked.

"I was a combat medic in Korea."

"I will go with you."

"I'm sorry, she's a two-seater," Will said. "Anyway, you

need to make arrangements for an ambulance to meet us at the airport. And for the hospital. Have the airport radio me; I'll give you my call sign. Then you and Lale can drive over."

The colonel Will bought *Blue* from had flown all over Turkey and had charts for the entire country. He'd been happy to sell them to Will, who would never have guessed he'd need them within a few weeks. When they got Timur stabilized, he'd get their course to Ankara set. *Best to get going as soon as possible.*

Lale ran up, and everyone made way for the boy's mother. She knelt beside Timur and lightly touched his cheek.

"*Anne, Anne,*" he said in a hoarse, groggy whisper. Mama, Mama.

∾

Kevin heard sniffling from Rob's side of the room. Was he bawling?

"What's wrong?" Kevin asked into the dark.

"I didn't mean to hurt him," Rob said. His crying, out from under the covers, was louder.

"*You* didn't hurt him. It's not like you shoved him off the roof. Did you?"

"No, but it was my idea."

"Well, it was a stupid one."

Rob sucked in a breath between sobs. "I know."

It sounded like Rob was choking. Kevin got out of bed, found a dirty T-shirt on the floor, and tossed it onto his brother's bed. Rob blew his nose hard. Kevin waited, listening to his brother's breathing. It began to even out.

"Really, what the fuck were you thinking?" Kevin asked.

"We were bored. We finished our drills, but there wasn't time to go fishing before dinner. I thought it'd be fun to get Paula's old bed out. You know, like a trampoline. We took turns bouncing on it, but then that got boring. I climbed up on the roof; it's not that high. I did a front flip off it and landed right on the bed. It worked just like I thought. It was fun." Rob paused. "I didn't think he'd miss the damn thing."

"Dumb shits."

"Yeah."

The boys didn't speak for several minutes. Rob sniffled.

"You want to sleep with Buddy tonight?" Kevin asked.

"Really?"

"Sure," Kevin said. "For tonight." He gave Buddy's warm body a nudge. It wasn't far to the edge of the bed, given how big Buddy had gotten and how small the bed was. The dog's front paws thumped onto the floor, followed by the rest of him.

"Here, boy," Rob said. He sounded a little happier already. "Hup. Jump up, Bud."

Rob's bed squeaked when Buddy leapt onto it.

"Settle, Buddy," Rob said.

Kevin knew the dog's routine and pictured him circling three times before curling up at the foot of the bed. He listened to Rob murmuring to the dog a while, and then the room went quiet.

There goes their baseball season, Kevin thought, *but they'll be able to go fishing.*

In a whisper, Rob asked, "Do you think he'll be okay, Kev?"

"I bet. Maybe you can call tomorrow. Find out how the operation went. When he called from the hospital, Dad said they were taking him in right away."

"Yeah," Rob exhaled loudly. "Shit. I hope he'll be okay."

"Me too. Guess you'll be reading to him a lot this summer, instead of playing baseball. Paula can load you up with books. That'll be fun, huh?"

Rob groaned.

Kevin laughed. "I'm kidding, doofus. Timur'll get good on crutches. It won't be the same as last summer, but it'll be okay."

"He's my best friend," Rob said. "The best friend I ever had."

"I know," Kevin said. "You're his too."

"You think?" Rob asked.

"Yeah, I do," he assured his brother. "Go to sleep. Maybe you can talk to Timur tomorrow."

∾

April 28, 1974

Dear Mom,

I'm sorry I missed so many letters. I've been really busy. Anyway, how are you? We're all fine, except for Timur, who broke his leg. Dad had to fly him to Ankara to get surgery. Oh, yeah, that was one of the things I forgot to tell you too. Dad got another plane.

I'm working at an excavation both days on the weekends now, that's why I've missed writing the last few weeks. It's hard work, but I like it. The site is called Bağvadi. It's pretty close to the house, so I can walk out there. They're excavating all the ruins closer to the dam first because they'll get flooded first. I help sieve sediment looking for artifacts. The sieves are so big that two people have to hold them while a third person shovels the dirt into them. The people I work with most are graduate students from Turkey and Britain and the States. They look through what's left in the sieve, and if something looks like it might be important, they call a professor over to check. So even though I'm just shoveling or sweeping with a little whisk broom or sieving, it's pretty interesting.

I guess that's all that's going on here. Kind of a lot, though. Miss you, Mom.

Love, Kevin

ᐧᐧᐧ

Will was just sitting down to a late dinner, dirty and tired from a long day in the field, when Rob slammed in the screen door and bounded down the hall to the kitchen.

"Timur's coming home!" he shouted, out of breath, his face flushed with excitement.

Will glanced up, and Paula caught his eye as she turned from the sink, drying her hands. She gave him the slightest of nods, and he knew he was supposed to say or do something to "connect" with his younger son, but for the life of him he didn't know what.

Paula crossed the room and grabbed Rob into a hug. "That's great!"

"The gruesome twosome united once again," Kevin said.

Rob squirmed out of Paula's grasp. "They're going to put a cast on tomorrow. And teach him to use crutches."

Rob had been going to see Borkan every evening during the weeks his friend was in the hospital. Borkan was kind enough to give the boy a detailed report about Timur each day and had even worked it out so the boys could talk on the phone a few times.

"Mr. Borkan's leaving tomorrow after work to go to Ankara to get him and Mrs. Borkan," Rob continued.

"I hope he's less klutzy with crutches than he is jumping off things," Kevin said.

"Kevin, really," Paula said.

"He's going to drive all night to Ankara, then back the next day?" Will asked.

"That's what he said. Can we ask him if I can go? I could keep Timur company on the ride home." Turning back to Paula, Rob said, "I promise I'll make up all my schoolwork. I'll do extra if you want me to."

If Will were in Borkan's shoes, he wouldn't want to deal with his son's friend. But with Paula's gentle urging, Will was learning that not everyone thought the way he did. And that sometimes he could, and should, think differently himself. Imagine that, as she liked to say. Actually, Will couldn't have a few short months ago, but he could now. So rather than just saying no, he considered Rob's request.

"Well, there'll be an overnight. And we don't want to make trouble for them." Will paused, thinking. "I could offer to cover a few days for Erdem, so he wouldn't have to drive sixteen hours of a twenty-four-hour day. That might be a good trade-off."

"Please, Dad," Rob said. "Can we ask him?"

Will looked from Rob's face to Paula's. She smiled and gave a big nod of approval. He could read *some* of her signs.

"You wouldn't get your day off this week," she said to Will. "But friends help each other out, right? And it would mean a lot to Rob." She rested her hands on the boy's shoulders and looked over his head at Will.

"*Please*, Dad," Rob added.

"Okay, son." Will pushed his chair back and stood up. He crossed the room and awkwardly put his arm around Rob's shoulder. (Paula had been telling him he needed to give Rob more attention . . . or was it affection?) "Let's go talk with him."

TWENTY-THREE

W ill returned to the office at midday on a beautiful, blue-
sky day in late May. The seasonal rains had dissipated,
and sunny spring weather had arrived. Will was on shift in the
field, but a pump had broken down. He'd radioed Kerry, the
maintenance manager, but it would take their crew a while to
get out there. Will figured he'd use the downtime to catch up
on paperwork. That way, he might not have to work quite as
late as usual that night.

Borkan came to Will's office door, but before he could speak,
the radio clipped to Will's belt crackled. "Ross, this is Authier.
The pump's hooped, man. I'm not sure it's reparable. Over."

"So get a spare, and get us back up and running. Over," Will
responded.

"I used my last spare a couple of days ago, and we haven't
gotten a replacement yet. We've got two partly back together in
the shop, but they won't be ready till tomorrow at the earliest.
Over."

"Will, take the rest of the day off," Borkan said. "You hav-
en't had a day off in weeks."

Kerry's voice came over the radio, "Awaiting instructions.
Over."

"Hang on," Will said into the radio.

"You'll reassign the pump crew for the day?" Will asked.

"Yes. Go ahead," Borkan said. "It's a beautiful day, take it."

"Ross to Authier. Tell the pump crew to radio Borkan for

instructions for the rest of their shift. You make sure we've got a pump that's running tomorrow morning. Over."

"Roger that."

"Thanks. Ross, out."

Will put the radio down on his desk, unclasped the buckle of his field belt, and dropped it behind him onto his desk chair.

"Thanks, Erdem. I think I'll go take *Blue* for a spin."

∾

Will knew exactly where he wanted to go. Along with the chart, he packed a site map into his flight bag, but he didn't really need it. He knew the Kayakale Dam site as well as any he'd worked on, except for seeing it from the air. That's what he'd do today. He expected to be surprised.

Will always said that flying provided a view that walking-around life could not. For him, that applied in more ways than one, but definitely with respect to seeing the geology. The footprint of the dam was altered well beyond its natural state—probably not much he'd get from it. But he was sure that observing the abutments from the air would be instructive. Besides, it would be fun.

After takeoff, he steered north of west. The airport was on the southeast side of Elazığ, and as *Blue* climbed, Will looked over at the city. Of modest size, though large for the region, Elazığ appeared up-to-date but unattractive. It lacked the charm of the smaller, older mountain and valley villages surrounding it. He was, however, appreciative of its modern conveniences— particularly its airport.

Leveling the plane, he fussed with the trim tab, still learning *Blue*'s subtleties. He laughed. Seemed there were always nuances to learn about the females in his life. He patted the plane's yoke. He hoped Paula wouldn't be miffed that he was out playing. The time had simply presented itself on a perfect day to fly. If she and the kids weren't in school, he would have asked if one of them wanted to come along for the ride. As it was, the afternoon was all his.

Elazığ disappeared over his right shoulder, and the peak of Bulutlu Dağı (Cloudy Mountain) appeared to the south. But it was free of clouds this brilliant day. He waggled *Blue*'s wings, getting the feel of how she reacted. He climbed, leveled again; he slowed, stalled, then throttled up to cruising speed. Though he'd flown several more hours in *Blue* than he'd expected to by now, to and from Ankara to get Timur to the hospital, that was not a time for play. Today was.

Forty-five minutes after takeoff, he flew over the village of Kayakale. Just beyond it, he steered right, to follow the Firat's course upstream to the dam site. He'd come to think of the Euphrates as the Firat, its Turkish name, during the months he'd worked on the dam that would control it.

The first structures he saw were the outlets of the diversion tunnels, the two 14.46-meter-diameter tunnels taking the flow of the Firat from behind the cofferdam upstream of the dam site to downstream of the construction. They ran northeast–southwest between curves of the river's course, a way to shorten the tunnel lengths that needed to be driven. Water cascaded from the tunnel outlets rejoining the river.

Though he couldn't see the trace of the Paula Fault, he knew it was just northwest of the northern tunnel, nearly parallel to it. The fact that they'd missed it driving the tunnel was sheer dumb luck, since the faults hadn't been mapped at that time. For the thousandth time, Will shook his head in disbelief at the geologic features, so important to the success of the dam, that were overlooked before construction started.

He slowed the plane to just above stall speed, prolonging his view of the muddy mess of the foundation excavation. Conditions would improve with the drier weather, but excavations were huge holes in the ground and bound to be messy regardless. He could see workers' hard hats flash in the sun as they craned their necks at the sound of *Blue*'s engine. He dipped his left wing at them, though he doubted they'd know it was meant as a wave.

He flew over the traces of two more faults, Lale and Kadriye. Just like the Paula Fault, he knew they were there but couldn't see them. They trended north–south, cutting across the river valley at an angle.

He could see the Didi Fault when he looked at the left abutment. When he named it, he hadn't known that the fault named for his daughter would be the most troublesome of those dissecting the dam's foundation. The shear zone of the Didi Fault was one of the major conduits for the groundwater that caused the karstic features, the huge voids in the subsurface, that had shut down construction. Unlike its namesake—the least troublesome of Will's children—the Didi Fault was a complex structure, an oblique fault, whose sense of movement was up and down and sideways. There were two other faults, Elif and Figen, similar in structure to the Didi Fault, and they were also problematic, but they weren't directly under the proposed dam alignment like the Didi Fault was.

From the vantage point of flight, he could see clearly where the Didi, Elif, and Figen Faults entered the left abutment. They all dipped to the east, Didi at about fifty-five to sixty degrees, and Elif and Figen at steeper angles. The Didi and Figen Faults had very wide shear zones where the rock had been ground up when the faults ruptured. Elif, between the other two, was a tidier fault trace and nearly vertical. These faults looked pretty much like Will had expected—no surprises, which pleased him. It meant he and his team had done a thorough job investigating them.

Will smiled at the memory of Paula's not-very-happy reaction to the faults being named after the females in their families. He was sure he wouldn't remember them as well if they were numbered, but he tried not to mention them by name at home.

Well past the footprint of the dam, he banked to the left, making a tight turn. He'd fly at least one more pass and take a look at the other side of the site. He followed the river back downstream, going as slow as he dared. He could see the Figen Fault, then Elif, where they intersected the abutment. But after that, the right abutment looked like hash, with the Kadriye, Lale, and Didi Faults intersecting it in very tight spacing. Though not impossible, it would make controlling leakage in this area a real challenge.

Will concentrated on the slope, trying to pick out the individual faults he knew were there. He was lucky—the sun angle was good for discerning the geologic features below. He did, however, notice one lineament that he didn't recognize. It ran parallel to the contour of the slope. Was it simply a contact of two formations, highlighted in the sun, or was it a fault aligned sub-parallel to the slope angle, and therefore, hard to pick out?

In minutes, he was past the dam site again.

He banked hard to turn back around so he could fly directly over that lineament. He climbed three hundred feet to give himself air room over it as he headed upriver. No, he definitely didn't recognize that feature from his many times up and down that slope, or looking at it from the other abutment. It was upslope of what would be the top of the dam, which was probably a good thing. Perhaps less likely to affect the dam, but that was at the surface. What was below the surface *could* affect the dam. He would need to understand what the feature was and what its orientation was both at the surface and in the subsurface before he reached any conclusions.

Although troubled by the introduction of another potential problem for Kayakale Dam, Will was also intrigued. This was what he loved most about being a geologist, reading the landscape and interpreting the story it had to tell.

He left the dam site behind, flying east toward Elazığ. He picked up the chart from the right-hand seat and decided to follow the left bank of the Firat, to where the Murat River joined it, not far upstream. At the confluence, the Firat flowed in from the north, out of the high mountains. He would follow the Murat east, and take a look at that part of the to-be Kayakale Reservoir on the way.

The merging of the two great rivers so close to Kayakale Dam was no small part of why that location had been selected. It would result in a reservoir of much greater proportions than if the structure were upstream of the confluence. Kayakale Dam would impound both watersheds. More bang for the buck was the logic in that choice, Will was sure. What they hadn't counted on was all the bucks it would take to make that particular site work.

∽

"You're early," Paula said when Will arrived home at five o'clock on a warm Friday afternoon. "Is something wrong?"

"More breakdowns. That failed pump last week was just the beginning. Stuff's been crapping out every day since."

"I guess the equipment's been working as hard as y'all have," she said.

"Round-the-clock for months. Kerry and his guys are wizards at keeping things going, but they're overwhelmed. There's a truckload of parts on its way from Ankara now. Borkan made an executive decision to shut down for the whole weekend. That way maintenance can catch up. And. . . ."

"And?" she asked.

"And the rest of us are off until Monday at noon."

"We get to see you for two whole days?" Didi asked,

wrapping her skinny arms around Will's waist and looking up at him hopefully.

"That's right, Dee," he said, patting her head. "Let's go camping. We hauled all our gear over here and haven't even gotten it out of the boxes."

"A 'benture!" Didi skipped around the living room.

"Where?" Kevin asked.

"Kerry told me about a great trout stream up the Firat, in the mountains," Will said.

"We're going fishing," Didi sang.

"But I can't go," Kevin said. "I work at the dig on weekends."

"Come on, Kev, if I can take a few days off, you can too."

"Tell them your family's going away for a few days," Paula said. "I'm sure it'll be all right."

Kevin looked down.

Rob laughed. "Hey, squirt, do you remember that time Mom dressed you up in that ruffly dress for an official girls' day out? By the time she got herself ready, hair curled and makeup and stuff, and she went to the patio door to get you from the backyard, you and your fancy dress and your white sandals were covered with mud. You were so proud of your handful of worms."

"I remember that," Kevin said. "You held them right up to her face and asked if she thought Dad would take you fishing if you brought the bait? Man, I'll never forget the look on Mom's face. It was like she was watching a horror movie."

Didi's eyes teared up.

"Stop it, boys," Paula said, hugging her. "She didn't mean to disappoint your mom. She's just a tomboy is all. I get it. I am too."

"And a daddy's little girl," Rob wheedled. "Oh, Daddy, can I go fishing with you, puh-leese?" he mimicked his sister's high-pitched voice. "Daddy, watch me digging worms."

"That's enough, Rob," Will said.

"It's okay, Dee," Paula said. She kissed the top of her head. "Rob's just teasing. That's what big brothers do."

Didi looked up at Paula. "I didn't like that stupid pink dress anyway."

"I don't like pink either."

"And I really like fishing," she said.

I don't, Paula thought. But she kept it to herself. She was more than happy to sit on a stream bank reading a good book on a pretty spring day while people who liked to fish did just that.

"We all do," Will said. "We can go for two nights."

"Can Timur come?" Rob asked.

"He's still on crutches," Kevin said.

"So?" Rob said.

"I think crawling in and out of a tent would be hard for him, don't you?" Paula asked.

Rob scowled at her.

"I know you don't like to leave him out, but I doubt his parents would let him go until he's better," she said.

"He's not sick," Rob said.

"No, but his leg's not healed yet either. You wouldn't want it to get hurt again, would you?" Paula asked.

"No. . . ." Rob conceded.

"Maybe we'll go again later on. When Timur can come too," she said.

"Come on, boys, let's go get the gear," Will said. "We'll get organized tonight, so we can leave early tomorrow."

"Can I come?" Didi asked. "I can help."

"We can all go." Will squatted down, so she could climb on piggyback. She smiled hugely at Paula over Will's shoulder.

TWENTY-FOUR

Will yawned and stretched. He reached to his right, forgetting that Paula wasn't beside him. His second thought, since the first was out of the question, was of coffee. He folded back the flap of tan canvas, crawled out of his tent, and inhaled, still feeling newly appreciative of the freshness of the mountain air, even though they'd been out of the city for months. He craned his neck to take in the view. The rocky slopes to his right ascended to a jagged ridge. To their left, the topography eased, sloping down to the river. They were camped near a small tributary of the Firat, probably spring fed. If he followed the creek bed far enough upstream, he might find where it bubbled out of the ground. He breathed in again, slow and deep. He wasn't sure he'd really looked around yesterday. He'd been in too much of a rush—to get packed up and out here, then to fish, and then to cook the fresh trout for dinner. He smiled at the irony of being in a rush to slow down.

There was no movement or sound from the other two tents—the one next to his, with Paula and Didi, or the one on the other side of camp, with the boys and Buddy. He'd let the crew sleep a while. They'd stayed up late last night telling ghost stories around the campfire. After dinner, Paula had surprised them with a bag of marshmallows and the first story. Either she possessed an active imagination, or the basement of her granny's "damp, gray house" was a truly terrifying place. Either way, she won the scariest story prize.

Will crossed the clearing to the folding table that defined the camp's kitchen. Two ammo boxes, tucked under the table, held the cookware and provisions. He opened the Coleman stove as quietly as he could and set the kettle to heat on a low flame. Then he made his way along the trail out of camp, toward the Firat. They hadn't explored in this direction yesterday, and he hadn't seen this particular reach of the river before. He knew this area would all be inundated when the dam was built. He felt a pang, even though it was his mission to make that inundation happen, and he believed in that mission.

When he could just see the deep green of the Firat, he stepped off the trail behind a boulder and contemplated the view of the river while relieving himself. Something upstream caught his eye. Was it a ruin? It looked like a wall, but that didn't make sense down in the riverbed. Maybe a bridge abutment? There were remnants of ancient river crossings throughout the valley.

He couldn't leave the kettle any longer, but now he had a plan for the morning. Exploring a ruin would be fun for everyone. Paula loved learning local history and used it in her teaching. Kevin had been working on a dig in the to-be reservoir for a couple of months and had learned a lot about the archaeology of the region. And even though Rob professed not to like history, he did like scrambling around on rocky ruins, even if he only let his excitement show when he didn't think Will was watching. Little Didi loved adventures of any shape or size. So did Buddy.

He hurried back to camp. Making coffee, he was as noisy as he had been quiet before. He wanted the crew up and going now.

Buddy let out a boof at the lid clattering onto the big pot when Will got oatmeal cooking, finally raising some activity in the tents. As he poured himself a second cup of coffee, he poured a first one for Paula, then reached the cup inside the flap of the girls' tent and held it steady until he heard a sleeping bag unzip, a rustle of fabric, and felt the cup's weight lift from his hand.

"My hero," Paula said.

"Me too," said Didi.

"I have a surprise for you," he said. "But you have to get up to get it."

"Better than coffee in bed?" Paula asked.

"Yup," he said, giving the tentpole a shake. "Come on."

Will hustled the crew through breakfast and dishwashing. The morning sun was still at their backs when they turned west from camp onto the trail that paralleled the Firat. Will led, his strides fast and long. He heard the crunch of Paula's boots and Didi's quick footfalls behind him. Farther back, Kevin and Rob talked and laughed, probably pushing and shoving each other.

He passed the boulder where he'd spotted the cut stone blocks, eager to see the structure—or what was left of it. About twenty paces farther, he stopped short. What had looked like a wall was the crumbling end of a failed dam. The buckled edge of wall that had made no sense now had context. Beside it lay the rubble of what had been, indeed, a wall—a wall that had held the Firat back, smaller to be sure, but not entirely unlike the one they were building miles downstream at Kayakale.

"Wow," Paula said.

"What's that?" Kevin asked, but didn't wait for the answer.

With Kevin in the lead, the kids and Buddy pushed around Will and Paula, clambering down the slope to the ruin. The sound of happy shouting filled the valley. Then a shrill whistle drowned out the shouts. Will turned to see Paula blowing through her right thumb and forefinger in another piercing blast.

The kids all turned, and Buddy too.

"Be careful," Paula called. "Stay away from the water. And watch out for Buddy."

"Another hidden talent," Will said. "You almost broke my eardrums."

"It comes in handy. Got their attention, didn't I?"

"You sure did," he said over his shoulder as he began to angle down the slope.

He could see the collapsed margin of the dam climbing in stairsteps of blocky risers up to what had been the left abutment. Where it was still complete, the full height of the structure looked to have been about twenty-five feet. It was topped with a wider, more finished layer of capstones, though some of them were missing. Despite the missing blocks, the juncture between the natural and man-made structures, where the dam met the bank, appeared to be intact.

Well ahead of them, the kids climbed up the dam, Buddy jumping and barking below.

"Whoa!" Paula yelled, and they all turned to look at her. "Go slow. And remember, three points of contact."

A chorus of okays was her answer.

"Good job, Mama Bear." Will smiled. "But let the cubs have some fun."

"I hope you won't be making another flight to Ankara anytime soon," she said.

"They're good," he assured her.

Will walked the contour to the top of the dam, then scrambled over to the upstream side. Observing the portion of the dam that still stood, there were no obvious issues. His eyes panned down what remained of the failed dam. He could see water flowing over the rubble to the point it got too deep near the middle of the river, but there was none on the other side— no remnants of the structure on shore, no debris, nothing.

Then Will shifted his gaze up the opposite slope, and the answer to the dam's failure fairly screamed at him. He'd broken his own rule by looking too close before looking at the big picture. And when he saw the big picture, it told the story loud and clear.

The slope comprising the right abutment had liquefied as a mudflow at some point in the past, surely causing the catastrophic failure of the dam. The landform looked like thick gravy congealed over lumpy mounds of mashed potatoes. The feeling of fluidity was unmistakable.

Pleased with himself for solving the mystery of the small dam's destruction, Will's mood shifted to dread within moments. The unstable slope would be submerged by Kayakale Dam's reservoir. It was a massive slide complex, the hummocky topography so indicative of movement, and yet it had been missed. Probably not overlooked, but not even looked at.

Those sediments had liquefied, become oversaturated, and flowed downslope. Where the water had come from, Will could only guess—perhaps a series of downpours of cataclysmic proportions; perhaps a winter of heavy snowfall followed by a warm, wet spring; or perhaps all of the above, plus an earthquake on the East Anatolian Fault or one of its ancillary faults. The filling of the small reservoir behind this dam might have exacerbated the situation. And it would have been a mere puddle, compared to the reservoir that Kayakale Dam would impound.

Will stood across the Firat, studying the slope, with the possibilities playing out in his mind. Simply impounding the reservoir might be enough to cause another failure. That was the worst-case scenario. There were numerous others Will could envision, like climatic events or earthquakes. There was reservoir-induced seismicity to think about as well. Kayakale's reservoir would be more than big enough to need to consider that. To Will, it seemed inevitable that at some point in the future that slope would again fail—perhaps catastrophically.

The words of the father of modern geology, James Hutton, echoed in Will's head. His first geology professor required the class to memorize them. In 1788 Hutton wrote, in his volume *Theory of the Earth*, "from what has actually been, we have data for concluding with regard to that which is to happen thereafter."

"That which is to happen thereafter," Will said out loud, looking across the river at some of that data.

If Kayakale's reservoir was filled to design capacity when the slope failed, the consequences could be disastrous—for Kayakale Dam and for the village downstream.

The case of Vajont Dam immediately came to Will's mind. In 1963, Vajont Dam, an 860-foot-high concrete arch dam in the Italian Alps, was overtopped by an 820-foot wall of water when the side of a mountain failed as a block slide into the reservoir. A third of the volume of the lake poured over the dam and crashed down the valley. Two thousand people perished, and numerous villages and towns were destroyed. Vajont Dam still stood today—a testament to the dam's engineering, the structure itself hadn't sustained much damage. But the reservoir was never refilled. The dam remained, a monument to the failure of scientists and engineers to heed Earth's warnings.

"What're you looking at?"

Will jumped at the sound of Kevin's voice. So intent on his observations and the thoughts they had provoked, he hadn't heard his son approaching.

"Sorry, Dad. What's up there?"

"Nothing good."

"I thought maybe you saw more ruins."

"No, but see that slope . . . the landform tells me it was a mudflow or a large, wet, complex landslide. That's what made this dam fail."

"It *told* you?"

"Come on, Kev, you know what I mean. No, it didn't literally tell me. But you know when the light's good for shooting. Right? You just *know*."

Kevin nodded.

"It's like that for me with the landscape."

They were quiet, standing together for a long moment. Then Will pointed across the river. "*That* could be really bad for Kayakale."

"But how?" Kevin asked. "It's so far away."

"If the whole slope failed and slid into Kayakale Reservoir when it's full, think about how much water would be displaced."

"I don't get it."

"Imagine dropping a really big bucket of mud and dirt and rocks into a full bathtub. What would happen?"

"The bathtub would overflow," Kevin said.

"Right. And that might damage the dam, which could cause the whole reservoir to be released downstream."

"That would be a huge flood, wouldn't it?" Kevin's brow furrowed.

"Yes, huge, for sure. And even if the dam held, but it was overtopped, it would flood Kayakale. Maybe villages farther downstream, too, depending on how big the wave was."

Kevin whistled under his breath.

"That's what I was looking at," Will said. "There are ways to handle it, just like we're fixing the foundation. Finding out about it now means we can solve the problem before it's a problem. But it's no small thing." He swept his arm in a wide arc for emphasis.

"You're going to tell them?"

"As soon as we get back."

∞

Kevin, Rob, and Didi built the campfire that evening. Dad and Paula were doing the dinner dishes, and talking. But Kevin couldn't hear what they were saying. He wondered if his father was telling her about that slope. He'd asked Kevin not to say anything, that he didn't want Rob talking about it with Timur before he could speak with Timur's father. Dad said he needed to think about how he'd explain the problem when they got back.

Kevin bent low to the ground and blew gently on the flames that were just licking at the twigs Didi had collected and proudly presented to them. Rob followed suit, except for the gentle part, and nearly blew the fire out.

"Easy," Kevin said.

"Shut up," Rob said. "I know how to light a fire."

"Oh yeah?"

"Yeah." Rob glared at him through the smoke.

"Don't fight," Didi said. She sat cross-legged on the ground with Buddy's head in her lap. "Buddy doesn't like it."

"How do you know?" Rob asked. "He can't talk."

"He does so, just in different ways than us," she said.

"That's stupid," Rob said.

"Maybe not. I think Buddy talks too, like she said, just in a different way." At the sound of Kevin's voice, Buddy thumped his tail.

"See?" Kevin said, reaching over to pat his dog's rump. "Good boy, Buddy."

"Have any of you gotten your weekly letter to your mom written yet?" Paula asked, crossing the clearing.

They all shook their heads.

"I didn't think so. Lucky for you, I brought paper and pencils and books to lean on, so you can do it right here."

"I don't have anything to tell her," Rob said.

"Sure you do. Tell her about camping and fishing and playing on the ruin today." She continued with a bribe: "We'll roast marshmallows after you get your letters done."

"Dear Mommy," Didi said out loud, drawing the words out for as long as it took her to print the salutation in big block letters.

"Shut up, squirt," Kevin and Rob said in unison.

TWENTY-FIVE

Will knocked on Borkan's office door. He didn't wait for a response before stepping into the room.

Borkan looked up from a pile of papers. "What are you doing here?" he asked. "Shouldn't you be sleeping? You start night shift tonight."

"I know, but I needed to talk with you," Will said. "We went camping this weekend, in the mountains just downstream of Kemaliye, but still in the reservoir area. I saw something that could be a real problem when the reservoir's impounded."

"What could be such a problem so far from the dam?"

"There's a large landslide complex, actually a mudflow, on a slope that'll be inundated. It caused the failure of what looked to be a small Ottoman-age dam. Maybe saturation of the slope from that reservoir caused it, or possibly rising hydrostatic pressures. Any number of other things could've caused the failure of that slope and the dam, like an earthquake on one of the nearby faults, or a big one on the East Anatolian Fault, or a wetter-than-normal rainy season, or a big snowpack followed by a warm, wet spring. But the point is that Kayakale's reservoir is going to submerge much more of that slope, more saturation, higher hydrostatic pressures, and the possibility of reservoir-induced seismicity too."

Will paused to catch his breath. He took the two steps up to Borkan's desk, placed both his hands down on it, and leaned toward his colleague. It was imperative that Borkan understand the gravity of this situation.

"You know about Vajont?" Will asked, leaning farther forward. "We could be looking at another Vajont here."

"Of course I know of Vajont," Borkan said. "The dam here is nothing like it."

"It doesn't have to be the same type of dam or the same geology to have similar implications. The issue is that a huge amount of material could slide into the reservoir. Whether it's a block failure like Vajont, or a debris flow or mudflow like what would probably happen on the slope I saw yesterday, doesn't matter. We've got to look at it."

"Further site investigation is needed, as you like to say."

"Yes, for sure. Was the reservoir area mapped?"

"I believe so, but that would have been before I came to work here."

"Can I see the maps? And the report that went with them?" Will said. "I've been so focused on the foundation, I never asked before."

"We'll have to go into the archives to find them."

"Erdem, the slope I found might not be the only one that has the potential to be a problem. We have to find out. You and I both know that the site investigation for this dam wasn't what it should've been."

"True," Borkan agreed.

"Lives are at stake."

"My family's lives. My village. Yes, I want to see this slope."

"I can fly us out there. It's good to see these features from the air. That's how I found the Kris Fault on the right abutment, remember? We can go one day this week. We'll watch the weather for a good window. I'm on night shift, so I won't have to miss a shift to do it."

"Sleep?" Borkan asked.

"I'll be losing sleep over this anyway. Might as well do something about it."

"If this is a problem, am I correct that it will not be a problem until the valley is inundated?"

"Yes," Will said.

"Then we have time."

"Yes."

"Good. We will have to think of the best way to get time allocated and funds authorized to investigate. *If* it is needed. My assistant will begin to search the archives immediately. I will make myself available to fly any time you say." Then he deadpanned, "At least it is not a flight to hospital."

Will answered with a wry smile of his own. "Different kind of emergency."

∿

Up in *Blue*, Will and Borkan surveyed not only the unstable slope Will already knew about, but the entire reservoir perimeter, taking three flights in all. After the first, Borkan agreed that they needed to see the entire zone. They found two other areas that presented concerns, though not as dire as the first, at least as far as they could tell from the flyovers.

No report, reconnaissance level or otherwise, on the proposed reservoir could be located. As they had before the presentation on the foundation, they spent hours in deep discussion. Will had never voiced his suspicions about the possibility of more than mere incompetence before, but he did now. It was hard to imagine someone intentionally sabotaging the dam's construction, intentionally endangering the village of Kayakale. What would you get from doing that?

Money. Money earmarked for studies, like drilling the foundation or mapping the reservoir area, could have been diverted. To send twin boys to a name university, with a big sister already at a fancy college, on a mid-level engineer's salary? Seemed more like a movie than real life. Even though he disliked Browning, Will didn't want to believe it. They found no evidence, but that kind of paperwork would be in Ankara, or New York, or destroyed. In any case, Browning wouldn't have left it at the site.

Will and Borkan strategized about what to do next and when to do it. That Browning would be defensive seemed a given. It would have been on his watch that the oversights, or worse, occurred. Borkan had good rapport with Browning; Will did not. They both had solid reputations with Heatley and his superiors in DECCO's New York office, but they understood the likelihood of repercussions if they chose to go over Browning's head.

"We have to do something," Will said, sitting on the front steps of the house with Paula, watching a luminous gibbous moon rise over the gorge.

"Yes," she agreed.

"We have a better shot of being heard by Heatley, but. . . ."

"There could be ramifications to going around Mr. Browning," she said.

"Right. Could be consequences to going through him too."

They sat in silence as the early summer evening cooled. One of the many things he appreciated about her was her comfort with quiet. He turned to look at her. Moon shadows played on the contours of her face. He reached for her hand, wrapped his around its warmth.

Without shifting her gaze, she said, "Will, what if you and Mr. Borkan went to the Ankara office and told Mr. Browning you think you've found features that could be a problem when the valley's inundated? Say you need to find the reservoir reconnaissance report, which must be there, since you can't find it here. *Ask* him for his help in defining the problem, and fixing it. Try to make him part of the process, instead of assuming he's going to be an obstacle to it? If you get him invested in it, he could go up the chain of command to New York. Then he could be the hero. Of course, you and Mr. Borkan would have to be willing for him to be the hero. Remember, his wife said he's ambitious. He wants to look good. Do you think he'd go for that?"

Will thought about it. "He might, if it really was just an oversight. . . ." He left the statement hanging.

"What? Are you saying Mr. Browning. . . ?"

"I'm not saying anything. Not anything we can prove, anyway."

"Wow," Paula said.

"Yeah, wow."

"Do you really think. . . ?"

"I don't know, Paula. I can't imagine it, but you know it happens."

TWENTY-SIX

"I'm going to fire you!" Browning roared across his desk at Will and Borkan. "Or you can drop this nonsense and keep your jobs. How dare you come here—not doing your jobs, I might add—and pull this shit?"

"We have a legitimate need to see the work that's been done on the reservoir area," Borkan said. "It is all of our jobs to make sure this project is completed safely."

"*I* say what your jobs are, Borkan. I knew he was a pain in the ass. . . ." Browning flicked his chin in Will's direction. "He was from day one. Now *you* too?"

"*He* made it possible to get construction going again."

"And you both should be at the site working on that construction right now."

"Mr. Browning, as professional engineers, you and I have a responsibility to protect life and property. Those letters behind our names, PE, they're like an oath. We must do that now. We must see the data we already have. There is ample time to do any additional work that's needed before we start filling the reservoir. May I ask why you are opposed to studying the slopes? To making sure this project is safe?"

"No. You may not ask."

Will and Borkan had agreed that Borkan would do the talking, but it was all Will could do to sit silently through this. He might not have those precious PE letters behind his name,

185

but he knew a lot more about Kayakale Dam than Browning did, and he sure as hell cared a lot more about its safety.

Borkan pressed on. "These slopes can be mitigated. This does not have to be a fatal flaw. But if we don't fully understand them, they could be. We cannot take that gamble."

He was covering all the points they'd gone over.

"There's no gamble," Browning said.

"You cannot guarantee that."

"And you can? What are the odds?" Browning asked. "About the same as little green men swooping down in their Martian spaceship and blowing the dam up. My bookie back home would love that bet."

"Did we not learn anything from the Vajont failure? DECCO and DSI must deal with this. It could cause Kayakale Dam to fail."

"This is nothing like Vajont. Besides, the dam didn't fail."

"Vajont is still standing. True. No reservoir, no power, but the dam is standing—a tragic monument," Borkan said. "Come to the field to look. Let us show you why this needs investigation."

"I spent years in that fucking backwater. I know it better than you ever will," Browning said.

"Do you?" Borkan snapped. "Then why have I been cleaning up the messes you left the whole time I've been there?"

Borkan's face was red; his fists were clenched on the arms of the office chair. He looked like he might launch himself across the desk at Browning, who had clearly gotten to him. Will had never seen his colleague and friend more agitated.

"I could fire you right now. For insubordination."

"Mr. Browning," Borkan said; then he paused to take a breath. "Perhaps you think this will threaten your *excellent* reputation? Admitting that you missed yet *another* problem at Kayakale Dam. I assure you that failure of the dam, or any part of the project—like for instance, a hillslope plunging into the reservoir—will destroy that reputation entirely."

"That's it!" Browning yelled, standing up and slamming his hands down on his desk. "We're done. You're both suspended for a week without pay." Browning looked down at his watch. "Starting now. If you haven't dropped this by the time the suspension's up, you're fired. Period. End of story. Now get out."

They stood, and as if they'd rehearsed it, they buttoned their suit jackets, still facing Browning, staring him down. Then they left his office and continued out of the reception area, the secretary calling, "*Güle, güle*," after them.

On the sidewalk, in the summer sun, they turned to each other. Will held out his hand. Borkan shook it.

"You were great," Will said.

"I'm afraid not."

"Can he do that? Suspend us without pay?"

Borkan shrugged.

"Well, I guess I'm going to take the time to think about what to do," Will said. "Maybe take my family someplace we haven't been before while I do. What are you going to do?"

"I must think as well. If we push this further, I suppose he could fire us. But if we don't and something happened . . . I would never forgive myself. I will need to speak with Lale, of course. This could mean another move. She would not be happy about that. We love Kayakale. It is our home. I had hoped to stay on as site engineer when the dam was operating."

"But she wouldn't want your village and your families endangered."

"No," Borkan said, his voice flat. "No."

∾

A few days past the longest day of the year, it was late by the time Paula noticed the shadows lengthening. She considered the time, wondering where Will might be and how his day had gone. He and Mr. Borkan had left early that morning, just before dawn, for the airfield in Elazığ. She'd stood on the porch to wave them off and stayed to watch the sunrise. Pensive. The feeling had lingered all day.

When she realized how late it was, she sent Kevin and Buddy to fetch Rob from the Borkans' or the ball field, wherever he and Timur were, and helped get Didi ready for bed. She heard the boys come in while she and Didi were reading. The door to the boys' room was closed by the time Dee was tucked in. Paula made her way to the porch steps and waited.

Will's face was grim as he crossed the patchy, dry grass between the Land Cruiser and the house.

"Browning didn't want to be the hero," he said. "But the good news is we're going on vacation."

"What? Vacation? I don't get it."

"Where're the kids?"

"Didi's asleep. The boys are in their room. Tell me?"

"Some . . . but I'm tired," he said, sinking down onto the step beside her. "I'll fill you in on the rest tomorrow, but the short version is that Browning suspended both Erdem and me for a week without pay. He said if we don't drop this after the week, we're fired."

"Can he even do that?"

"We don't know. But I'm going to take the time. Think about what to do next," he paused. "We might as well have some fun while I'm thinking it all over. Where should we go?"

"I have no idea. I can't even think. Someplace we haven't been before?"

"That's what I thought. Someplace new. Since it might be our last chance."

"This isn't what I expected. . . ."

"I don't know what I expected," Will said. "But we had to try."

TWENTY-SEVEN

B uddy nudged Kevin awake, like he did every morning. Let-
ting the dog out, he found Dad and Paula packing the car.
"What's up?" he asked, standing on the porch in his pajamas.
"Good. You are," his father said. "It's a long story . . . I'll
tell you on the way. We're going on a vacation to the coast, the
Mediterranean, for the rest of the week. Run over and tell Dr.
Young that you'll be away from the dig again. Back Monday, I
think. We'll see."

That's weird, Kevin thought. He knew that his father and Mr.
Borkan had gone to Ankara to talk to the DECCO boss about
that slope.

But going down to the coast—to the Mediterranean Sea—
now that sounded pretty great. Playing at the ocean versus
sieving dirt at Bağvadi in Kayakale's summer heat was a good
trade-off, even though Kevin wouldn't admit it to anyone, having campaigned to stay on at the dig after school was over.

When he and Buddy got back, Dad looked up from a cooler
he was filling from the fridge. "Pack for five days," he said. "We
can do laundry if we're gone longer. Get Buddy's stuff ready too.
Paula's helping Didi, and Rob's gone to see if Timur can come."

"Buddy and I call the wayback," Kevin said when the crew
gathered around the Land Cruiser to load up. He knew shotgun
wasn't an option. That was Paula's now. And Buddy was too big
to fit anywhere else anymore. He was happy to let Didi, Rob,
and Timur duke it out in the back seat.

Before they finished lashing everything down on the roof rack, Kevin grabbed one of the sleeping bags and tossed it inside. He climbed in, settled back against the bedroll, and patted his leg. Buddy jumped in, and as Dad swung the tailgate closed, the dog spun three tight circles, lay down, and rested his head on Kevin's thigh. His warm brown eyes looked up at Kevin, and one eyebrow went up, then the other. Kevin rubbed Buddy's silky ears, looking out the back window as they headed out of the compound.

Kevin remembered the first time they'd driven in on this road. It was eleven months ago yesterday, now that he thought about it. He couldn't even say Kayakale correctly then. He remembered how Dad made them all practice saying *teşekkür ederim* over and over in the car that day, minding their manners in Turkish. And now they all spoke the language.

A lot of other things had changed too. The most recent one was how Kevin viewed the landscape. Since the morning when he stood beside his father looking at that failed Ottoman dam, he'd been seeing the geomorphology, as Dad called it, differently. Seeing it more literally—geo meaning "the earth" and morphology meaning its "shape." His father had lectured to them about rocks and stuff for years—as long as Kevin could remember. As a kid, he'd hung on Dad's words, but the last few years he'd pretty much lost interest, until that day.

Seeing the mudflow, he could imagine it liquefying like his father had described. He could picture the mass of mud and rock surging down the slope and destroying that dam. It made sense how his father said he read landscapes and told their stories. Standing there, Kevin saw the story in that slope, and it was interesting. And important.

Now he watched the passing landscape, trying to see things he hadn't before. But he didn't. Then again, Dad had gone to school a long time to be able to do that. Kevin understood that now. It had taken him years to grasp the process of taking and developing pictures. He was just beginning to get an inkling of that about drawing. And archaeology too—what to do and what it meant.

Seeing Dad, how he was always looking at the geology, whether he was at work or not, you could tell how much he loved it. What could be better than loving what you do most of the time? Kevin knew so many kids back in Moorestown whose fathers hated their jobs, and his hadn't been happy working at the port in Philadelphia either. He was way different here—totally into it. Paula was like that about teaching, for sure. And the professors and grad students he worked with at the dig were like that about archaeology. Kevin hoped he'd be able to spend his life doing something he loved.

"Hey, y'all," Paula said, rustling a map and rousing Kevin from his reverie. "If we take a little detour up here, we can go through Kahraman Maraş. They make the best ice cream I've ever tasted. What do you think?"

"To resist the siren call of the sea, it better be some really special ice cream," Dad said.

"Turn north at Narlı . . . I'll tell you when," Paula said. "It has a secret ingredient, but I'm not going to spoil the surprise. Don't you either, Timur."

"Another interesting fact is that the Turkish Parliament changed the city's name from Maraş to Kahraman Maraş just last year. In February," Paula continued. "Kahraman means 'hero or heroic,' and they added that in honor of the brave people there. After World War I, the French army occupied the city, but the residents put up fierce resistance to the occupation, so they became heroes in Turkey's War of Independence. And now their city's name proclaims it."

"How do you say it?" Didi asked.

"Kahraman Maraş?" Paula sounded it out: "Kar-a-mon mar-osh."

Can't help being the teacher, Kevin thought. *There's the thing about loving what you do.* And he felt kind of bad about all the times he'd complained to Dad for doing it, in his case, talking about geology. He wondered if he'd do the same thing to his kids. *Yikes,* he thought, *kids?*

Didi sang it over and over. "Kar-a-mon mar-osh . . . kar-a-mon mar-osh."

Over the back seat, he saw Rob and Timur elbow each other, whispering and snickering.

"Jeez," Kevin said under his breath, and thought that maybe you don't have to have kids.

"You're so lucky, being an only child, Tim," Rob said.

"I don't know. . . ." Timur answered.

"Kar-a-mon mar-osh!" Didi chimed in.

"Maybe," Timur said.

His father navigated the Land Cruiser through the narrow streets of the city center. When he parked on a side street, they all piled out and trooped toward the square. Kevin and Buddy brought up the rear. As the crew turned the corner, Dad hung back.

"I didn't want to talk about what happened in front of Timur," he said. "I don't know what his father's told him or wants him to know. And I don't really want to let Rob and Dee know yet, because I'm not sure what I'm going to do. Gus Browning suspended Mr. Borkan and me for a week."

"What? Why?" Kevin asked.

"Because he's mad that we found another problem at Kaya-kale. Another one that he missed. He doesn't think it has merit, from what we told him, and he refused to come to the field to see it. He said if we don't drop it, he's going to fire us."

Kevin stopped and turned to face his father. "What are you going to do?"

"I'm not sure."

"But if it'll make the dam unsafe, don't you have to tell someone? Someone else? Someone who'll listen?"

"I'm considering that. I'm also considering whether I can do the project more good by staying on, somehow."

"Shit," Kevin said.

"Yes," his father agreed.

Kevin noticed that Dad didn't say anything about him swearing for once.

"I'm going to think about it these few days away. I have to decide by Monday."

"Paula knows?" Kevin asked.

"Yes."

"What does she think?"

"You can ask her yourself. I wanted to tell you. To make up for last year. You're growing up, and I need to trust you."

Kevin was speechless. *Wow*, he thought, looking at his father, who was gazing intently at him. *Did Dad really say that?*

"Come on. They're going to wonder where we are. Keep this to yourself for now?"

"Okay," Kevin said. "Hey, Dad. Sorry . . . that this is happening."

"Me too, son."

Though distracted by his father's news, licking his cone, Kevin had to admit the Kahraman Maraş *dondurma* was delicious. It was vanilla, but not just vanilla. He tried to analyze it while working on his double scoop. It had a hint of something—honey, maybe. And a gooey, kind of chewy, texture that slid across your tongue and down your throat and coated them with sweetness. It was different from any ice cream he'd ever had before.

"That's worth the trip," Dad said, as if he hadn't just told Kevin what he had. But his father was good at hiding things. *Like moving here last year.*

Even though Kevin didn't like the way he'd done it, he did

like *here*. Turkey. Kayakale. And all the places they'd explored—
like Nemrut Dağı, Mt. Erciyes, Cappadocia, and Istanbul. He
was pretty sure he'd like the Mediterranean too.

The Land Cruiser rolled through the countryside, and
his father pointed out that they were losing elevation, leaving
the mountain ranges they'd been weaving through all day and
descending to the delta of the Ceyhan River as they approached
Adana. Today, Kevin got it. The gradient of the river gentled, its
velocity slowed, and it dropped its sediment load, forming the
delta. It spread like an apron draped down the mountain front,
and Kevin saw it, maybe almost like his father did.

∽

Will picked a *pansiyon* in the village of Kızkalesi for their seaside
getaway. It turned out to be more interesting than just a place to
stay. The inn was owned by an American couple, Joe and Skipper,
who had quit their jobs five years before, sold their house and
everything in it, bought a thirty-two-foot sloop, and set off to
sail around the world. They'd gotten all the way to the Med,
fallen in love with the southeastern Turkish coast, and stayed.
Will thought that was a bold tack to take in life, and he liked
and admired them from the moment they met. He could imagine the thrill of being in the middle of the ocean on a small boat,
and he hoped their hosts would tell some of their sea stories.

In the morning, Skipper pointed out their boat, *Sparrow*,
swinging on a mooring buoy. It had pretty lines, and Will
guessed it might move through the water like a dancer. Though
not a sailor himself, he had the idea that boats might be like
planes and possess distinct personalities. Will wondered if Joe
and Skipper felt the same way about their boat as he felt about
his planes.

When the Ross crew all made it to the dining room, Joe
announced they'd be having breakfast American-style, rather

than Turkish, that morning. His face was flushed, and he was smiling as he pushed through the swinging door from the kitchen, carrying a pot of coffee in one hand and a pitcher of juice in the other.

"We decided having so many Yanks here was a good reason to break out the waffle iron," Joe said. "How do waffles and scrambled eggs sound?"

He was met with a chorus of approval and the sound of chairs scraping on the floor as everyone found seats around the big table.

Will was pleased that their hosts joined them after they brought heaping platters of food to the table. But rather than the sea story he had hoped for, Joe and Skipper related the tale of the two castles just a short walk down the beach from the *pansiyon*.

Korykos, the larger of the two, rose above a spit jutting out from shore, standing guard over the long, low coastline. And Kız Kalesi, the Maiden's Castle, stood on the small rocky island about a thousand feet offshore.

The legend started with a soothsayer's prophecy that the Byzantine King of Korykos's baby daughter would die by snake-bite. In response to the dire prediction, the monarch built an impenetrable palace where the princess would live safely tucked away from the world and its snakes.

"Alas," Joe said, with a wave of his arm for dramatic effect. "The curse comes to pass anyway."

"Isn't that how these stories go?" Skipper added, raising her eyebrows.

"The villain was a subject who felt slighted by the king. He swam out to the island, carrying a venomous snake in a basket of fruit. When he presented the plump purple grapes to the hungry princess, the snake"—Joe jabbed his hand in the air like a viper striking—"killed her."

"But, really," Skipper said, "how impenetrable can a castle be if any strong swimmer can get to it?"

Joe and Skipper finished the story as they cleared the breakfast dishes. The castles, they said, stood as monuments to the moral of the story: don't imprison someone in the name of protecting them.

Will didn't put much stock in the yarn Joe and Skipper told, but thought it'd be fun to explore the castles. After breakfast, they all trooped down to the beach. Will and Kevin decided to swim over to the island, and Buddy appeared more than ready to join them, prancing on the shore, delighted with his first taste of the ocean. Rob said he thought he could make the swim, but he wanted to ride the boat with Timur, Paula, and Didi instead.

They clambered over and around the ruins for hours. Kevin pointed out how they had been built, at least partially, from previous structures. There were segments of columns from older Roman structures in the walls, their circular cross sections incongruous within the stone block layers. The princess's castle, Kız Kalesi, covered most of the tiny island. It was just wide enough for the crew to walk around the perimeter, but not much more. They lunched on a flat, rocky spot looking out on the blue-green sea, as small waves broke on the jagged rocks immediately below them on the unsheltered side of the island.

It was a beautiful place, one of so many they'd found in Turkey. Will didn't want to leave. He wanted to see more of this country and do more of the work he loved. But how could he go about his business as if he didn't know of the potential danger upstream of the dam? The question clouded his mind despite the clear, sunny day.

The afternoon slipped away with Paula, Kevin, and Didi sketching. Rob and Timur wandered off, and, after a while, Will saw them down the shoreline, tossing rocks into the waves. Squinting at the sun sparkling on the sea, Will wished he'd brought his camera. But it would have distracted him from the problem at hand, and that's what he'd come to contemplate.

When Paula caught his eye and pointed to her watch, he knew she was signaling that they should head back. Despite mulling it over all afternoon, the answer Will sought was no less murky.

"Come on, crew," he called. "Time to go. Let's all ride the boat back across."

He led the way around to the lee side of the island. When they got there, they all started laughing. The tide had ebbed, revealing the remnants of a cut stone causeway between the two castles. They could walk right to the king's castle.

"So much for myths," Kevin said as they passed under the arched gate that welcomed them back on the mainland.

TWENTY-EIGHT

Paula rose early, leaving Will's bed to go to her room to shower and dress. She was sure she was only kidding herself that the children didn't know that they slept together. She didn't think they knew much beyond the sleeping part, but she might have been kidding herself about that too. Toweling dry, she thought about making love with Will the night before. Paula fully believed there was nothing wrong with who she was for Will or what she was doing with him. Still, the early programming recorded in her psyche rewound and played over in her mind—that she was *bad*. "Sinful" is what her granny would have said.

But bad sure feels good, she thought.

She figured she'd just have to live with the conflicting voices inside her head. Maybe everyone else did too—each with their own particular messages from their own particular pasts. Sometimes it was quieter in her head than other times. Depended on the day. Some days, good days, *her* voice spoke loudest.

"Let's make today a good day," Paula said, tousling her hair and smiling at herself in the mirror. Then she went in search of coffee.

"Morning," Skipper greeted her. She set a pitcher of fresh-squeezed orange juice on the table and arranged the butter dish and jars of jam.

"It looks beautiful," Paula said.

"Thanks. We love this."

"You can tell. You and your husband make a good team. Did you figure it all out sailing around the world together?"

"Living in a small, constantly moving space for months on end does provide its lessons, but with watches and all, on ocean crossings, you just kind of cross paths with each other. As long as everything's okay, that is. But when things get intense, like changing sails in heavy winds, stuff like that, teamwork means everything. Innkeeping seems pretty easy in comparison." Skipper paused. "By the way, Joe and I aren't married. That doesn't make a difference to you guys, does it?"

Paula wondered if Skipper saw the relief on her face. "Will and I aren't married either."

"Unless it's a big deal to one or the other or both of you, what's the point?" she asked. "We happen to feel that *not* being married makes us stronger. We're together because we choose it every day, not because it'd be a horrible mess to split up."

"And no one here minds? You *are* running a business, so what other people think matters, right?"

"Well, we don't advertise that we aren't married. I'm not even sure why I mentioned it. Maybe you looked like you needed to hear it."

"Maybe I did," Paula said, looking down.

"Coffee?" she asked.

"I thought you'd never ask."

"Come on," she waved for Paula to follow her into the kitchen. The swinging door squeaked as it swung back behind them.

Joe was cinching the tie of a crisp blue-and-white striped apron around his waist. "Guess those hinges need oiling again," he said.

"I'll put it on the list. Is the coffee ready yet?" Skipper asked.

He tipped his head toward the pot. "Just finished perking." Then Joe turned to Paula, his eyes warm and welcoming under bushy eyebrows, and said, "Skipper and I were talking last night. Will seems awfully interested in sailing, and we haven't had *Sparrow* out in a while—"

Paula interrupted him; she couldn't help herself. "Are you offering to take us out on *Sparrow*?"

"Only if you guys really want to go."

"I know I'd jump at the chance. I bet the others will too."

"We'll ask at breakfast," Skipper said.

And that's how they ended up going sailing for the very first time.

∾

Paula stood at the water's edge, her hands resting on Didi's shoulders. Joe rowed the dinghy back and forth four times to get everyone onto *Sparrow*, even Buddy. Paula and Didi were his passengers on the last trip, and when they got to *Sparrow*, Joe held the tippy little rowboat steady while she boosted Didi onto the deck. Looking up at everyone as Paula prepared to climb aboard herself, they all looked happy. The blue eyes of the Ross family, ranging from the color of the sky to the seawater surrounding them, all seemed to sparkle that morning.

"Welcome aboard our fair little ship," Skipper called over the rumble of the engine. "Looks like a great day for a sail. Joe and I'll teach you as much as you want, or as little. In other words, if you want to, you can just go along for the ride. But first things first—safety. On *Sparrow*, we all wear life jackets underway—that means when we're moving."

She smiled and went on, "Seafaring has very specific language, and you'll learn some of it today. Like all these ropes." She swept her hand, indicating the tidy coils that seemed to be everywhere. "On a boat, they aren't called ropes. They're lines."

Joe came up out of the little stairway that Paula thought must lead to the living quarters. His arms were filled with life jackets of various sizes. They got everyone into one, and Skipper went from one to the other, checking fit and tightening a buckle here and there.

"What about Buddy?" Kevin asked.

"They make life jackets for dogs, but we don't have one," Skipper said. "When we're underway, let's clip his leash to that pad eye"—she pointed to a metal fitting—"and put him in a sit- or down-stay. If he seems comfortable, he can sit up and watch what's going on, and if he's nervous, he can lie down and, hopefully, go to sleep. How does that sound?" she asked Kevin.

"Good," he said. "Thank you for letting him come."

In the few minutes before Joe cast them off from the mooring buoy, they had already learned about ten nautical terms.

"It's a lot to remember, I know," Skipper said. "But don't worry, there won't be a quiz. I just wanted to give you some basics so you'd get a sense of what Joe and I are talking about."

While they motored past the island with the princess's castle, Joe went forward and uncovered the sails. Skipper explained what he was doing while they watched.

As they came around a point, the wind, which had been nearly still, picked up. Just when Paula noticed it, Skipper's right hand reached over the wheel and pulled back on the engine's throttle, slowing the boat.

"Ready to set the main, Joe?" she asked.

"Righto," he said, heading for the mast.

There was a lot of clicking and clattering of the fittings on the sails and lines through pulleys, as Joe hoisted the sail.

"Hoist the jib," Skipper said.

And Joe raised the sail in front.

Then the magic happened. Skipper eased all the way off the throttle and turned the wheel. The sails filled, billowing out in graceful white arcs against the bright blue of the sky. *Sparrow* tilted slightly and slid forward, skimming the small waves.

"Will, please turn that key off," Skipper pointed to a panel just ahead of where he was sitting.

And then, the real magic happened. *Sparrow* sailed along—the only sounds were the *whoosh* of the breeze, the chuckle of water on the hull, and the quiet where the sound of the engine had been.

Without realizing she was speaking, Paula breathed, "Ohhhh. . . ."

Skipper laughed. "I know," she said. "I love it when the engine goes silent, when it's just *Sparrow* and us and the wind and the water. I never get tired of it."

There were no words. It was wonderful, in the truest sense—full of wonder.

And yet, it all made sense when Skipper explained how the physics of sailing worked. They did sailing circles, demonstrating all the points of sail. Everyone was having a grand time. Even Buddy—he sat tall, grinning his big goofy dog grin, his ears blowing in the breeze.

Kevin stood up on deck, then looked over his shoulder, and shouted, "Coming abaft of the beam!"

"Avast!" Skipper played along. "One hand for you, one for the boat, matey."

Holding on, Kevin made his way back to the cockpit and hugged his dog. "Isn't this fun, Bud?"

Joe made adjustments to the sails, sometimes at Skipper's command and sometimes on his own. They didn't talk much; their teamwork was seamless. Skipper made helming look easy, but they soon found out it wasn't, because she invited each of them to take a turn.

Paula hadn't gotten to fly with Will yet, but his face was a picture of concentration and joy as he steered the lovely *Sparrow*, and she thought that might be how he looked aloft.

Didi was the last one to take the helm. Skipper waited until the boat was back in the lee of the point that protected Kızkalesi from the prevailing west winds, and Joe had dropped the jib, easing the boat's speed. Didi stood on the helm seat, confident, with Skipper guiding her as she sailed *Sparrow* on the balmy breeze and rippled sea.

Paula's favorite photo of Dee was taken that day. Kevin caught her in just the right light, and whenever Paula looked at that picture, she saw the intelligence, courage, and joy that, for her, defined Didi.

"Okay, Didi, we're going to do this together, sail *Sparrow* right up to our mooring," Skipper said. She slid closer and put her hands on either side of Didi's. "Joe, get the boat hook and show the boys how to nab the ring. Then prepare to drop the main."

"Aye, Skipper," he said.

"You love this, don't you?" Paula asked.

"It shows?" Skipper grinned at her.

Didi beamed as *Sparrow* nudged up to the mooring.

"Now, Joe," Skipper said.

Paula marveled at how effortless they made it look. Of course, it wasn't, but that was what artists did. A painter could make light shimmer out of a canvas. A dancer flew without wings. A poet made words sing. And a sailor rode the wind with a grace Paula could only aspire to. What a magical day it had been.

∾

That evening, Paula sat on the beach holding hands with Will. Didi was asleep, exhausted from her big day. The boys were supposed to be getting ready for bed too, but she could hear laughter coming from their open windows.

"Did you like it?" Will asked, squeezing her hand.

"I *loved* it. I've never felt anything like that."

"It's like flying. Maybe even better. You don't have to worry about running out of gas. The wind's your fuel."

He put his arm around her, and she leaned into him. They sat together in silence for a beat or two.

"Can you imagine crossing oceans in a boat that small?" he said. "I've heard of people doing it, but I never met anyone who did. And they don't really seem out of the ordinary."

They watched the sunset shade to the blue of evening. "I can see us doing that," he said. "If Browning fires me, we should buy a boat and sail the Med for a few years. Explore it all, then cross the Atlantic and go from there. Would you go with us?"

"You think it'll come to that?"

"I don't know, but it's a tempting backup plan."

"We don't know how to sail," Paula pointed out.

"What better way to learn?" he asked.

That was Will—not always right, but never in doubt.

"Well, as the teacher of record here, I'll just say that getting thrown in over your head isn't necessarily the best way to learn."

"Sink or swim. . . ."

"Exactly," she said. "That's pretty black and white. Maybe learning to 'swim' is a good idea before jumping in the deep end. Metaphorically speaking. Although the reality of sinking a sailboat wouldn't be metaphorical at all."

He laughed. "Point taken."

"Besides, I hope DECCO will come to their senses and listen. I really do." Then uncharacteristically without doubt herself, she added, "But if they don't, give me enough time to serve notice, and you've got yourself a first mate."

She wouldn't let Will and his family, *her* family now, sail away without her.

TWENTY-NINE

Kevin was having the best time, even though he knew why they were there—that his father might lose his job for doing what was right, trying to protect people. The decision seemed as crystal clear to Kevin as the jeweled waters of the Mediterranean. His father said it wasn't so simple, that he was considering whether he could do what needed to be done as part of the project team, rather than by making a big pronouncement and getting fired for it. But Kevin saw it purely as a matter of wrong or right.

While his father was figuring out what to do, they had been swimming and sailing, and today they'd go snorkeling. At breakfast, Skipper and Joe told them about the scattered remains of a wreck close to shore, and they had masks, fins, and snorkels for everyone, except Rob and Timur said they'd pass. Timur couldn't swim much yet, and he was worried that kicking with fins might hurt his leg. They said they were good with hanging on the beach tossing a baseball. They'd brought their gloves, of course.

The two buddy pairs, Kevin and Dad, Didi and Paula, suited up and stepped awkwardly backward through the small waves washing up the beach. Dad gave Paula and Didi their first lessons in snorkeling while they were still in really shallow water. His father was holding Didi, and Paula was right beside them. As they practiced putting their faces in the water, looking around, coming up, and clearing their snorkels, Kevin swam out to where the water was about ten feet deep. He skimmed along, hands behind his back, listening to the hollow sound of his own breath in and out of the snorkel, diving and surfacing. The cool water slid over his body. He bent at the waist, kicked his fins up, pulled down through the water with sweeping strokes. He held his nose around the rubber of the mask and puffed, cleared his ears as he dove, felt the slight pop. At the bottom, he hovered over the tips of seagrass swaying in the current, and his hair stirred in the same rhythm. He felt part of this world.

When it was time, fluid as the water, he thrust his arms up, forced them down, and pulled himself to the surface in one smooth move, looking up at the sky shimmering above the column of water. As he broke the surface, squinting in the sun, he blew hard into the mouthpiece of his snorkel, spouting out the water it contained. He paddled his fins beneath him to keep his lean body upright. He imagined how the water arced out of the snorkel, how the sunlight would've caught it, how it rained down in droplets, each one radiating ripples. He wished he could have shot it, wondered what that picture would have looked like.

But you can't be two places at once, he thought. And here was where he wanted to be.

"Hey, Kev." Dad swam up to him.

"Where are they?" Kevin asked.

"They're going to stay closer in, look at the fish, get used to snorkeling. We can take them out to the wreck later if they want. Ready?"

Treading water, they oriented themselves, looking toward shore at the inn, then out toward the island. They headed in the direction Skipper and Joe suggested. Using their fins like fish, they propelled themselves, side by side, quiet and companionable.

"There," Dad said through his snorkel, pointing ahead.

Kevin didn't see anything and wondered if his father was somehow reading the sea floor like he read the land. But with a few more kicks forward, Kevin glimpsed what Dad must've seen through the blades of seagrass. Pottery. Lots of it. Most were pieces about the size of his hand, though he knew that the water made things look bigger.

Like synchronized swimmers, they dove.

The sandy seafloor was littered with pottery shards. He reached the bottom and scooped up a handful of sand. Small shards were so plentiful they seemed like part of the sediment itself. The ship's hold must've been filled with urns and amphorae, all shattering when the ship ran aground. The wood hull had decomposed, leaving only the slivered clay remains of the cargo. He picked up bigger pieces, looking for painting or patterns, signs of the age or culture they came from.

A small, stout fish, silver gray with three black stripes top to bottom and bright yellow eyes, darted out of the grass and bumped his mask, shooing him from its territory. Kevin poked his finger at it, then followed it with his eyes as it looped up and back to thump his mask again. He liked the little guy's determination, so he let the fish have his way. He needed to surface anyway.

Dad was on his way down as Kevin was on his way up. They waved as they passed.

He cleared his snorkel and took a few more deep breaths before diving again. He scissored his fins, reached and pulled with his arms, heading back to the bottom. Then he saw it. A red-brown handle curving out of the sand. He descended, steering toward it. He reached it, reached out, and it felt like the lives of those who used it tingled in his fingertips when he touched it. He jiggled the handle but it didn't move. He dug around it with his right hand, trying to lift it with his left. It shifted a bit, and his fingers slid from the handle onto a narrow neck. It was an amphora, maybe whole. The fine sand jammed under his fingernails, but he ignored the pain and kept digging. He dug, jiggled, pulled, working the jug free from the seabed that held it captive. For how long? Hundreds of years? Maybe thousands? Sand swirled in the water around him.

Kevin's heart pounded. A last tug and the amphora broke free. He hugged it to his chest in the cloud of sand and water that engulfed him, and kicked for the surface.

Too late, Kevin realized it was too late. Unable to hold his breath a second longer and unable to see the surface in the churning water and sand, he inhaled a lungful of seawater. He choked, coughed, and gagged, then gasped in more. His body twisted, contorted against the assault. His chest heaved against the amphora, clinging to it, kicking, still believing he'd make it to the surface. His legs thrashed him upward. His stomach expelled the salt water and sand he'd swallowed, then he choked the vomit in again. His right hand clawed up through the water, reaching for the surface. It was too far. He felt his eyes bulge. His fingers unfurled. His treasure slid from his hand. It bumped his legs as it fell away.

Then Kevin knew. You *can* be two places at once. He watched his body sink through the water. It settled beside his beautiful find. And here was where he wanted to be.

∽

"No!" Will screamed through his snorkel when he saw Kevin sprawled upon the sandy bottom. He bolted for the surface to breathe, gulped air, then dove. His son lay like a perfect sea star, limbs splayed, as he so often did while sleeping. Will needed this to be a very short nap. He told himself he knew what to do, how to save a life. And he knew there wasn't much time to do it. He scooped his right arm under Kevin's shoulders, his left under his knees. He pulled his feet up and under him and pushed off the bottom, creating a cyclone of sand and seawater through which they rose.

Bursting to the surface, Will swung Kevin's limp body onto his back, his left arm under Kevin's chin. Adrenaline powering them toward the shore, Will's right arm pulled strong strokes and his legs lashed the water. *Hang on, Kev, hang on*—an internal chant accompanied the thunder of Will's breathing. When his heels brushed the bottom, he yanked his fins off, stood up, lifted Kevin in his arms, and charged out of the water.

Will dropped to his knees, Kevin's body lurching to the ground in front of him. He pulled Kevin to a sitting position and whacked his back as hard as he could. He turned him onto his side and thumped his back again. A slurry of sand and mucus slithered out of the corner of Kevin's mouth.

Will laid Kevin flat, tipped his head back, opened his mouth, made sure his airway was clear, and pinched his nostrils. He clamped his mouth tight over Kevin's, forcing down the gag reflex that rose at the taste of vomit, and exhaled hard into Kevin's lungs. One, two, three. He stacked his hands atop Kevin's sternum and was about to start compressions when his son's chest heaved. He coughed, choked, took a rasping breath, coughed again.

Will wrenched him upright, pounded his back harder, and more sand and snot and seawater and puke dribbled from his mouth. Kevin drew another breath, then choked out more slime. His hand came up and wiped at his chin. He gulped air, then choked on it. With Will supporting his back, he sat mostly upright, legs sprawled out in front of him, coughing and coughing and coughing.

But you can't cough unless you're breathing.

Will stared at his son's contorted face. "Oh God, oh God," he intoned.

Kevin was breathing. He was alive.

Will felt, rather than saw, someone approaching. His eyes flashed on Paula sprinting toward them. Rob and Didi were on her heels, with Timur half running, half limping behind.

The spasms racking Kevin's body lessened, and he inhaled a deeper breath. He coughed, then spit. And looked at Will. "What's the secret ingredient?" he asked, his voice hoarse.

"What?" Will said.

"The secret ingredient? In the Kahraman Mariş *dondurma*. What is it?"

"What the hell?" Will said, rocking back on his heels, his hands landing flat on the wet sand behind him.

Kevin slumped, but Paula caught him.

"A kind of flour made from the roots of wild orchids. It makes it thick and kind of gooey," she said, kneeling down and supporting Kevin's back.

"Are you crazy?" Will said.

"What?" Kevin asked.

"Why do you ask?" Paula said.

"Am I missing something here?" Will said.

"He's disoriented," she said.

"I am?" Kevin asked. "Why?"

Will was stunned. Was there brain damage? Hadn't he gotten Kevin breathing fast enough?

"Kevin, honey," Paula said. "I think you almost drowned. Is that right, Will?"

He nodded.

"You've had a big shock. You may not even remember it right now. But you're here . . . your dad saved you."

"Really?" Kevin said.

Will nodded again.

"Wow," Rob said. "What's that like?"

"Do you feel okay?" she asked.

"My throat hurts," he said.

"Maybe we should go to a doctor and make sure everything's okay," Paula said.

"Yes," Will said.

"Okay," Kevin said. "I guess. But what about Buddy?"

Paula's fingers brushed at Kevin's bangs. She touched him so tenderly, Will felt like he might cry. He blinked hard.

"Skipper and Joe are watching Buddy," she said.

"Who?" Kevin asked.

"Buddy's fine, Kev. We'll take care of him while you're at the doctor's," she said.

"Can you stand up?" Will asked.

Kevin pedaled his legs in the sand in front of him. "I think so, but I can't walk with them." He pointed at his fins.

"See, he's coming around," Paula said, as if she'd read the worry running through Will's mind. "It's going to be okay."

∾

Will called the *pansiyon*.

"*Merhaba*," Skipper answered.

"It's Will. I told Paula I'd call. Is she there?"

"Yes, hang on," Skipper said. Will heard her asking Joe to get Paula. "How is he?"

"Looks like he'll be fine. We're lucky," he said. "I'll let Paula fill you in, okay?"

"Of course." Then, "Joe, come on!"

Will held the line.

"Hello? Will?" Paula said. "What took so long? Is everything okay?"

"Yes. We went to the hospital in Adana, but their X-ray was down. They suggested we go to the clinic at Incirlik. They called ahead to tell them we were coming. They took X-rays of his lungs and his cervical spine. They were normal. They took some blood too. They want to keep him under observation overnight. Pulmonary edema can happen for hours after . . . after a near drowning."

He heard her exhale. "What's pulmonary edema?"

"Fluid in the lungs, which he obviously had some of. If it's severe, it can cause respiratory failure. But they think he'll be okay. They just want to be sure."

"How does he seem?" she asked.

"Still a little out of it. But they told me not to worry about that, that he'd resurface, in a manner of speaking. The doctor said except for babies drowning in bathtubs, teenaged boys are the most frequent drowning victims. He said their bodies grow so fast that their brains can't keep up, and they get out of sync. He said that Kevin's body didn't signal his brain that his lungs were out of air until it was too late for him to get to the surface in time."

"That makes sense. Kevin's usually so careful."

"He was concentrating on that amphora. In the car, he remembered it. He said he wanted to go back for it."

"What did you tell him?"

"That we'd talk about it later."

"How're you?"

"Exhausted. Hungry."

"Maybe kind of shaken up?"

"I wouldn't admit it, would I?" Will smiled in spite of the day he'd had.

"No, you wouldn't."

Will could hear the smile in her voice too.

"So, what now?"

"Get something to eat, then find a place to crash for the night. We'll be back tomorrow."

"Will, you were great today."

"He's my boy. What else could I do?"

"Still, you were great. And I love you."

Will took a deep breath. "Thank you, sweetheart. I love you too. See you tomorrow," he said and hung up.

∞

Will's hand trembled getting the key into the ignition. He sat for a minute, rested both hands on the wheel, and stared through the windshield at the building where his son slept—peaceful and breathing evenly, at least when Will left him.

He realized in that moment, in a way that literally shook him to his core, that he almost lost Kevin today—his beautiful boy. Kevin's mere being, his arrival in the squirming, squalling package of baby boy he was, helped Will make himself the man he didn't necessarily believe he could be. A good man, he liked to think. And for the second time that day, he almost cried.

Instead, he gripped the wheel hard. Rejecting emotion as a basis for this response, he blamed fatigue, hunger, and coming off the hours-long adrenaline rush that had carried him from the moment he saw Kevin on the seafloor until now. Just now, when Will felt certain that Kevin was safe. He reached down and turned the key. He looked over at the clinic one more time, then over his shoulder, and backed out. He'd get some food. Then some sleep. He'd be fine and back to himself in the morning.

Wings Grill and Bar, located right outside the gates of the air base, was the first place Will came to where he could get some food. He pulled over and went in. He'd been in his share of base bars, though not in a very long time. He immediately felt at home in the loud, smoky atmosphere. He dropped onto the last empty barstool, uniformed men on either side of him.

"Hi," the man on his left greeted him. "You a civilian employee here? New?"

"No. I don't work at Incirlik," Will said. "My son's at the clinic. He almost drowned today. He's okay, but they want to observe him overnight. Make sure."

"Wow, that's something. What happened, man?"

Will found himself telling this stranger the whole story. He didn't know why. It just poured out—where he worked and why they were there, the adventures of the past year and the last few days. And then what happened that morning, ending with Kevin on the beach taking his first ragged breaths after nearly drowning.

The man gave a low whistle. "You deserve a drink," he said. He waved the bartender over. "Hey, Mike, I want to buy this man a drink. He saved his son from drowning today. And I'll have another."

Will was just about to say he didn't touch the stuff, like he'd said whenever this came up for the past sixteen years. But why be unfriendly? One wouldn't hurt. And he could use a drink. His hands vaguely quivered on the bar in front of him, though he hoped the others couldn't tell. It had been a hell of a day.

"What'll you have?"

"What's he having?" Will tipped his head toward his new friend.

"He likes the local stuff, rakı."

"I'll try that," Will said. "Thanks, uh. . . ."

"Rich," his seatmate said. "Always happy to celebrate, uh. . . ."

"Will," he said and shook Rich's hand.

The bartender put a glass half-full of clear liquid down in front of each of them and a small carafe of water between them. Will watched Rich pour the water into the rakı, filling the glass, and he followed suit. The rakı eddied into a cloudy white as the liquids mixed, like a swirl of smoke in the air when a candle was blown out—like Kevin's life could've swirled away in the sea and sand.

"Here's to your son," Rich said.

Will raised his glass and drank, licking the sweet anise from his lips after he swallowed. "To my son," he said.

PART IV

THIRTY

Will sat alone on the Kızkalesi beach in the middle of the night. Wavelets swished onto the shore below, and the moon shone above. Shadows played on the weathered white limestone of the castles. He drank from a bottle in long, slow swallows. Had their outing to those castles only been three days ago? It seemed like a lifetime. And it could've been—Kevin's. Will reflected on the legend of Kız Kalesi. Even kings, with all their power, couldn't protect their children from their fates. He'd just been lucky. If he'd been facing away from Kevin rather than toward him in that fateful moment, he might have been too late. He shook his head, dispelling the thought. Then he drank until there were no thoughts.

∾

June 30, 1974

Dear Mom,

How are you? I'm fine. (*Except for almost drowning on Friday*, he thought.) Rob and Didi are good too. We're on the coast of the Mediterranean Sea this week. Timur's along too. We're having a great time. (*Except for almost drowning that is*, he thought.) The first day, we explored some ruins, which is pretty much a theme around here. The second day we went sailing. The people who own the little hotel we're staying at are Americans who took their sailboat across oceans. And it's only 32 feet long!

217

Can you imagine? They invited us all to go sailing on their boat that day. It was neat. Then the next day we went snorkeling. Dad and I went farther out than the others and explored what was left of an old shipwreck. There wasn't really anything left of the ship, but its hold must've been full of clay pottery jars, because the whole seafloor there was covered with pot shards. I found an amphora and tried to dig it out of the sand, but I had to leave it on the bottom. (*Because I almost drowned*, he thought.) I tried to get Dad to go back for it with me, but we had other stuff going on today. (*Resting, because the doctor said I should after, well, you know*, he thought.) We leave tomorrow.

That's all that's going on. (*Except for almost drowning*, he thought one last time, at least the last time while writing that letter.) Miss you, Mom.

Love, Kevin

∽

Kevin turned out the light in the boys' room. They were supposed to get to sleep, because they'd be leaving for home early the next morning.

Rob's voice came from across the room. "For once it was you making the bonehead move," he said.

"Yeah," Timur agreed.

"How the hell do you *forget* to come up for air?" Rob asked.

"I was busy," Kevin said.

"Too busy to *breathe*?" Rob laughed and Timur joined in. Even Kevin smiled into the darkness. That did sound pretty stupid.

"Were you scared?" Rob asked. "Did you think you were gonna die?"

"Do you really want to know?"

"I do," Timur said.

"Me too," Rob said. "What was it like?"

Kevin thought for a minute; then he took a deep breath, and he was aware of it, breathing.

"I'm not even sure I remember it all," he said. "But when I realized I was out of air, I did kind of panic. That felt scary. And I tried to get to the surface, but I just had to breathe before I got there, and I sucked in a bunch of water and choked on it, I think. But I don't know if I was really thinking anymore by then. It was all just sort of happening. But then, it was kind of amazing, it was like I was hanging in the water, watching myself, watching my body. It went limp, my body, and started sinking, and it got to the bottom and settled there, real gently. And I was watching it all. I didn't feel panicky at all. I felt fine. I felt like I was right where I wanted to be, kind of suspended, in the ocean, in time. It was like when you have a flying dream, and you're magically hovering in the air. . . ." Kevin paused. "Then I don't remember anything else. Until the beach."

"Dude, did you see the white light?" Rob asked.

"Are you being an asshole? 'Cause if you are, fuck you. You said you wanted to know, so I told you. Maybe I did make a bonehead move, but you could try not being a dick, for once. And just in case you weren't, on that off chance—no, I didn't see any light. But that time, that time floating in the sea and in space, that was amazing, and I'll never forget it."

THIRTY-ONE

Will went directly to Borkan's office, tapped his knuckles twice on the door, then reached for the knob to let himself in. The door was locked. *Odd*, Will thought. He glanced around the office. It looked like the junior staff were all in the field, as usual, their desks unoccupied. He checked his watch: two o'clock. Too late for Erdem to be at lunch, too early for him to have left for the day.

Will needed to talk with him, to brainstorm how they could make the dam, and the reservoir, safe—*and* keep their jobs. Kayakale was home. Will didn't want to leave, and he didn't want to uproot his family again, especially after what had happened. He needed things to settle. He needed for his family to get their feet back under them. *He* needed to get his bearings. Now was not the time for a complete change in course.

Will let himself into his office. It was just as he'd left it, a neat stack of field reports on one side of the desk, waiting to be filed. The other side was clear, for now. By the end of the day, he expected it to be piled with his staff's field reports from the past week.

He saw the envelope when he pulled his chair out to sit down. It said, simply, "Will Ross" in Erdem's impeccable handwriting. Will sank into the chair, holding the letter, unopened, in his hands. He tipped his head back, contemplating the ceiling panels. After several minutes, he took the letter opener from his desk drawer and sliced the envelope open. He slid the handwritten pages from it and unfolded them deliberately, as he was sure Erdem would have folded them and sealed them and left them for him. It was dated June 26. Will counted back the days, five days before, last Wednesday. He thought for a moment, remembering their day at the Kızkalesi castles.

Dear Will,

You are a valued colleague, and you have also become my friend; therefore, I would have preferred to tell you in person what I will say in this letter, but I am departing for Ankara tomorrow, so this will have to do. I will submit my resignation from DECCO, effective immediately, to Gus Browning upon arrival in Ankara.

My intention is to seek a job with DSI. I feel I must do all I can to ensure the safety of the dam. This is my responsibility, both as a professional engineer and a son of Kayakale village. Based on Browning's words and deeds, I do not believe I can do that within the ranks of the prime contractor. Perhaps I can within the ranks of DSI, the owner of the project and the regulator of Turkey's hydroelectric program. That will be the first avenue I explore going forward.

Staying in Kayakale and working at the site would be my personal preference, as you know. Upon reflection, however, I cannot make this decision based on my desires. Nor will I indulge in a surreptitious plan to investigate the safety issues you and I have identified. That type of investigation is the kind that Browning, as my predecessor at Kayakale Dam, may have conducted, and I will not put myself in that same category of engineer. Though I believe my reasons would be in the right and his were not, it would still besmirch the title and the profession.

Matters concerning the safety of a project on the

scale of Kayakale must be paramount, and public. Turkey cannot step into its rightful and deserved place in the world if we do not operate as such. I am going to Ankara to try to take my place in that process.

I have, of course, discussed this at length with Lale. Like me, her preference would be to stay in Kayakale. We missed our families very much in the years we were gone, and we now confront that prospect again. However, neither of us could face ourselves, each other, or our families if a catastrophe befell Kayakale Dam that could have been prevented.

So with a heavy heart, I again leave my home. But I leave with the hope of making Kayakale Dam safe.

Whatever your decision, I trust it will be well considered. It has been a privilege and a pleasure to work with you. I will never again take for granted the geologic framework of any foundation that an engineered project is built upon, and in that way, you have made me a better engineer. I also appreciate your great acts of friendship, particularly flying Timur to Ankara when he was hurt. Words of thanks do not seem adequate, but it is what I have to offer.

Most sincerely,
Erdem Borkan

Will stared, his eyes blank. As if in slow motion, he placed the pages down, set his elbows on the desk, leaned forward, and held his head in both hands.

"Shit," he said. "Shit, shit, shit."

Will hadn't been a hundred percent sure of his decision, but he'd been inclined to stay on the job, to see if they could deal with the problem from within the project team. And he realized now, he'd counted on doing that *with* Erdem Borkan.

The letter was formal, eloquent, even noble. Like Erdem himself, now that Will thought about it. His colleague sounded assured of his decision, though it was not the one he wanted to make. Will asked himself if he was rationalizing, thinking he could do what was right *and* stay.

He raised his head and shook it. He couldn't believe he was in this position. He'd been certain that when he and Borkan explained the situation, they'd be given the go-ahead to study it, take it on, and solve it, like they had with the dam's foundation.

He checked the time. He had to decide by the end of the day. The week was nearly up. He had two and a half hours.

∾

Will left a phone message with the receptionist in Ankara right before leaving his office. He said, simply, "This is Will Ross. Tell Mr. Browning I'm on the job. He'll understand. *Teşekkür ederim.*"

He thought about it as he traversed the path from the office to the house, the path he had walked so many times in the past year. Was it a year? Today was the first of July. So, yes, just a few weeks shy of a year now. It had been a good year—until he found that damned slope. But not finding it wouldn't change the fact of it, just the fact of knowing about it. A scientist could never believe that not knowing was better than knowing.

Will hoped Borkan, quiet and proper but smart and tough, would indeed land a job with DSI. As DECCO's client, DSI could insist that the reservoir area be fully evaluated, could insist that Browning be replaced. Will hoped there was hope. His decision was to sit tight and see.

Preoccupied as he mounted the stairs to the house, Rob blindsided him, slamming out of the screen door, swinging.

"I hate you!" his son screamed, landing a few punches to Will's chest and gut before Will got hold of his wrists. They struggled, Rob yelling and twisting in an effort to escape Will's grasp. Paula and Didi rushed onto the porch as they scuffled.

"What the hell?" Will shouted, moving his grip to Rob's shoulders and shaking the boy. "What's wrong? Stop this. Tell me what's wrong."

"Will!" Paula said. "Be careful."

"You know what's wrong. It's your fault!" Rob panted.

"What are you talking about?"

"Timur's moving away! His mother told us his father quit. She's packing up their house. It's your fault."

"What?" Paula said.

"I just found out myself, Rob. Erdem left a letter at the office."

"You knew! You put him up to it, didn't you? Now, Timur's moving away. I hate you! I'm never going to speak to you again. Ever!" Rob wrenched himself from Will's hold. He bolted down the stairs and across the square, running toward the Borkans' house.

"Cripes." Will looked over his shoulder at the nearby houses and the neighbors poking their heads out their doors. "At least we know where he's going," Will said. "Let's go inside."

He could stand a drink about now, though he'd wait until the rest of the crew went to bed.

∾

Will spoke with Borkan on the phone a few days later. No news on the work front as yet, but Will wished him well—for his friend's sake, the sake of Erdem's family, the sake of the safety of the Kayakale project, and, he would admit it, for his own sake.

Through Paula, Rob asked to stay at the Borkans' house. The timing of their move was uncertain, and Lale had extended an invitation to Rob for as long as she and Timur remained in

Kayakale. Will was sure that Timur was as unhappy as Rob about their impending separation. The depth of the boys' friendship was evident, and Will did feel for them.

But it wasn't just Rob; the whole crew seemed on edge. If Paula asked him one more time if he was okay, Will thought he'd lose it. Work, which was busy as ever, in fact more so without Borkan, was a welcome excuse for him to dodge all the damned emotions at home.

A week after getting back, Will switched onto night shift. The first night was always the hardest and he dragged himself home that morning. Kevin was drying the breakfast dishes when Will walked into the kitchen to grab a glass. All he wanted was a quick drink, a shower, and sleep.

"Hi, Dad."

"Hey, Kev."

"Could I ask you something?"

"Sure."

"Do you want to talk about it?"

Will almost groaned. "I don't think so. Do you?"

Paula came up behind Will, wrapped her arms around his waist, and rested her chin on his shoulder, looking over it at Kevin.

"I just thought you seemed kind of, I don't know . . . distracted? And I thought you might be worried. So I was wondering if we needed to talk about it. It was kind of a big deal."

"Yes." Will had to agree with that. But he didn't even want to think about it, much less talk about it.

"I guess I just want you to know I'm not freaked out or anything. I feel fine," Kevin said, drying his hands and folding the towel. "And there's this . . . after I started for the surface and couldn't make it, after the choking and stuff, something happened. It was like I was watching my body. I watched it settle to the bottom. It was like being suspended in time and space, but I wasn't scared. It was like when you have a dream that you're flying. Maybe it was like your best times flying, you know, Dad?"

Paula stepped around Will and hugged Kevin, murmuring something to him about how glad she was that he hadn't been afraid. Kevin's eyes were on Will while he returned Paula's embrace.

Did Kevin want something from him? What? He loved his son, more than anything. He wanted to help while Kevin found his way through the aftermath of what had happened. But did this mean his son was going to end up as some la-di-da, spiritually enlightened type?

He kept himself from rolling his eyes. He wanted to do the right things, say the right things, but he didn't know what those things were. A drink sure wouldn't hurt right now. It would make all this talking about *it* a lot easier to take.

THIRTY-TWO

Paula ran more in the weeks after they got back to Kaya-kale than she had in a long time. The finish line of a race was a worthy goal, but in Turkey, Paula ran by and for herself. Moving her body through space always helped move her toward solutions or resolutions, of specific issues or less specific feelings. It had been her salvation from the time she was a teen. The problem that summer: Paula didn't know what she was running through. Not at first.

She had come to love the dry, mountainous Turkish landscape, so different from the rolling green hills back home. There was a stark beauty to it. The contrasts in the landscape resonated with the contrasts she felt, between what Will and she shared before and at Kızkalesi, and what she felt, or didn't, after the trip.

So much had happened. Kevin had almost died, Mr. Borkan had made the decision to resign, and Will had made the decision not to. There was a lot going on for Will, and Paula was doing her best to understand. But she had felt so close to him before; and afterward, he seemed so distant. He was avoiding her, avoiding all of them, even when he was home, and he wasn't home much.

Kevin went back to work at the dig, so Paula didn't see much of him either. Remarkably, he didn't seem the worse for wear after nearly drowning. What he did seem was disappointed in Will. He confided to her that he believed his father was wrong in not taking a stronger stand for the dam's safety, even if it cost him his job. Even if it meant that the Rosses had to move, like the Borkans, which Kevin admitted he didn't want to do. To Kevin, Will's choice had cost his father his integrity. He told her he had just begun to trust his father again, even understanding him in a way he couldn't have a year ago, and now that trust and understanding had been shattered. Again. Kevin wouldn't even engage in a conversation about the nuances of his father's decision.

Rob had pretty much moved in with Timur. They'd been inseparable for nearly a year and the Borkans' move was going to be rough on them. Paula got why Rob wanted to spend as much time with his friend as he could. She didn't agree that Timur's having to move was Will's fault, but as long as she'd known Rob, that had been his position. If he could blame something on his father, he would.

Paula noticed that Didi seemed to be walking on eggshells. She wanted to make everything okay for everyone, but no one could do that. Paula spied her hugging Buddy a lot, and she hoped that helped.

And Paula . . . well, she took to the hills.

∿

Will got up when his alarm went off, for day or night shift. When he rose, he did his push-ups and sit-ups. He worked with his field team, reviewed shift reports, compiled data, and wrote progress reports.

Days passed, then a week. And another. Like before, Will made sure to eat dinner at home at least once a week to appease Paula. He worked long hours, taking shifts in the field, then catching up on the backlog of paperwork that piled up, page by page, file by file. It filled the time until he could take his next drink.

At first, he drank in hiding. Will knew how to do this. Years ago, before Kevin was born, he'd done the same thing month after month, year after year. But he couldn't rationalize it now—like he had years ago—and he kept telling himself he'd stop.

Soon, he wouldn't question whether he'd made the right choice to stay on the project. Soon, he'd be able to get through a day without thinking of Kevin almost dying. And then he'd stop.

But he didn't. He drank. And drank and drank. Scotch. Vodka. Rakı. He found out who to go to for what he needed, whenever he needed it.

As the days and nights wore on, he needed more, and he started feeling lapses. Not at work, never at work—at home, where he let his guard down. He could tell from the way his family's eyes followed him that they were seeing something. But it would be okay, because he would stop.

Will opened the door to the boys' bedroom one night. Buddy raised his head and thwapped his tail, and Will smiled. Kevin slept, his limbs splayed, like he so often did, and, in that moment, Will saw his son spread upon the sandy seafloor. He began to shake, and his throat closed. He couldn't breathe. He shut the door with a trembling hand and hurried down the hall. Then, remembering Paula asleep in his bed, he continued out the front door and down the porch stairs. He ran the few remaining steps to the Land Cruiser. He'd stashed a bottle under the seat.

Relief washed over him at the first long, warm swallow. He pulled a deep breath into his hungry lungs. His hands steadied. Just one more night, he told himself. I'll stop tomorrow.

But he said that night after night after night.

∽

Kevin sat at the kitchen table after breakfast. It was Sunday, the day he wrote to his mother back in New Jersey. He scribbled the date on his notepad, followed by "Dear Mom." Then he wavered, his pen poised over the page.

July 21, 1974

Dear Mom,

How are you? I'm fine. I'm pretty sure it was a year ago today that we left for Turkey. So that means it's a year since we've seen you. Then again, we didn't see you that day, because Dad picked us up at 11:00, like always, and you were never up that early, since you'd have been hungover, like always.

You know, I'm never going to take a drink. Not one. Not ever. I hate alcohol. I hate what it does to people. I hate that it makes them not care. And you know what else? I hate alcoholics. That means I hate you. And Dad too.

I thought life was finally okay, even better than okay. Good. I was happy, Mom. I gotta tell you, it's been a relief not taking care of you. You were supposed to be taking care of us, but you're really kind of a big baby. You're a lot like the girls at Moorestown High. You probably consider that a compliment, but I don't mean it as one.

I don't get why you started drinking so much. And I don't remember Dad ever drinking, so why'd he go and start? I just don't understand. I never got why Dad did things the way he did, but I got to where I understood what he did. Getting us away from you was the right thing to do. I see that now. No kid should have to clean up his drunk mother's puke or put her clothes on after she passes out naked in the living room after screwing her asshole boyfriend in the middle of the fucking house. But now we're starting that whole scene all over again.

So where are we gonna go now? Not back to you. Maybe Paula would take us. Even though she's not our mother, she acts more like one than you did. But she doesn't seem to see what's happening with Dad. Is it because she's that crazy about him? Is that why they say love is blind? If that's true, I don't ever want to fall in love either. Not fucking ever.

I guess I could leave. Dad was sixteen when he enlisted. Left home and never went back. But it was just him. I can't leave Rob and Didi in this mess. I won't.

I don't know what I'm gonna do, Mom. That's what's new here.

Love and fucking kisses, Kevin

P.S. Even though I write you all these nicey-nice letters, and I always tell you I miss you, I don't. Not really. So there.

Kevin was breathing hard when he finished. He hadn't realized how mad he was. He read back over it, and even though he was angry, parts of the letter made him laugh, but it was bitter laughter. He knew he wouldn't send the letter, but it sure felt good to write it. He ripped the pages off the pad, wadded them up, and shoved them into his pocket.

He skipped sending a letter to his mother that week. He couldn't bring himself to fake it this time.

∽

Paula tossed and turned on a hot night in late July. When the light of the waxing moon passed across her face, she opened her eyes, untangled herself from the clammy sheets, and got up. Will wasn't in bed, either.

She looked in on the kids. They were all asleep, covers thrown off, sweaty hair stuck to their foreheads. Only Buddy raised his head when she opened the boys' door. He panted a few heavy breaths, then laid his head back down.

The concrete floor felt cool under her bare feet. At least something felt cool. Hoping for a breeze, she headed down the hall for the porch. Maybe Will had done the same.

He turned and smiled when Paula sat down beside him on the bottom step. Then he lifted a bottle and took a swig. He held it out to her.

What the. . . ? she thought.

"No, thank you," she said.

"You drink, though," he said.

"But you don't."

"I guess I do, honey" he said, his words slurred.

"You're drunk?"

He nodded slowly and turned away from her. The moonlight lit his profile.

"Why?" Paula asked.

"Why not? Ask any drunk. We drink to celebrate, we drink when we're sad, we drink to someone's health. Or someone's death. Or almost death. Or life. *L'chaim.*"

"Oh, Will."

"Baby, don't be like that. It isn't the end of the world." He snorted an odd laugh. "But maybe it feels like it some days." He shook his head slowly. "I keep thinking I'll quit again."

"So why don't you?"

"Easier said than done. Ask any drunk." And as if to punctuate the point, he lifted the bottle and emptied it.

"When?" she asked.

"What does it matter?"

"I want to know."

"The night that Kevin almost"—he hesitated—"drowned. I stopped to get dinner. There was a bar. I told an airman the story. He wanted to buy me a drink. I almost said what I've said for all those years. Fifteen? Sixteen? Then I thought, why not? One drink won't hurt. Now I know why not. I never could take just one drink. But it had been so long . . . no problem . . . I didn't think it would be. I was wrong, baby." He barked a short, harsh laugh. "You know I don't say that very often, but I was wrong. And you know . . . it's funny. Kevin almost drowned, and now I'm the one who's drowning."

He turned back to her, a twisted smile on his chiseled face. "I love you, you know. You won't leave us, will you?" He stroked her cheek, planted a boozy kiss on her lips. "I *love* you."

"I love you too," she said, trying to hold his gaze, but his eyes flickered away.

She looked up at the moon.

"Will? What made you stop last time?"

"Crashed. My motorcycle. Drunk. Damn, I loved that bike. A fifty-one Indian." His voice was dreamy. "Kevin was just a baby. I almost died. I wanted to see him grow up. So I quit. Cold turkey."

"Don't you want to see them all grow up?"

"Baby, don't be like that."

After a while, he rambled on, "Maybe I'm like my mother . . . more than I care to admit . . . just can't let it be, when things are good . . . she never could let me be . . . happy. Don't think she was herself . . . maybe not ever . . . so she couldn't stand if I was. Always screwing up any good times . . . running off any people who cared. Damn . . . am I doing that? Am I doing that to my kids? Am I doing that to you? Shit. . . ." He folded his arms across his knees and laid his head down.

"I'm not going anywhere," Paula said, wondering if she'd made a double entendre of sorts. Shit, indeed. She remembered Will saying, "Shit, shit, shit," when that rockfall rained down on them early on, at Nemrut Dağı. What was raining down on them now?

"I need to stop," he mumbled, his head still down.

"Yes. Is it possible you didn't want to make the decision that week? That you used what happened to Kevin as an excuse? To take a drink? To not decide?"

"Anything's possible."

"Maybe you need to. Now," she said. "Decide. Did you really make the choice in staying, in not standing up to Browning? Not making a choice *is* making a choice. Just not a conscious one."

"Things were so good, and then they weren't."

Again, they sat in silence. The moonlight made the silver strands in Will's rumpled hair shine. Paula reached over and smoothed it. She absolutely loved him, and seeing him like this pained her. She couldn't begin to imagine what it felt like to him.

"I'm tired." He stood, then made his way slowly up the stairs.

Paula stayed behind. Contemplating the moon. Feeling the warm air of the summer night moving in and out of her lungs. Absorbing the fact that Will had been drinking—for weeks. How could she not have seen it? She felt stupid. And sad.

She heard echoes from her past. Mama, in the kitchen, kneeling down to hug her. Unsteady at best, visibly shaking at worst. "Don't be like that, baby girl," she would say. "Don't cry. Mama's gonna stop." Paula hadn't understood what she needed to stop, and she would feel so stupid. And sad.

She lingered to watch the moon set, feeling the darkness after. Finally, she noticed how hard the concrete felt. She rose stiffly, climbed the stairs, and made her way down the hall. She struggled to convince herself it would be all right. That he *would* stop. He said he was trying to. She wanted to believe him.

∽

Paula started out running on the trail one morning, then took off cross-country. It was early, not too hot yet. She picked up the pace, then pushed up a hill and took five quick steps at the top, like her high school coach always told them to. She almost ran right over Kevin. Buddy barked sharp and loud.

Breathing hard, she gasped out, "It's okay, Buddy. It's just me."

Kevin looked up and lifted a hand in a wave. He was sitting cross-legged in front of a fire ring. He poked at the embers of a small campfire with a stick.

"I thought you were home, asleep. It's your day off."

"Nope," he said.

"Kind of early for marshmallows, isn't it?"

"Yeah. I wrote something I didn't want anyone to see." He smiled up at her, but it wasn't his usual sweet smile. More sardonic than sweet. "But it felt pretty good to write it. And *really* good to burn it." He jabbed at the pile of ashes.

"So. . . ." She paused. "Do you want to talk about it?"

"Oh. You know? Took you long enough."

"Thanks, Kev," she said. Sweat dripped into her eyes, and she rubbed at them. "I didn't feel bad enough already."

"Sorry." He leaned his elbows on his knees and rested his chin in his hands. "What are we going to do?"

"I don't know." Paula sank down to sit across from him. "I don't think *we* can do anything. He has to stop on his own. We can only be responsible for us. I stopped sleeping in his room. Oh. . . ." She paused again, embarrassed this time. "I suppose you knew, though."

He nodded.

"Anyway, that felt like condoning it. But I'm not moving out. I want to be with you and Rob and Didi, for as long as you want me to. I was kind of hoping forever."

"That didn't make him stop?"

"I'm not sure he even noticed." And then she began to cry.

"I'm sorry," Kevin said. "Hey, Buddy, go see Paula." He pointed at her. "Make her feel better."

And Buddy tried. He stood and stretched, ambled over and gave Paula's salty cheeks several swipes with his soft pink tongue. She hugged the dog, looking over his back at Kevin. "You know, he's not just an alcoholic. He's so smart. And a great geologist. He's interesting and courageous and fun. I know you and he have had your ups and downs, but he loves you so much. He tries to be a good father, but he never had a good example to follow. Right now, it's hard to see anything but the alcoholic. For me too."

Buddy circled once, then settled down on the ground beside her.

"Seems like it cancels out the good stuff." Kevin broke the stick he was holding in two. "Do you think Rob will ever speak to him again?" he asked.

"Do you think he's noticed that Rob's back, and Timur too?" she asked.

Kevin shrugged.

Mr. and Mrs. Borkan were both in Ankara now, looking for a place to live. They'd let Timur stay with the Rosses in Kayakale, so the boys could be together until school started or something else changed, like where Mr. Borkan would work or where they would live. Everything felt so vague, yet so on edge.

"Nice of you to give Timur your bed."

"I don't mind sleeping on the floor. How about you, Buddy?" Kevin said.

"He was getting too big for the bed, anyway," Paula said.

They sat together, not talking, for several minutes. Paula stroked Buddy's flank. It was comforting.

Kevin finally said, "It's not just about us. He's never said another word about that slope. The one that could fall into the reservoir. How can he not care about that anymore? I don't get it." He shook his head.

"I don't either, Kev." She searched for the right words to say, but they all felt hollow. Then, she tried: "He told me he's going to stop. He did before, when you were a baby, so he *can*. He said he's trying."

"Not hard enough."

THIRTY-THREE

Will climbed the office stairs, tired and dirty from a long day in the field. What a difference it would make if something good would just shake loose or some obstacle shift: if Borkan signed on with DSI, maybe he'd be reassigned back to the site; if Timur didn't have to leave, maybe Rob's iciness would thaw. Maybe Kevin would ease up on Will, if he saw that the right course to a destination isn't always a straight line. Not that Kevin was open with his disapproval; he was simply ignoring his father's existence, which felt even worse to Will. There were just too many ifs and maybes these days.

He trudged up the stairs and into his office, riffled through the papers on his desk. Some he'd left there, some were new ones his team had. He hoped for a message from Borkan that wasn't there. Damn. He could use a drink. But not before he finished the shift reports.

Almost two hours later, Will headed for home, trudged up the stairs, and down the hall straight to the kitchen. He took a glass from the cupboard, went into his bedroom, closed the door, and pulled a bottle from a drawer. The metal cap snapped when he twisted it off. He sank onto the edge of his bed, poured, and drank, finishing the glass in two swallows. He poured another.

Bottle in one hand, glass in the other, he meandered to the living room and settled into his easy chair. Buddy looked up from the corner where he was curled up. The dog rose, stretched long and languid, then padded over to Will's chair, and rested his head on the armrest.

"Good dog, Bud," Will said.

Through the screen door, he could see Rob and Timur tossing a baseball out on the square in front of the house, graceful silhouettes in the waning light of the evening. He filled and emptied the glass of scotch until there was no more. He dozed.

∽

Buddy's barking jerked Will awake. He knocked the glass from the arm of the chair, and it exploded on the concrete floor.

"Damn it, Buddy. What're you barking at?"

Buddy scuffled by the screen door, his nails slipping. Will squinted, trying to get the dog in focus in the dim light. He hauled himself out of the chair and crunched through the broken glass. He swung, hitting the dog across the head. Buddy whined, then squealed when Will's kick landed in his rib cage.

Then Didi was there, bending over the dog, covering him like a blanket. Where'd she come from?

"Buddy," she said, "Buddy."

"Get outta th' way. Buddy was bad. Gotta be taught."

"Daddy, *please*," she said, looking up at him. He pulled her off the dog and flung her out of the way. He heard a thud, and her body crumpled in a heap.

"Shit," he said, starting toward her, but Buddy was on him before he took a step. His teeth sank deep into Will's calf. Will howled, and the screen door slammed behind him. A blow landed out of nowhere and his knees buckled, but he was pulled back up to his feet and shoved against the wall.

Buddy snarled, and Kevin growled into Will's ear, "Get the fuck out, and don't come back."

Then his son dragged him across the room and pushed him out the front door.

∽

Will saw light. It was the murky orange-red light you see through your eyelids, and even that hurt. It was going to be a whopper of a hangover.

I have to quit, he thought.

His mouth felt like the desert, dry and gritty. When he tried to lick his lips, he couldn't open them. He needed water. He inched his way toward the edge of the bed, knowing not to open his eyes until he absolutely had to. When he slid his leg under the covers, pain tore through it.

"Shit," he said, lips ripping as he did.

He reeled off the bed, hit the floor, tasted blood. He breathed in. It hurt. He slit his eyes open. Where was he?

He moved his head slowly, trying to orient himself. Colorful walls—Paula's old place behind the schoolhouse? He scanned the room, stopping at her feet in front of the chair in the corner. He raised his eyes. She sat with Didi in her lap. His daughter's head was bandaged and rested on Paula's chest.

"What happened?" he croaked.

Paula's arms tightened protectively around Didi. "You don't remember?" She stared down at him, not blinking. "No," she answered her own question. "You wouldn't, would you?"

"Is she all right?"

She rocked Didi, kissed the child's head. "She's alive, if that's what you mean. You didn't manage to kill her."

"Oh God," Will whispered. He pulled himself to his knees, knelt there, hands on the floor, head in his hands. He crawled to the bathroom. He vomited, his throat burning. He collapsed onto the floor, curled into the fetal position. The tiles felt cool on his throbbing head and the shredded skin of his leg.

He tried to remember what he'd done, but there was nothing. Nothing. He'd almost killed his little girl and had no idea he'd done it—no idea he'd done anything at all.

He pressed his forehead into the cold hard tiles and began to cry.

THIRTY-FOUR

Paula had kept Didi awake that whole night, which Kris had said to, so the little girl slept most of the next day. As the afternoon shadows lengthened, Didi roused. She was hungry, and Paula assumed that was a good sign. She asked for and ate a grilled cheese sandwich. Then she curled up on the living room floor to cuddle with Buddy and fell asleep.

Paula decided she could leave Didi under Kevin's watchful eye and went back to her old place, carrying two tote bags. She tapped on the door and when no answer came, let herself in. Will was where she'd left him late that morning, in the bathroom. Only now, he was sitting up, wedged between the wall and the commode. She wondered if he'd been there all day. His chin, covered in two days of whiskery stubble, rested on his chest.

"You look like hell," she said.

He raised his head. "And feel worse."

His eyes were bloodshot, his clothes bloodstained, and a dark crusty scab scored his right cheek.

"You should," she said. "I brought some clean clothes and towels." She held them out to him. "Get up and shower. That'll help. Then I'll make you something to eat."

"Not hungry."

"Too bad. You have to eat. Are you drinking water?"

He nodded, then lifted the plastic cup she had kept on the sink and took a sip.

"Drink more. Water," she said.

"Yes, water," he said. "Paula. . . ."

She waited.

"Go to the office. Please. Find Refik and tell him I'm sick. I'll need a few days. My leg," he said, his hand fluttering toward the wound she'd bandaged that morning. "He'll know who to tell and he can fill in for me. Just a few days. . . ." His voice trailed off.

"Okay. Yes," she said. It wouldn't be lying; he was sick. "Now get up and shower."

The bathroom door squeaked, and Paula turned from the pot she was stirring. Will emerged from the bathroom. He looked a little better.

"Chicken noodle soup," she said. "You should be able to keep that down."

He sank into one of the chairs at the tiny table.

"You're going to have a scar," she said.

"Good," he whispered. "Every time I look in a mirror, I should know what I did. How is she?" His voice quavered.

She switched the stove off and crossed the room to him. He put his arms around her and leaned into her. Paula held his head and stroked his hair while he cried.

҄

Will couldn't remember ever crying—not when his stepfather blinded his pony, not holding his friends as they died on the battlefields of Korea, not through all the pain after the motorcycle crash, not even when Kevin nearly drowned. He'd come close, but he'd always held the tears back. Now he couldn't. The dam had been breached, and years of emotions poured out.

Despite being inundated with unfamiliar feelings, Will could see more clearly than he had in months. He knew what he had to do.

Holed up in Paula's place, he got himself clean.

He puked and shook and ached. He made himself swallow more water than he thought his gut could hold. Some days, aspirin helped the horrendous headaches. Some days not. He forced himself to eat, though some days the mere thought of food sickened him.

Every day, he yearned for the one drink that his body told him would make it all better. Every day, when the cravings hit, he made himself remember Didi with her head bandaged, curled up on Paula's lap, and he didn't give in. He told Paula where he'd hidden the booze, and she dumped it all.

After the first, worst days, he went back to work. He was still limping from Buddy's bite, but he managed to hide the tremors and nausea. The sweat and stink that permeated his field clothes couldn't be concealed, but it was summer, and they seemed to pass without much notice.

He tried to sleep, knowing his body needed rest. Sometimes he could.

And he cried. A few tears might leak down his cheeks, and he could wipe them away before anyone saw. Alone, the tears flowed for what seemed like hours. And Will finally let them. He let himself cry for all the pain, all the years of not crying.

He pushed himself through the days. It took almost as long to get clean as it had to get polluted, but soon he'd be ready to do what he needed to do.

He didn't know what would happen after that—if he'd lose his job, if he'd have to move his family, or if they'd go with him if he tried to. He didn't know if his children would forgive him. Or if Paula would stay with him. He had to leave that to them. Will began to discern, for the first time in his life, what was his to control. And what wasn't.

∾

Will hesitated after pulling the door of the tiny apartment closed behind him. He blinked hard against the afternoon sun, and the tears. Always more tears. He paced carefully forward, his leg still hurting, its skin stretched taut across the healing wound. He was headed toward the house, and his family.

Didi and Buddy played together on the square, and as Will approached, Buddy stopped mid-frolic, swiveled, sat, and sniffed in his direction.

Didi followed the dog's gaze. "Daddy!" she cried and ran to Will, throwing her arms around his waist. "Where were you?"

Buddy trotted toward them. A growl rumbled in his throat.

"It's Daddy! Don't growl!" She reached out, and the dog advanced with his tail wagging.

Will exhaled, and the clenched feeling in his chest eased.

"I had to be away for a while, sweetie," he said, kneeling down and pulling his little girl into a hug. "I'm so sorry."

"It's okay, Daddy," she said. "I missed you."

"Me too you," Will said, appreciating the feel of her soft hair against his cheek, the grasp of her wiry little arms around his neck.

When she started to wiggle free, he held her at arms' length, wanting to look at her just a moment longer.

"Where's Paula?" he asked.

Didi pointed to the front door of the house as she ran off with Buddy.

Will knocked and watched Paula walk up the hallway toward him through the screen door.

"Hi," she said.

"May I come in?"

She pushed the door open.

"I'm sorry. I'm so sorry," he said.

"I know. You've told me about a hundred times."

"I just told Didi. She doesn't seem to know what for."

"No," Paula said. "She doesn't remember. Kris said that's not uncommon."

"But she's okay?"

"Seems to be."

"The boys? I need to talk with them."

Paula nodded. "You will," she agreed. "But don't expect too much. They're mad as hell."

"Are they here?"

"Not now, no."

"When should I come back?"

"Let's play it by ear," she said.

"What will I say?"

"Start with 'I'm sorry,' I think. No reasons. No excuses."

Will studied her kind eyes, grateful for her steady gaze. "There is no excuse," he said.

∾

A few days later, on August 29, 1974, the day before Turkey's Victory Day holiday—which seemed appropriate to Will, as each day he stayed sober was a small victory—he came off day shift, knowing it might be his last at Kayakale Dam. It was time, and he was ready. He walked slowly across the compound, but rather than stopping at the apartment or the house, he climbed into the beat-up Land Cruiser and drove to Kayakale village.

The village's one pay phone, blocky and newly painted red that summer, was in front of the post office, and Will parked beside it. He didn't want anyone on staff to hear this conversation; the distance to town and the shelter of the phone booth was a better bet than a closed door at the site office.

Will checked his watch. Quarter to seven. He counted eight hours back, quarter till eleven in the morning in New York. He'd catch Heatley well before he left for lunch. He pulled the piece of notepaper from his shirt pocket and unfolded it. He dialed the myriad numbers needed to make a call to the States, then reached into his pants pocket where he carried the coins that he'd put in the car the night before for this purpose. When the operator instructed him to, he dropped one coin after the other into the slot.

"Mr. Heatley's office," the secretary answered. Will recognized her voice from the many times they'd talked when he was arranging the move to Turkey last year.

"Hello, Belinda. This is Will Ross. I need to speak with John on an urgent matter regarding the safety of Kayakale Dam."

"Oh!" she said, the surprise in her voice vibrated through the wire. "Please hold a moment. I'll connect you right away."

Waiting, Will flipped through the field book where he'd made notes and sketches about the unstable slopes, starting with the one near Kemaliye that he'd found on the camping trip. Was it really just a couple of months ago?

The phone line clicked.

"Heatley."

"John," Will said, "we need to talk."

THIRTY-FIVE

Will remembered the feeling—almost like floating on air—when he would drop his pack at the end of an endless field day as an undergraduate intern in the rugged White Inyo Mountains on the California–Nevada border. Working for the US Bureau of Mines, that pack would have been loaded with samples bound for the assay lab, weighing sixty pounds or more.

This evening, so many years later, covering the distance to the Land Cruiser after an hour on the phone with Heatley, he felt that same sense of weightlessness. The burden Will had carried was finally set down. Now it was Heatley's, and all Will could do was wait to see where his boss would take it.

Back at the dam site, that light feeling persisted as Will sprang up the steps to the house. He forgot to knock, something he'd done since Paula had allowed him back to visit.

"Hey, everyone," he called. "Family meeting!"

Kevin scowled at him. "I hate family meetings. They suck."

"Language," Will said, at which Kevin looked down, mouthing the words "fuck you" with what appeared to be the clear intent of being seen.

"We have news!" Paula interrupted. She pointed across the room at Rob and Timur, who stood with their arms draped across each other's shoulders, beaming.

"Baba is going to work for DSI. Here!" Timur said. "We don't have to move!"

"We've been looking for you. To tell you," Paula said. "Where were you?"

Then everyone was talking over everyone else. Rob was cheering. Didi was chirping. Buddy chimed in with a few boofs. Will was trying to ask Timur about what Erdem had said, and the boy was trying to answer.

A blast penetrated the din, and Will looked over to see Paula lowering her hand after delivering one of her signature whistles. "Whoa, y'all," she said, looking back at him. "What's your news, Will?"

∿

Just a year ago, before meeting Paula, Will would've scoffed at the notion of considering metaphors on a daily basis. But there he was, thinking about figurative dominoes toppling. After months of everything going sideways, the dominoes were finally falling in the right direction.

Borkan had been summoned to DSI's headquarters in Ankara for a job offer hours before Will called DECCO's New York office. DSI had decided a full-time, on-site presence was needed at Kayakale Dam, and Erdem Borkan had convinced them he should be that presence—first domino.

The second domino was Will's conversation with Heatley.

That resulted in a telex to DSI from DECCO New York that very evening—the third domino. It acknowledged a potential but mitigatable threat in the reservoir. To Will's eye, it appeared that a lawyer had been involved in composing the memo, but he could only guess at what transpired between the time of his call and the telex being sent, six hours later.

In the following days, dominoes fell fast and furious. Clerical staff in Ankara and New York combed the archives for studies of the proposed reservoir. Gus Browning was reassigned from his project management role and recalled to New York. The project manager position was split into two jobs, one financial and administrative, the other technical. A senior accountant was named as the executive project manager, the former role, and moved from New York to Ankara in a week's time.

Will was appointed to the latter position, the technical project manager, which would be based at the dam site. The Ross family would be calling Kayakale home for the long haul.

No record of a reservoir investigation was ever found, not even falsified results—like the borehole logs that had been fabricated for the dam's foundation. Will would always wonder if Browning figured he'd gotten away with it once, assumed he would again, and didn't even bother to cover his tracks. And Browning would have pulled it off, if it hadn't been for those equipment breakdowns, which led to that unusual weekend off, which led to the Ross family's camping trip, where Will observed the first evidence of slope failures.

Will had to admit that Browning was smarter than he'd given the guy credit for; his tracks were, apparently, hard to find. It took months of forensic accounting to uncover his embezzlement of the funds earmarked for the reservoir work, at which point he was fired. Will was never provided with details of that analysis, and no legal action was taken against Browning. When Will asked about it and whether Browning would be stripped of his license to practice, Heatley said the corporate lawyers had decided not to pursue the matter. They didn't want to expose DECCO to litigation—admission of wrongdoing or some such legal argument. Heatley added that they would have no further discussion of Gus Browning, and Will should consider the conversation they were in the midst of strictly confidential.

Although Will questioned the wisdom of Browning's being allowed to continue working as an engineer, he rationalized that Browning's engineering skills weren't necessarily the issue; rather, it was his integrity. But wasn't integrity integral to professionalism? At the end of the day, however, Will felt darn lucky that DECCO hadn't been ousted from the project, and he decided any battle about Browning's future wasn't his to fight.

That lesson again—realizing what was under his control and what wasn't.

After all the dominoes fell, the dam began to rise. The foundation had been probed, plugged to the extent possible, and prepared. The lifts began to be laid in the rock-fill portion of the dam, and concrete formed up on the gravity dam side. Though a year later than planned, DECCO hit full stride for the most concentrated construction work during a perfect weather window, a long dry autumn followed by a mild winter. Construction was nearly back on schedule by mid-1975.

Even Paula, who was more than a little ambivalent about the future effects of the dam on the landscape, the ecosystem, the people, and the culture, acknowledged to Will that the feat of engineering happening before their eyes was impressive.

Meanwhile, studies of the reservoir area moved forward. As Will and Borkan had acknowledged from the start of the process, there was time to get it right. Investigation, then mitigation, all completed before reservoir impoundment began.

Reflecting later on the two years in Kayakale, it would occur to Will that only when he had risked everything he wanted most, both professionally and personally, did he get what he wanted most. It was the act of deciding on those risks that *was* his to control.

THIRTY-SIX

August 22, 1976

Dear Mom,

How are you? I'm fine. Maybe getting a little nervous, but Dad always says it's hard to tell nervousness from excitement. I finished up at the dig on Friday, and I finished packing everything that was left yesterday. It all fit in a duffel and my backpack. There's Buddy's crate, but that's for when it's time to load him onto the plane, poor guy. I hope the flight won't be too hard on him. The vet gave us a sedative to give him in those soft treats he likes, so he should sleep most of the way. Thanks again for finding the apartment. It would've been hard to get everything arranged from here without your help. I really appreciate it. Did my trunk come yet? It should be there by now. Before Buddy and I get there, for sure.

Kevin's pen hovered above the page. He looked up and across the kitchen at Buddy. "Oh!" he said. "This won't get there before we do. I didn't think about that."

He swallowed the last of his sweet, milky coffee, while Buddy crossed the kitchen after one last lick of his bowl.

"Hey, boy, don't let me forget your bowl. Guess we'll start writing letters to the crew back here next Sunday. What do you think about that?"

He stroked his dog's head, fondled his soft ears, and blinked back tears. It seemed very real all of sudden. Leaving.

A week from tomorrow, Kevin would be a freshman at the Maryland Institute College of Art, or MICA as it was called. His father had been amused by the mineralogical acronym, saying that Kevin couldn't escape his geological background even going off to *art* school. There was no doubt he'd placed special emphasis on *art*, but despite the sarcasm, Dad had not stopped Kevin from submitting applications to the colleges he did, all art institutes.

∽

That afternoon, a few short hours before their departure, Kevin sat on his bed with his back against the wall, surveying the room. The mattress was so thin he could feel the springs poking his butt, but that was nothing new. It had been saggy from the get-go. Photographs he had taken and developed and sketches he had drawn filled the walls on his side of the room.

The collection made for a collage of images, and memories, from the three years Kayakale had been home, and he had mined it for his portfolio. Kevin understood he had a lot to learn to master his chosen crafts, to discover the art he felt moved to make. Still, he felt proud of the work he'd done so far. He had applied to several schools with it, handled the inevitable rejections, and celebrated the acceptances to MICA and the Milwaukee Institute of Art and Design, before choosing MICA.

It was a very good thing he had reconciled with Mom, and he was grateful for the help she had given him in the upcoming relocation. She had found the affordable, dog-friendly apartment above a freestanding garage within walking distance of the school. It was especially nice that home would be close to a huge park and the trails near Druid Lake, where Kevin could take Buddy for the long rambles they both loved.

Flipping through the snapshots Kevin's mother had sent, Paula proclaimed the apartment "Kevin's garret," and said it was perfect for a promising young artist and his four-legged muse.

Of course, it was important for all sorts of reasons that Kevin, Rob, and Didi had reconnected with Mom; she was, after all, their mother, even if embracing that role didn't seem to be the highest priority for her. Kevin felt what he thought was love for her, though he saw them as having little in common. She seemed stuck in a high school mindset, something Kevin had graduated from, if he'd ever been there in the first place. For him, the reconciliation had only become possible when she had finally quit drinking.

It was too bad it had taken her boyfriend dying, driving drunk on New Year's Eve on his way to pick Mom up no less, to scare her into sobriety. Afterward, his mother had admitted to him that she and Russell had gotten drunk together while Russell was driving, any number of times. She knew it could have been her that night, and she had stopped.

Several months after the accident, she had written the three of them a long letter, apologizing for all she'd put them through after the divorce and before his father took them to Turkey. It didn't change what had happened, but it helped to hear it anyway.

After almost a year of steady letters and phone calls back and forth, the three of them had decided they wanted to go to New Jersey to spend Christmas with her last year. Their father had agreed, and it had all gone well. Kevin thought it must have helped her get through the anniversary of Russell's gruesome death too.

His mother was doing better now—she'd gotten a job as a receptionist at a dentist's office, then started dating her boss. Mom liked having a guy in her life, and she seemed happier in her most recent letters. He hoped the new boyfriend wasn't an asshole. He'd find out in a few days.

During that Christmas trip, Kevin had also been able to visit MICA. He remembered pacing the platform, waiting for the southbound train early that cold, gray morning. Relieved to board for the two-hour ride to Baltimore, he'd settled into a seat, his breath fogging the window when he leaned close to peer out as the train groaned forward and gained speed.

As usual, he'd failed miserably at trying to read the landscape, like his father could, as it flashed by the train window, but the contrasts with Kayakale were unmistakable—in the land forms, and in the heaviness of the humid smoggy air, and the colors, smells, and sounds of the urban corridor the train had carried him through.

With all his mental meanderings, the trip flew by faster than the passing scenery, and Kevin was surprised when the conductor announced that Baltimore's Pennsylvania Station was the next stop. He'd triple-checked around his seat to make sure he hadn't left anything, while butterflies, as Paula called them, started fluttering in his stomach.

"You don't get anxious about things you don't care about," Paula had said. "And you *should* care about the studies you're embarking on."

Kevin appreciated the way she'd expressed it—studies you embark on—like it would be a journey, an adventure.

Walking briskly, he'd made it to MICA in ten minutes flat. There, his jaw had dropped at his first in-person look at it. Kevin had seen pictures in the institute's catalog, but in the midmorning sun, the white marble edifice fairly sparkled. It was beautiful, and as he mounted the front steps, he felt reverent.

Warmth swirled around him when he pushed into the entryway door. He gazed up at the leaded glass skylight towering more than two stories above. It flooded the space with natural light, and as a photographer, Kevin pictured how that light would shift throughout the day and with the seasons.

"Hello, young man."

Kevin jumped and turned. He raised his hand in a half wave to a white-haired man in a blue uniform who lumbered toward him. "Hello," he said. "I'm applying to come here for the fall, and I was kind of close by. May I look around? Did I need to make an appointment?"

"No, no. You're fine to come in," the guard said. "We're open, but there's hardly anyone around. Only saw one young lady on my rounds. Sketching." He tilted his head up to the mezzanine. "Better to visit when classes are going, see what it's really like."

"Yes, sir," Kevin said. "But I live in Turkey, and we're only stateside for the holidays."

"Well, then you won't be hopping on a bus for a second visit, will you, young man? Go ahead and explore. The galleries are open. Here's a brochure."

"Thank you."

The man nodded and continued, "The studios are all locked, but there're windows in their doors, so you can peek inside."

"Thank you," Kevin repeated, then took a deep breath and made himself ask, "Do you think I could see the darkroom, sir?" Desire to see it outweighed his desire not to be a nuisance.

"I guess I'll just have to say yes to such a polite request. Tell you what, I'm about to take my coffee break, so look around on your own awhile, then come get me." He pointed to a tiny office off the foyer. "I'll be in there. Come back around, and I'll take you down to the darkroom. It's in the basement."

Then the guard walked off, brandishing his arm in a sweeping arc, as if ushering Kevin farther in. Kevin accepted the invitation and headed for the central marble staircase. He had read about the award-winning architecture and the replicas of Greek and Roman statues that students sketched and painted and photographed in their first-year studies, but the words and pictures had not done justice to the space. He made his way around the second floor, pausing at paintings and sculptures in the hall and galleries, thinking about how he might photograph or draw them, and what he might find within himself to create.

Leaving the last gallery on that level, he turned left and headed for the staircase opposite the one he'd come up, anticipating the promised tour of the darkroom. He nearly tripped over the girl, feeling rather than seeing her seated on the floor in front of him at the last second.

"Whoa!" he said. "Sorry . . . I didn't see you."

"How could you miss me?" She laughed, her voice lilting, with an accent that sounded both British and not.

Where was she from? he wondered.

She was right, she sat directly in his path, her back against the stone railing that overlooked the first floor, her legs outstretched, crossed at the ankles in turquoise-and-black leather cowboy boots. Kevin's eyes traveled from her colorful boots to ribbed black tights, to a red knit skirt, gold turtleneck sweater, and finally, her burnished complexion, deep brown eyes, and black hair pulled severely back.

"Hi," he said.

"Hi yourself."

"Are you a student here?"

She tipped her head down to the sketch pad in her lap, and with the movement, a cascade of long thin braids poured over her shoulder. "You think? Are you?"

"I'm applying. For next fall."

"Nerve-racking, isn't it?"

Kevin nodded. "Do you like it here?"

She patted the floor to her left. "Love it."

"What are you studying?" he asked, setting his backpack down and sitting beside her.

"Sculpture. That's the plan, anyway."

"But you're drawing."

"Need to get it right in two dimensions before you venture into the third. I only got a B in Forms Foundation. That's not good enough. When you get here, you go from being the best artist in your whole school, to just one of the pack. It's humbling. And motivating. For most of us, anyway. Two in our class dropped out before break."

"Really?"

"I know . . . why would you work so hard to get here, and then just quit? I don't get it. I'm Andréa, by the way." She twisted to reach out to him with her right hand.

Kevin took it, shook it, and introduced himself. Without realizing he was going to, he blurted out, "You're beautiful."

"Thanks, handsome." She laughed again, her musical voice resonating.

Kevin felt his cheeks flush and probably blushed harder for noticing it. He looked down and saw that his hand was smudged with the charcoal she'd been drawing with.

"Can I see?" he asked, pointing to her sketch pad.

"They're just small studies." She held it out to him.

He considered the different views she'd rendered. They were good, her strokes solid yet somehow soft. She'd played with shading to create illusions of light and shadow.

"Where else did you apply?" she asked, reaching to take the pad back.

"Here and RISD, Columbia, Chicago, Tyler, RIT, and Milwaukee."

"No 'insurance' school then?"

"Milwaukee, maybe? It's newish, so maybe sort of, but no, not really . . . I'll wait a year and try again if I have to."

"Me neither. But I got in, here and Tyler."

"And you love it."

"Absolutely! It's. . . ." She stopped, glanced at her watch, another colorful bit about her with a bold purple band.

Kevin thought she must want the interruption to end.

"I'm sorry," she said. "It's been really nice talking, but I've got to go. Meeting my mum for lunch."

She tore a corner off her notebook page, scribbled on it, and held it out to him. "Write?" she asked. "Tell me where you decide to go."

"Okay," he said, watching her leave in a graceful swish of textures and colors. He smiled at the scrap of paper in his hand. In addition to her address, she had given him one of her sketches, the outer curve of the statue's hand.

Back on the first floor, after seeing the well-appointed dark-room, which was almost as thrilling as meeting Andréa, Kevin strolled the perimeter of the great hall. The shifting tones of afternoon light reminded him to check the time, and lucky they did, or he would have missed his northbound train. Safely aboard, he had leaned back in the coach seat, swaying with the rhythm of the train. He closed his eyes and imagined himself studying in that marble temple to art.

Kevin returned from the memories of that winter trip to the dry heat of the Kayakale summer afternoon—MICA and Andréa both on his mind. He bounced off the not-so-springy springs and rose from his bed, and *that* brought up another memory—of Rob and Timur using one of those smaller-than-single beds as a trampoline on an April afternoon during the first year they lived there. Timur was lucky he'd only broken his leg. Also lucky the nasty fracture had healed so well. You didn't get off scot-free from many stupid decisions, which made Kevin think of his own brush with fate that same year.

"You were lucky too," he said, addressing himself.

He wished Buddy were there, rather than being alone with all those memories. Buddy made everything better, like he had since the moment they'd found each other just before dawn in the hills surrounding the dam site on Kevin's first morning in Kayakale.

Didi was out walking him now. That kid was sure going to miss Buddy. The whole family would, but once they'd confirmed that Kevin could get him through customs, there was no question about his dog going with him.

They would overnight in Sivas that night, then drive the rest of the way to Istanbul the next day. Kevin and Buddy were booked on a nonstop flight to JFK early Tuesday morning. The family had all agreed it would be easier on their beloved pet to fly nonstop to the States, and that would make the extra hours on the road worth it.

So this was the last afternoon Kayakale would be Kevin's home. His father would complete his work on the dam in a year, maybe two, and move on, like he always did. Dad seemed to find *home* in his work, wherever in the world it was. Kevin wondered if he would find *his* home in his art. He didn't know yet, but he was going to find out.

THIRTY-SEVEN

Will stayed on the job long after Kayakale Dam was completed. As the reservoir began to fill, he supervised expansion of the network of wells that already peppered the site, to further define the groundwater regime and observe any changes in it.

He learned about applying an old technology in a new way—using a microseismic array to monitor reservoir-induced seismicity. Or, as he translated it for the executive project manager who needed to sign off on the budget, a system to track earthquake activity triggered by the increase in hydrostatic pressure exerted by the water impounded in the reservoir. The project included installing seismometers to measure ground motion and seismographs to record those measurements, and contracting a seismologist to design the network and interpret the data. Fascinating stuff to Will, if not to his accountant project management counterpart.

Another task became a daily ritual Will loved, especially since the intensity of fieldwork had eased, and so had the physicality involved with his job. He hiked the nearby tributaries, a different drainage each morning, repeating the circuit the next week, over and over. Will thought of it as making his rounds.

He would occasionally meet local children on those walks. *Ne yapıyorsun*, they would ask him. What are you doing?

Su arıyorun, he would answer. Looking for water.

They would laugh. There's no water here, they'd respond. *Su yok!* No water!

He would laugh with them, then tell them that he thought he'd keep looking anyway.

They would shake their heads and wave as he moved on.

It began with a trickle. More came as the months went by. Only in one drainage, a tiny tributary of Kayakale Creek (itself a small tributary to the Firat), close to the troublesome left abutment of the dam. By the time it stabilized, there was enough flow to support a fish hatchery. So they built one, for rainbow trout. Making lemonade out of lemons, if Will ever saw it.

As Kayakale Reservoir filled, the water surging farther and farther up the Firat and Murat valleys, Will took *Blue* on weekly overflights to check the slope mitigation measures he and Borkan had risked their jobs for. They all seemed to be holding, even after big storms. A good sign, but time—with its seasonal wetting and drying cycles, and all the geologic hazards the area was susceptible to—would be the real test.

On one of those flights, Will squinted ahead through the whirling propeller, then shook his head as if to clear his vision; the reservoir had risen halfway up a house that he *knew*. He'd even sat there, visiting and drinking chai, by the very door small waves were lapping up against. Will found himself choking up, thinking about Okan, the man who had lived there. Will had met him and his brother when the slope mitigation work was beginning. He'd hired them as laborers, gotten to know them, enjoyed their company. They'd hunted ibex together in the mountains that towered over their town. Then, busy as he always was with work, Will had lost track of them. When had they relocated, and where?

The week before, the reservoir had not yet reached Kemaliye, but now a full third of the quaint hamlet was under water. The lump in Will's throat remained, even when he'd flown well past the village, soon to be submerged. He wanted to believe the positives of the project outweighed the negatives, but seeing the inundation shook him.

In the end, Will chose to make his peace with the professional decisions he'd made at Kayakale. He had done his best and was proud of what had been accomplished, though he understood it was not nearly as black and white as he'd once thought. He also knew hazards could never be completely mitigated and risks never completely eliminated, so he waited and watched.

THIRTY-EIGHT

Paula pulled her bandanna from her back pocket and dabbed away the sweat on her forehead before it dripped into her eyes. In the seven years she'd lived in Kayakale, she was sure this was the hottest day ever. Not the best day for packing, but this was the last of it.

Kerr-rip-thwack, kerr-rip-thwack—she hit a steady cadence with her tape dispenser, sealing up the boxes. Hands on her hips, she surveyed her handiwork—sorting, packing, and shuttling the house contents that they weren't giving away off to storage.

In the kitchen, she soaked the bandanna under the cold water tap and wiped her face, sighing with the simple pleasure of cool wet cotton on hot skin. She tied the dripping cloth around her neck, shivering a bit at the cold trickle down her back.

Paula looked forward to getting back to the sea breezes on the Med. Being able to dive in as the day warmed when the afternoon winds stilled. What had started as a casual conversation on the beach five years before, after their first sail with Skipper and Joe, had become a dream.

And starting tomorrow—Monday, August 20, 1979—the dream of living on their sailboat would become a reality. The date had been marked with a big red *X* on their wall calendar for months. Paula slid her fingernail under the thumbtack holding the calendar to the kitchen wall, and after glancing once more at the *X* on their momentous day, folded it closed and made space for it between some files and books in her already over-stuffed briefcase.

In 1972, back in Dudley Gap, she hadn't had time to mark her calendar, time to contemplate what might come next when she left West Virginia for Turkey. But she *had* dreamed, having submitted an application with the Calvert School for just such a possibility, preferably in a faraway place. When it came, the stipulation was that Paula would be on-site within a week.

Never sorry that she'd leapt at the chance, still she'd felt at sea, tossed about, for months after her whirlwind arrival in Kaya-kale. But now, Paula felt rock-solid in her preparations for actually going to sea. Her inner foundation fortified over the years.

The past Friday had, finally, been Will's last day on the job. Yesterday, he and Erdem left for Ankara with Rob and Timur, who were off to college at the Colorado School of Mines in Golden. The two of them would have a week to settle in as roommates in the freshman dorm. A friendly face would meet them at the Denver airport. Refik Kaptanoğlu was a year into a master's program in geological engineering. Will seemed as pleased and proud about Refik matriculating there as he was about Rob and Timur.

It sounded like the campus was nestled into the foothills of the Rocky Mountains, and Paula hoped the boys would strike a healthy balance between their studies and skiing, which they'd both gotten into on trips to Mt. Erciyes, even learning to race. They still loved baseball, and harbored a season-long rivalry between the Phillies and Mets throughout each summer, but they'd broadened their horizons to include a wintertime passion.

Paula had gone into Rob's room while he packed. There was something she wanted to say. It had come to her, for herself, working on the boat during the two months since school, and her professional capacity at Kayakale, had ended.

She'd cleared her throat, and Rob looked up from his duffel bag.

"What's up?" he asked. "You're not gonna get all huggy, are you?"

"Worse," she laughed.

"Nope," Rob said. "Can't be worse than that."

"I just wanted to say something that occurred to me while I changed the oil in *Cygnus*'s engine, of all things. Here goes . . . my life might be half over, and it took me this long to really understand that it's a do-it-yourself project."

"Umm, okay."

"I'm telling you because I hope you don't have to wait so long to figure it out. I hope in college you'll find and follow the path that's right for *you*. Not the one your dad would've wanted, or the one he wouldn't have, but *your* path."

That boy, a young man now, had the deepest blue eyes— indigo, really. So different from his father's, but no less stunning. He blinked them at her, their white-blond lashes glittering around the dark pools. Good thing he was going off to a male-dominated school, Paula thought, or he'd be fending off smitten girls right and left.

"Thanks," he said. "Changing the oil, huh?"

With his question, Paula's attention came back from coeds to the conversation. "That, and all the other things I've been working out. Replacing the bilge pump. Installing a foot pump for water in the galley. Sailing singlehanded! Especially that. Not that I want to cruise solo long-term; it's about sharing the experience, like we all have since we bought *Cygnus*. But it feels amazing to handle her on my own. It's . . . it's *empowering*. I want you to feel like that."

"To be at the helm?" Rob smiled at her.

"Yes, of your life! Yes!"

Rob tilted his head. "That actually sounds like pretty good advice, Paula. Thanks."

"Can I hug you *now?*" she asked, opening her arms and taking a step toward him.

"Nah. When we leave, okay?" Rob dropped the balled-up socks in his hands into his bag.

Two months earlier, at the end of June, the last of the American staff, aside from Will, had departed. So had their kids, most of Paula's remaining students. Rob and Timur, who had taken his last two years of high school at the on-site school to polish his English, had gotten their diplomas in elegant leather cases from the Calvert School. Didi would've been the only pupil left in the schoolhouse come autumn. But the decision to move onto *Cygnus*, a stout cutter-rigged sailboat, and cruise the Med for a year or two had been made long before.

Since they'd hatched their plan, she and Will had been tucking away as much of their respective paychecks as possible. Skipper and Joe, their sailing mentors, had explained that live-aboard cruising costs what you have. If you have lots of money, you'll eat out, rent cars for shore excursions, and tie up at marinas to grocery shop and do laundry. If you don't, you'll eat beans and rice, or fish you catch yourself; skip shore excursions or take buses to them; and lie at anchor, rowing to and from onshore errands. Your cruising kitty could go a long way, and so could you. Skipper and Joe had gone halfway around the world, with enough left over to buy their little inn.

They also recommended doing as much of your own sail repairs and engine work as you could, both for the sake of self-sufficiency and to stretch your cruising budget. With that in mind, since late June, Paula had been back and forth from Kayakale to Kızkalesi, where *Cygnus* swung on a mooring near *Sparrow*. Their mismatched flock of a swan and a songbird, as Joe had quipped.

Will was on the job, busy tying up loose ends, so Paula got *Cygnus* ready to move onto full-time. She was surprised Will let go of controlling every detail; not the most self-aware of men, even he would admit he liked to be in control. But Will was more invested in casting off sooner than in managing all the prep himself. His confidence in her reinforced the partnership they'd forged as captain and first mate over the two years they had cruised on *Cygnus*—not only learning to sail, but getting to know the boat's systems and her quirks.

In this process, Paula suspected she'd begun to draft the next chapter in her life's story—the story she'd been composing since she'd found a way to go to college, then to Turkey, and then into her relationship with Will. And, perhaps most notably, in her relationship with herself. She didn't know what the end of this chapter would be, but she was ready to live into it. It felt perfect that it would unfold on *Cygnus*, Latin for "swan" but also a deity of balance between love and reason.

Paula had written a letter to Kevin about it. She trusted he would understand the feelings she was struggling to express on paper. It would've been better to talk with him face-to-face, of course. She missed their quiet chats. She missed *him*. And now Rob was leaving the nest too.

She was relieved Didi wouldn't be fledging any time soon, though at nearly eleven, she was growing up fast. Paula would be homeschooling her on the boat. What an amazing classroom the Mediterranean Sea would be—for all three of them. Paula believed life was full of lessons. If you paid attention, education didn't end with graduation.

∽

Paula eased the jib and cleated the line. As usual, the wind diminished in the late afternoon, and although she thrilled to a brisk beam reach as much as the next sailor, she also loved it when the wind and sea calmed and *Cygnus* slipped through the riffles that remained.

Didi looked up from the chart, where she'd just penciled an *X* after siting their location and having Paula check it. "It's time to turn to starboard, Dad. See those small islands?" She pointed ahead. "We take them to port. Then it's about three miles to the anchorage."

They would stay for a night or two in a one-boat anchorage notched into the coast on the west side of the wide gulf south of Antalya. They'd happened upon it by chance on their first sailing vacation two years before, and this would be their third stay. It was sheltered on three sides, the holding was good, and the scenery was spectacular with rugged hills rising sharply above a narrow strip of rocky beach.

"What course?" Will asked.

Didi measured one more time, and said, "Two-five-five degrees. Right, Paula?"

"Looks good."

They had only lived aboard a few weeks, but in that time Didi had been learning navigation. Paula took the lead in most of her schooling, but Will was showing her the ropes on reading charts and plotting their passages. If they planned to weigh anchor the next day, the three of them would study the charts, review the tide and current tables, and sketch out a sail plan. At breakfast, after listening to the updated marine weather on their VHF radio, they'd go over the plan and fine-tune it. Didi seemed to be a natural, and she fairly beamed hearing her father's praise. With no work pressure on Will and no brothers around to steal her thunder, it looked like Didi would finally have what she'd longed for most—her father's time, attention, and approval.

"Aye, aye, Didi," he said. "Ready to bear off to a broad reach?"

"Ready," Paula said.

After adjusting the sails, Paula sat down and sighed along with the breeze coming across the port quarter. The September sun was bright and the sky azure, all accented with a few picturesque, puffy clouds. So far, the reality of full-time cruising was every bit as lovely as the dream.

"How's our course look, Dee?" she asked.

"Spot on." She'd picked up that phrase from her dad.

"But we're slowing down," Will said.

"Well, yes, the wind's easing."

"We should motor on in."

"Why? What's the rush? Let's sail a while longer," Paula said.

"The wind's getting fluky."

"Let me try," she said.

"Okay, all yours." He stepped aside as Paula slid behind the wheel. "I'm thirsty. Does anyone want anything from below?" he asked.

Didi tucked the chart under the dodger, made her way aft, and whispered to Paula, "I like sailing better than motoring too."

"I know." Paula smiled. "It just takes a gentle touch. Some finesse."

"Some what?" Didi said.

"We'll add that to your vocabulary list."

A few minutes later, Will climbed out of the companionway and looked one way then the other. "Are we moving? I mean, forward?" he asked, smirking.

"Very funny."

"I estimate that we'll be at the anchorage in an hour, Dad."

"Excellent. Really, babe, I can't seem to hold a course when the wind is so light. Can I get you anything? A drink? Want some?" He held out a bowl of carrot sticks.

"Thanks," Paula said, and took a few with her right hand

while her left rested on the helm, making only the slightest of corrections.

Didi helped herself, echoing her thanks.

Cygnus sailed along so quietly that all Paula could hear was the crew crunching their carrots. Then, *pffft, pffft*. Blows! She swung her head around. Where had it come from? Sound could be so deceptive traveling over water. *Pffft*. Again. And again. Then she spotted them and pointed. "There!" Paula cried.

The sea's surface rippled over a school of tiny fish. Their silvery scales caught the sunlight when they leapt from the water. And hungrily behind them came a pod of dolphins. There must've been a dozen, maybe more, headed directly for *Cygnus*. Talk about leaping—they soared in graceful arcs. They whirled and corkscrewed through the air, water flying off their sleek skin and raining down on the surface.

Didi squealed, "Lookee!" like she used to years ago, and scrambled onto the deck. Will followed her.

Paula kept one hand on the helm and held the other over her heart, exclaiming, "Oh my! Oh my!" over and over.

It was the first of many magical moments of their liveaboard life, amid the banality of deck swabbing, engine maintenance, rig inspections, and the endless cleaning and polishing that summed up cruising life—an equation whose parameters they would live within for two years.

PART V

THIRTY-NINE

Will jerked awake at the screech of feedback from the plane's loudspeaker.

"We are beginning our initial descent into Ankara's Esenboğa Airport. We are expecting turbulence and will therefore collect all service items at this time. Please return seat backs and tray tables to the upright and locked positions, and recheck the security of seatbelts," said a formal, accented female voice.

While the announcement was repeated in German and Turkish, Will surfaced from the nap he'd fallen into, counting the hours he'd been traveling since Erdem's late-night call requesting him to mobilize to Kayakale. There were twenty-eight of them.

It was six years since he'd been to Turkey last, and on that trip for a post-earthquake investigation in Erzincan following the March 13, 1992, magnitude 6.8 event, there had been no time for an excursion to his old stomping grounds. It had been almost a decade since the Congress of the International Commission on Large Dams, or ICOLD, was held in Istanbul. Not to mention the twenty-five years since he and the kids had moved to Kayakale in the summer of 1973—*twenty-five years!* Imagine that, as Paula would say.

The promised turbulence jounced Will back to real time and to the situation at the dam as he understood it from Erdem's description. He'd driven from Flagstaff to Phoenix, then flown to JFK to Frankfurt and, finally, was on descent into Ankara.

Refik, a senior engineer with DSI now, would be waiting in the terminal, and they would waste no time heading out on the last leg of the journey to Kayakale.

Will and Erdem had been trading emails for weeks. At first, they discussed the planned but rapid drawdown of Kayakale Reservoir in order to accommodate the expected influx of meltwater from a heavy winter snowpack, followed by a warmer and wetter-than-normal spring. After the drawdown, as the reservoir had risen with the runoff and rainfall, the fishery operation near the left abutment had observed incremental increases in total dissolved and suspended solids in its inflow. Nothing problematic, but anomalies to be noted; and both he and Erdem thought the water quality data should be reported on a daily basis, rather than their usual monthly reports. The TDS and TSS remained elevated but had begun to stabilize—until thirty hours ago.

That morning, the hatchery manager had seen a problem before he even looked at the data. He told Erdem he didn't need measurements to know the numbers would be off the charts— the inflow was *visibly* muddy. He had shut down the valves; they'd get by on recirculation until pumps from the Firat downstream of the dam could be set up for their water supply.

But that wasn't why Will was now onboard not only this flight, but as a consultant to DSI—at the same time the hatchery manager was ringing Erdem, a technician conducting routine monitoring on the dam's crest had noticed what appeared to be some kind of disturbance in the water near the shore upstream. He radioed his supervisor, who joined him with a pair of binoculars. They still couldn't tell what was happening, but something sure was, and it was getting bigger. The foreman dispatched a crew along the shoreline trail, and he and the technician took to the lake in a utility boat. The water was disturbed all right— like pulling a plug out of a bathtub disturbed—with one large vortex and three smaller ones.

Data started pouring in. Springs that typically ran inter-mittently registered flows ten times higher than their highest previous measurements, and new springs were observed in Kayakale Creek.

Erdem had alerted DSI headquarters in Ankara and begun emergency drawdown procedures. The reservoir level had to be reduced to elevations below those that precipitated the issues. Trying to convey urgency without tipping into panic, there had been no doubt in Erdem's mind that the situation could become dire if immediate measures were not taken. At the end of the call, he requested authorization to bring Will back to the site, and it was granted. As soon as he hung up with Ankara, Erdem phoned Will and Paula's home in Flagstaff, despite the hour, which was nearing midnight there.

∽

"Hello?" Paula said, trying not to sound as sleepy as she was. What time was it? Was it bad news? Why else would someone call so late?

"*Merhaba.* I am sorry to call you at this hour. . . ."

She recognized Erdem's voice. "You must need Will."

"*Evet,*" he said.

Will squinted his eyes shut when she turned the bedside lamp on. He yawned and sat up, asking, "Who is it?"

"Erdem."

"Uh-oh," he said, reaching for the phone.

She watched him, the phone tucked between his chin and shoulder, interjecting an occasional "I see" and "Go on."

Then Will climbed out of bed, keeping the phone in place. He went to the closet, retrieved a suitcase, placed it on the foot of the bed, opened it, and began packing, starting with the field clothes that he'd laid out for the next morning.

"Uh-oh," she stage whispered.

Though not usually in the middle of the night, Will had packed for the field on the fly numerous times during their years together. Paula typically didn't know the details of the projects and their problems, but this time she did, and she knew that people she cared for could be in harm's way.

"This can't be good," she said when Will finally signed off.

"It's not, but hard to say how bad it is at this point."

"How long will you be gone?"

He shrugged. "They're asking for a week, so I'm packing for three." He grinned at her.

"The voice of experience," she said.

"I'll drive. Will you work the car phone to get me onto the first flight to Ankara?" he asked. "If we head out now, maybe I can make one of the early departures headed east. Could save a whole day."

"I'll go make the coffee." She headed to the kitchen.

"The big thermos," he called after her.

They were on the road in twenty minutes' time.

∽

The semester had just ended at Northern Arizona University, where Will had been teaching for the last eight years, so he wouldn't have to worry about getting classes covered. Good thing his grades were posted already. He was down to one grad student, and had given her a quick call from the Phoenix airport, letting her know she'd need to recruit another student or her boyfriend or just go it alone for the rest of the week in the field. The plan had been for Will to help get her started on her summer research, but plans change on projects all the time—a lesson she'd need to learn. Might as well learn it now.

"Be a geologist!" he'd said before hanging up, hoping she would understand what he meant.

"Professoring," as Will thought of it, had become less

rewarding as he noticed a not-so-subtle shift in both undergraduate and graduate students' attitudes. It seemed their
expectation was to pay their fees and get their B's. Thinking
critically, learning the scientific process and how to apply it, did
not seem to be their priority. When Will was in grad school,
he and his cohort could be found in their offices and labs at all
hours. Not these days. These kids treated school like a nine-to-
five job, punching out at the end of the day. They also wanted
to be spoon-fed answers, resenting it when they weren't—
not grasping that framing the right questions and seeking the
answers to them was what being a scientist was all about.

It was disheartening, and Will had begun to consider leaving
academia to go back to full-time consulting. Though dismayed
to hear of the problems at Kayakale, Will relished the challenge
of solving them.

While he'd packed, he and Erdem had talked through some
of the possible causes of the increased flows, the new ones, and
the disturbingly high sediment contents in them. Clearly, fine-
grained deposits were eroding from somewhere, but where? It
seemed like a plug of sediment had been acting as a "stopper"
and it had been "pulled." Metaphorically, as Paula would say. Or
fine sediments could be winnowing out of a coarser matrix, but
again, from where? And would that process have resulted in the
sudden and violent vortices they'd observed?

Will could draw some parallels to a pumped storage project
he had worked on a few years back, but there, leakage from
the reservoir had increased gradually. Over a period of years,
not hours, as had just occurred at Kayakale. The differences
in the structures were more notable than their similarities—
at the pumped storage facility, the reservoir was completely
clay-lined, and as the finer-grained clays had flushed out of
the liner into the coarser-grained sediments the liner had been
constructed upon, the liner had cracked. No definitive answer

came to mind for Kayakale, but contemplating all the possible failure mechanisms bore consideration.

The reservoir reaching a record-high elevation almost certainly factored in, as it was one of the few changed conditions. Had the fluctuations in pool level—first the rapid drawdown, then the even more rapid increase—resulted in a pulsing or pumping action that had loosened the sediment plug Will was picturing?

The "drain" that the "stopper" had been extracted from was presumably indicated by where the vortices were located. Nearly a thousand feet upstream, it was not undermining the dam itself, suggesting that the structure was not in jeopardy, at least for now. Will fervently hoped that was the case.

Curtailing the leakage that had spiked so precipitously could be difficult, but that was, essentially, an efficiency matter. Important, but not perilous. The crux of the problem was this: the leakage was moving through an undefined pathway, or pathways, in the subsurface. You can't control something you haven't defined. And control *had* to be regained. Along those lines, Will wondered how the emergency drawdown was going. Lowering the reservoir was imperative, for safety first, but also to provide access to the areas they needed to investigate.

Deep in those thoughts, Will was surprised by the thud of the landing, the skidding of rubber on the runway.

"Turkey," he said to himself. "Made it."

FORTY

"What's that?" Will said, more a voiced thought than a real inquiry, as there was little doubt the small building just inside the entry gate to Kayakale Dam was a mosque. It was plain to see in the clear moonlit night.

"A mosque," Refik said.

The tenor of his brief response sounded flat to Will, but it had been a long day and concerns about the work ahead weighed on them. It was possible he was reading something into Refik's tone that wasn't there.

"Well, yes," Will said. "Since when are there mosques on government sites?"

"For a few years now. Things are shifting. Didn't you see how many more women wore hijab when we were in the airport?"

"I didn't, no. But I don't tend to notice what people wear."

"Seems as much political as spiritual to me," Refik said.

"Maybe we'll talk about those shifts sometime. Things are shifting in the US too."

"I read an article in the *New York Times* that said some states are trying to put 'creation science' into their school curricula," Refik said. "Is that one of those things?"

"You get the *New York Times*?" Will asked.

"It's been online for two years. I subscribed right away."

"That's practical. Paula and I get the *Times* too, but still in paper. And yes, that would be. Looks to me more like controlling

people than uplifting them—their clothes, their bodies. . . ."
Will paused. "And their minds."

"It's human nature to control things. Engineers are all about
control," Refik said. "Maybe our judgments about it just depend
on what it's applied to."

"Maybe so. But in the States, there's that small matter of the
separation of church and state, which is supposed to be one of
our central tenets." But Will realized he was too tired to engage
in an intellectual exploration of the issue, or anything else, after
so many hours of travel.

Refik pulled up and parked in front of the house the Rosses
had lived in. The headlights glinted off the front windows.

"They got the old place ready for you," he said.

Will stared through the windshield. Lots of good times there,
and one horrible, if hazy, scene crossed his mind. He shook his
head to dispel the image.

Instead, he reflected on his introduction to Refik. "I just
said I don't notice clothes, but remember our first day working
together?"

"*Botları! Botları!* You sure were wound up about hiking
boots." Refik laughed.

"I was. You'd have slid right off the trail in those shiny shoes
of yours." He thought back and chuckled. "But you ended up with
good solid field sense, and we ended up a darn good team. And
did I ever thank you for teaching me most of the Turkish I know?"

"Must be why your grammar's so shaky. You did the same
for me with English. And connections for grad school. *And* I still
think of how you look at things when I'm approaching a problem, and try to teach that to our young engineers."

"You know, Refik, I think that's the best compliment I've
ever been given. *Teşekkür ederim.*" Thank you.

"*Birşey değil.*" You're welcome.

They sat in silence a few more moments, perhaps with their respective recollections, or simply too weary to talk.

"Remember dragging in from night shifts?" Will asked.

"I do much better sleeping at night and working by day. But I *am* looking forward to working with you again, even if we end up doing marathon days. We've got to get this figured out."

"Yes," Will said, nodding. "Yes, we do."

"Erdem's office. Oh seven hundred. The coffee will be ready."

"Good." Will clapped Refik on the shoulder and climbed out. "See you at seven sharp."

∾

Will sent for a geophysicist and a karst hydrogeologist to join the project team. They, along with those assembled by DSI, were able to puzzle out the subsurface conditions that had caused Kayakale Reservoir to start emptying like a bathtub whose plug had been pulled as the spring of 1998 blazed into a hot, dry summer—fine weather for all the work in the field.

The three weeks Will had packed for turned into three months. One week in, it was clear Will would miss the Pacific Northwest vacation he and Paula had planned. Paula would go without him, and she sent her sailing résumé to the charter company, so she could take over as the captain. She invited her best friend to be first mate on the adventure. Will felt a twinge of envy at that, but he was immersed in his work, and when the time came, he barely noticed the date when Paula and Judi cast off from Anacortes.

Two weeks into the project, also after talking it over with Paula, Will pulled a metaphorical plug of his own, giving notice at the university. He would get his last grad student through the program, but passed along a number of names to the department chair as possible replacements, both consultants looking to leave corporate life as Will had and postdocs who had planned for careers in academia. Will hoped they would fill his position with another engineering geologist, even if they went with a temporary appointment. That was how Will had found his way onto NAU's faculty. If you were good, and lucky, it could turn into a full-time gig.

Will loved the phrase "you can't stop the wind, but you can adjust your sails," and that was how he viewed career decisions. The wind had shifted, and he'd left corporate consulting behind when DECCO was auctioned off in pieces to the highest bidders. There were two reasons the course change to the halls of academia had seemed right. First, he loved his profession and wanted to foster its next generation through teaching. Second, he thought he'd be able to pursue the science that sparked his particular interest, rather than the research clients needed done. But he'd found the continual scrambling for funding took more time than the research itself. Not to mention, he'd thought he would like the slower pace afforded by academic life, the time to delve into a subject, but the truth was he missed the sense of urgency provided by tackling problems that *had* to be solved.

If the causes of the vortices in the reservoir were not discovered, the dam could fail. If the seismic history of a site was not understood, a much-needed power plant would not receive its permits. If the tectonic framework and site-specific geology of a proposed particle physics research facility were not fully characterized, the structure would not be sited, much less built. And those were just three examples from Will's career in consulting.

Thinking harder and faster was motivating. And faster mattered these days; at sixty-three, Will no longer had all the time in the world. He got clear about what he really wanted to do professionally with the time he did have, starting with solving the problems now facing Kayakale Dam.

What the team found was a wide and deep honeycomb of karst features in the subsurface below the reservoir. It was similar to those that had plagued the foundation work during construction but not directly connected to them. If there'd been a connection, they'd have found this network back in the seventies. Still, Will questioned himself about whether they *should* have, but he recalled how hard they'd pushed to get the time and money to do the work they *had* done where the potential hazards were unmistakable. There was no way a detailed study of the wider reservoir area, especially one as extensive as Kayakale Dam's, would have been authorized if an imminent risk was not evident.

And that risk had been blanketed by sediments. Young in geologic age but old enough to obscure any surface expression, they covered the entrance to what turned out to be a cave larger than the Moby and Babe cavities in the foundation area combined. Under those surface deposits, clay had sealed the cave's entrance—until the reservoir level exceeded its elevation, a first since impoundment, and eroded that seal away, resulting in the larger, more turbulent vortex. Fractures, also with infilled sediments, intersected the roof of the cave, and the smaller vortices occurred through those joints when the clay had been flushed out.

With the sediment plugs in place and the lake level below the potential conduits, the massive void remained hydrologically isolated from the reservoir, but when those two conditions changed, the connection was made and the lake began to "drain" through it—that bathtub metaphor again.

The new springs in Kayakale Creek were part of the karst network that had not been discovered before. But in addition to water flooding through the newly defined features, more water was also streaming through the previously studied system, causing the increased volume and turbidity of the flow into the fish hatchery.

It took extensive geophysical surveying, mapping, and dye tracing to disentangle the many threads of the complex structure of the subsurface—following each strand until its origin was located, and quantifying how much of the substantial leakage was coming from which part of the geological framework of the site.

Erdem dubbed the huge void the Sorun cavity. *Sorun* meant "problem" or "issue" in Turkish. The next step was designing a solution for the aptly named Sorun cavity.

The team had a concept before they dispersed to their homes across Turkey and around the globe. Not only had the dimensions of the cave been defined, but the condition of the rock, specifically in the roof, had been as well. It was highly fractured and, therefore, subject to collapse given the size of the void it spanned—talk about potential for the metaphorical bathtub to empty.

Going forward, the reservoir level would be held below the elevation of the cave entrance, but that could only be guaranteed under ordinary operating conditions, and they all knew contingencies had to be in place for extraordinary situations, as had occurred that spring. With all those considerations in mind, the plan took shape.

First, the weak rock above and around the cave would be grouted. Then a shaft and a series of large-diameter boreholes would be driven into the cave. Through them, Sorun would be filled successively with hundreds of thousands of cubic meters of rock, gravel, sand, and, finally, clay slurry. The lake bed in that area would be cleaned of loose sediments, its irregularities smoothed with cement, then covered with concrete slabs. After the void was filled, the boreholes and shaft would be plugged with cement, as the cave's natural entrance had been.

Concurrent with the Sorun mitigation, additional grouting would be undertaken in the zones of the Moby and Babe cavities in an effort to scale back leakage to the stable volumes they'd seen in previous years, and particularly to stop the loss of fine sediments from the subsurface. That operation would be conducted from a barge, since both Moby and Babe were much closer to the dam, in an area where the reservoir could not practically be lowered. This would all be done to prevent water from flowing into and through the caves to the springs downstream—in effect, plugging up the drain whose stopper had been pulled. Only later, as they monitored discharges over months and years, would they know if they had ultimately succeeded.

ᕦ

Will rinsed the clinging bits of shaving cream from his cheeks. He'd trimmed his beard the night before and this morning tidied up the edges with a shave. Grabbing his towel, he straightened up, dried his face, then combed his hair, still wet from the shower. He barely ran the comb through, and it fell along the line where he'd parted it for decades. In a flash of memory, he saw the younger man who used to stand before this same mirror: his hair and beard light brown, bleached lighter still during summers in the field. Now, it was more salt than pepper, his beard silvery white. Paula said he looked distinguished, running her fingers through his hair.

It would be delightful to see her, to feel her hands in his hair, in just a few days. This time away had brought home for him how much he still enjoyed her company, still loved the music of her laugh, still relaxed under her strong hands when she massaged his shoulders after a long day carrying a field pack, and still thrilled to her "rubbing his arm."

What would've happened to that younger man without her? Paula had never given up on him, even in his darkest days. He traced the scar on his right cheek with his finger, thankful for the reminder, the warning, Kevin had left there for him.

Awakening early this last morning in Kayakale, he had sat on the stoop and watched the rising sun, just as he had his first morning here all those years ago. That morning he'd hoped to see fifteen-year-old Kevin loping toward him across the dry grass of the square. This morning, he looked forward to seeing forty-year-old Kevin tomorrow in New York.

FORTY-ONE

Kevin leaned across the car and hugged Andréa as close as he could over the gearshift. "I love you too," he said.

She kissed him, then tilted her head back and smiled as she rubbed the smudge of lipstick off his cheek with her thumb.

"Keep me posted," she said. "On everything."

She didn't really need to say it; she had to know he would.

"I will," he promised anyway. After all those years, they were still best friends, ever since she'd broken up with him after they'd dated for two years at MICA, explaining to him that aside from their passion for art, what they had most in common was their taste in men. Andréa, in her indomitable way, had helped him not only *see* himself for who he was, but *love* himself for it. A simple thing, but not an easy one.

He unfolded himself from her roadster, grabbed his backpack from behind the seat, and waved as she drove off. He'd come from Ithaca on the early train so they could meet for lunch before he needed to get to JFK to meet his father. She would meet them that evening as well, at the Jazz Standard for dinner and the show. Kevin's whole family adored Andréa, sometimes visiting just with her if they were passing through and Kevin couldn't make it down.

Andréa was the only one, possibly the only thing at all, Kevin missed about life in the city. In much the same way as when he was taken to Kayakale as a teen, he had been surprised by how much better—healthier and happier, inside and out—he felt living closer to nature. He had not realized how much he'd missed it, having lived in the city for such a long stretch, until he had it back.

On the other hand, he'd been keenly aware of missing a dog, not having had one since Buddy. Kevin knew big old goofy Buddy could never be replaced, but still he had longed for the empty space in his heart to be filled, and Rosy had. A golden retriever named for the pinkish hue of her lush coat, she could've been bestowed with it for her disposition. Al had been converted, becoming a dog person, with the first clumsy swipe of her oversized paw at his unsuspecting hand. Rosy had added new dimensions of love and joy into their lives, and soon they would be stretching those dimensions even further.

Like Kevin had with Buddy, he and Rosy rambled together for miles—hiking in spring, summer, and fall, cross-country skiing in winter. He smiled thinking of how delighted she seemed when he could keep up with her, gliding downhill in the snow.

It would only be one night, and Kevin would enjoy Dad's and Andréa's company, the music, even the bustle of the city. Still, he knew his heart would sing when he stepped back inside the cottage door late the next day. For in that little stone house in the woods, with Al and Rosy, Kevin had found *home*. A place of everyday wonders—waking each morning beside the man he loved, his senses singing with the seasons while tramping the forest trails with Rosy (the tender green of spring shoots, the heavy wetness of warm summer mornings, the pointillism of the turning leaves, the low leaden skies of winter), the smell of roasting root vegetables with the tang of balsamic vinegar, the swing of his axe and trickle of sweat down his neck despite the cold as he split logs for the woodstove. It was a place where Kevin was becoming a man he was truly happy to be, not contingent on what magazine bought his photographs or which gallery hung his work, but how he felt inside.

The blaring horns of taxis jockeying from lane to lane brought Kevin back to the sidewalk where he stood. He checked his watch, then headed into the terminal, following the signs to International Arrivals. The board indicated that his father's plane was on approach. Kevin took a deep breath and rubbed his clammy hands on his pants, glancing down to see if any sweat showed on the khaki. He shook his head, then shoved the hair out of his eyes where it had fallen. Would it ever be easier with his father? He'd turned forty a few months back, and it wasn't yet, though not for lack of trying, each in their own way. Perhaps that was part of the problem; their ways were so different. But Al kept reminding Kevin of his good fortune at having a father to be a bit uneasy with; he wished his own father was alive to hear their happy news. They were adopting a baby!

EPILOGUE

The phone startled Paula awake. Boone too. He barked short and sharp, scrabbling to his feet.

"Hush," she said. "It's Didi."

It had to be. Light filtered in around the shades, dawn coming early in June. Her old Baby Ben read half past five. Didi was the only one who called that early.

Paula fumbled for the phone. "Hi, sweetie." She yawned.

"I woke you; I'm sorry," Dee said, "but it's important. You know how I check the USGS website every morning?"

Didi had studied archaeological geology for her graduate work. From that she got interested in paleoseismology and that led to seismology. Before she went to work, she checked the earthquake catalog online. She only called when there was a quake in Turkey.

"Where?" Paula asked.

"It's the closest one yet to Kayakale. We should start the phone tree, make sure Lale and Erdem are all right."

"Oh! That close?"

"I'm sure they felt the shaking. It was shallow, but far enough east they should be okay. Still, you should call. I'm headed out to the field again. I won't be in cell phone range for four days. Call me then with news, okay?"

Didi was a ranger naturalist at Grand Canyon National Park, and these days she was working on a project deep in the canyon on the Unkar Delta.

"Yes," Paula said. "Want to come hang out with Boone and me after that?"

"I want to. Not sure I can swing it, though. We'll talk . . . gotta go now. It's getting late. Love you."

"I love you too. Be careful out there."

The line clicked. Getting late at 5:35 a.m.? Imagine that.

Before she climbed out of bed, Paula's hand skimmed the smooth, cool sheets on the empty other half of the bed. Tears flooded her eyes. As they slid down her cheeks, she swiped them away, but more followed as she padded barefoot through the little log house she and Will had built together.

She let Boone out, and then in, rubbed his ears the way he liked, and scooped kibble into his bowl, all the while telling herself she shouldn't have asked Didi to come. Again. She was so busy, and Paula didn't want to be a nuisance. But it wasn't that far to Flagstaff, and her visits helped. Both of them, Paula liked to think.

The aroma of coffee filling the kitchen, she opened her laptop and googled the earthquake—June 23, 2011, at 10:34 a.m. local time, 5.4 magnitude, and 5.7 kilometers deep. The fault ruptured over three miles below the surface of the earth. She knew from Will and Didi that an earthquake less than ten kilometers in depth was considered shallow, but it still boggled her mind.

She left a message for Rob. He had trouble sleeping—so much on his mind, what with managing the Elwha Dam removal project on the Olympic Peninsula and all. *All* being the emotional struggles he still hadn't faced up to; at least, that was Paula's take on it. Not that removing dams and restoring ecosystems wasn't a worthy cause, but she wondered if Rob had found his way to a career in deconstructing dams largely because his father had constructed them. In any case, he turned his cell off at night. He'd be up soon, and she'd ask him to call Timur, who lived in Boston, but worked just across the Charles River at MIT. Despite dwelling on opposite sides of the continent, they were still best friends. Timur's call should come from Rob.

Kevin, an art teacher, would be at school already. She would call him later. The only one of the kids (who were, of course, no longer kids but in their forties and even fifties) to have settled in with a family of his own, he lived with his boyfriend, Al, and their adopted children in Ithaca, New York. Kevin spent a lot of time being a gymnastics and hockey dad—his son Paul was a gymnast and his daughter Amy a hockey player. Kevin often called from their practices, but she missed seeing him more. She missed them all.

∼

Paula ignored the pile of thesis proposals on the kitchen table the next morning. Again. Her graduate students were waiting on comments, but she guessed they'd have to wait a little longer. Good thing she had a few more days to get them reviewed. It was still so hard to concentrate. No one told her that part, that her mind wouldn't work right, and for so long. During the semester, she'd somehow made it work. But without a schedule to keep, Paula wasn't even going through the motions.

Instead, she paged through the *New York Times*. In the world news, there it was, an article on the earthquake. It had occurred on a segment of the East Anatolian Fault, its epicenter the town of Içme in Elazığ Province. Paula had never been to Içme, but Will had. It was located in one of the three areas where, during the summer of 1974, Will had identified slopes that could jeopardize the safety of the Kayakale Dam project. That particular trouble zone was in the far eastern part of the huge reservoir.

She read on, sipping coffee and feeling the weight and comfort of Boone's snout on her foot. She reached down to fondle his ears, and he sighed.

According to the article, the shallow depth of the fault rupture made it more dangerous for its magnitude on the Richter scale. There had been severe shaking at the surface, and the small villages in the epicentral area had suffered heavy damage. The mud-brick homes common there couldn't withstand much ground motion before collapsing.

But it was the last paragraph of the story that really got Paula's attention—the shallow earthquake, coupled with above-average precipitation that spring, resulted in the failure of part of the shoreline of Kayakale Reservoir—just like Will had predicted. The article also noted that the failure could have been disastrous, if the area had not undergone slope mitigation during construction of the dam in the 1970s. The report said the dam itself did not sustain any damage.

She smiled. Will would have been gratified to know that the engineering measures he and Erdem fought so hard for had worked.

According to the article, there were no fatalities and very few injuries, unlike other earthquakes in recent years on the East Anatolian Fault. Since 2003, a series of quakes had occurred on the fault zone, generally from east to west, moving progressively closer to Kayakale. Will had described the rupture pattern like a zipper unzipping westward. Yesterday's temblor was the first to strike the reservoir. He had marked the epicenters of the larger seismic events, on both the North and East Anatolian Fault Zones, on a map. Paula decided she would keep adding notations to that map. He'd have liked that. Will never lost interest in the projects he'd worked on around the globe.

Paula's smile faded, gazing across the table at Will's chair. She ached at his absence. Really, it hurt inside; she wouldn't have believed that, until she felt it. At the same time, it felt like he was all around her in their home and in all the places they loved. She started to cry, something she seemed to do more than not during the seven months and eleven days since he'd died.

The final days played out in her mind. They often did, over and over.

A friend reminded Paula that Will only had to live it once. "How many times have you?"

Too many to count.

What he thought had been a bit of prostate trouble, not uncommon in a man his age, turned out to be colon cancer. Not late stage, but not early, either.

Paula came home to find him at this same table—Boone sitting with his head on Will's lap, Will's sturdy hand stroking it. Will had looked up at her, his clear blue eyes more intense than usual. "Paula," he'd said, as if he just wanted to hear her name. "Paula. Sit down, please. There's something I need to tell you."

He'd reached over and taken her hand in his. She remembered the strength of his grip, his skin's familiar roughness. He relayed what the doctor had said, then his interpretation of it.

"I might get through it, and I might not. The surgery will be ugly and the treatments after it uglier. I never thought I'd go like this," he'd said.

"What did you think?" she had asked.

His crooked smile twisted when he answered, "I thought I'd crash and burn."

Then he did.

Before he had decided on the final course to pursue with surgery and treatments, he went down with his plane in icing conditions in the Organ Mountains of Southern New Mexico, flying to meet a colleague who'd invited him to see a fault trench near El Paso. Paula didn't think he'd done it on purpose. She believed he really wanted to see that trench. To have life be normal one more time, before whatever was coming next— hospitals and all. But she would never know for sure.

Folding the newspaper, Paula wondered if Will would've lived to see this day if he'd had the chance to fight the cancer. Lived to know that his work had mattered, that it had saved lives.

She could hear the echo of his voice in her head—Will telling her that whether he was getting paid to do geology or not, it was the lens through which he viewed the world. And she remembered one of the entries in the cherished notebook he had left for her. Reflections, he called them. It said, "This Earth, though not a sentient being, is a marvelous mechanism, and was not created for mankind. We are part of the passing scene, and ought to be damned well impressed with the opportunity. Life is life, and amazing. Death is death, and unknown, for now. Here's to life, Paula, my love, and the great times you and I have found in it together."

And they had. Maybe, one day, she would write their story.

AUTHOR'S NOTES

Though many of the places described in *No More Empty Spaces* are real, Kayakale Dam and the village by the same name are fictional. However, many dams like the fictional one were built under the auspices of the Southeastern Anatolia Project, often referred to as GAP (Güneydoğu Anadolu Projesi in Turkish).

In Chapters Eight and Twelve, Wallace Stegner's *Angle of Repose* is mentioned and/or quoted from, as Paula has a habit of reading Pulitzer Prize winning novels, which that book was in 1972. At that time, it was not widely known (as it is now), that Stegner not only borrowed heavily from the personal histories of Mary and Arthur Foote in creating the characters of Susan and Oliver Ward, but plagiarized a good deal of writing from Mary Foote's work. *A Victorian Gentlewoman in the Far West, Reminiscences of Mary Hallock Foote* was not published until 1972, the year after *Angle of Repose* appeared, so the "defense" presented was that Stegner did not violate copyright law. This issue is not addressed in *No More Empty Spaces*, as Paula would not have had this information to consider (nor did I until 2022, years after including the references to Stegner's work in my manuscript). Though I have chosen to retain the references, I felt it was important to acknowledge that what Stegner did was wrong, despite the legal fine print. Paula, as a character, is a woman coming into her own, and had she known what is now understood about *Angle of Repose* she would have found Stegner's appropriation of Mary Foote's work reprehensible, as do I. For more information, read Sands Hall's April 2022 article in *Alta*: "The Ways of Fiction Are Devious Indeed," Finding Current Relevancy—and Outrage—in the Accusation of Plagiarism that have Long Haunted a Classic of the West: Wallace Stegner's *Angle of Repose*.

In Chapter Twenty-Four, Will refers to the unstable slope he views across the Euphrates River as a mudflow. A geology colleague who specializes in landslide studies informed me that the term mudflow is no longer used in this work, rather the slope that Will observed would now be called a debris slide with a flow component. I elected, however, to leave the term as drafted, since Will would have been using a term that was acceptable in the profession at that time, the 1970s.

In Chapter Thirty-Six, Kevin brings Buddy, his beloved dog, with him when he leaves Turkey to attend college in the United States. I chose not to research whether this would have been possible, or not. I simply couldn't imagine Kevin without Buddy and asserted my authorial prerogative to make that happen.

Though the real Sixteenth Congress of the International Commission on Large Dams (ICOLD) took place in San Francisco in 1988, for the purposes of the fictional timeline in Chapter Thirty-Nine, that conference was said to have been conducted in Istanbul. In reality, the Ninth ICOLD Congress was held in Istanbul in 1967.

READING GROUP GUIDE

The following questions are included to enhance your group's reading of D. J. Green's *No More Empty Spaces*.

1. How did this narrative's multiple points of view enrich the reading experience for you?

2. Have you ever been to Turkey? What did you learn about Turkey from this novel? Does a setting in another country increase your interest in a story?

3. Much of this book is about geology and how it affects our daily lives. Did the book change how you think about that? Discuss.

4. Do you think what Will did, taking his children to Turkey, can be characterized as "kidnapping" (since his ex-wife does not seem to care that he's taken them)? Is what he did best for the kids?

5. Paula is a feminist at a time when feminism was growing. How does she learn to chart her own course? Do you think she helps all the kids do the same? If so, how?

6. How do flying and sailing matter to this story, especially in a story that is so centered on the ground beneath us?

7. Why are Kevin's letters used in the novel?

8. What was your first impression of Will? Did that impression change over the course of the novel? Why?

9. Did the ending surprise you? Why?

10. How does this novel depict families?

11. This book begins in the 1970s, which were not so long ago. Yet our world is vastly different now. Do you consider this book historical fiction? Why or why not?

12. A theme in this novel is control—of oneself, others, and of the world around us. What do the characters wrestle for control of, and how?

13. Another theme is integrity. In what ways do the characters' integrity affect the plot?

14. What does the title mean? How does it work for this novel?

15. How does the book's cover evoke themes from the novel?

ACKNOWLEDGMENTS

It took years to bring *No More Empty Spaces* from my heart and mind to the page, and though the writing is solitary, getting a book out in the world is not, so there are many to thank.

The first is someone who is no longer here to read this, Norman Ross Tilford. Wanting to understand my late husband more deeply led me to imagine Will Ross. Thank you, Norm, for that and so much more. Part of who I am today is inspired by you, the love we shared, and the adventures we embarked on in our much too short time together. Also thank you for lending some of your words from letters written to me long ago, for Will to speak in these pages.

Thank you to my literary agent, Liz Trupin-Pulli, who believed in this book, and in me as a writer, from your first reading of the manuscript on. Your input made this a better book, and your encouragement has made me a more courageous writer.

Huge thanks to the She Writes Press team—to publisher, Brooke Warner, for "green lighting" *No More Empty Spaces*; to my editorial manager, Lauren Wise, for your thorough and kind attention, both to the manuscript and its rookie author; to copy editor, Christine DeLorenzo, and to proofreader, Jennifer Caven, for finding and fixing the many little things that add up to big things; to Krissa Lagos for searching out the perfect title within the manuscript's pages; and to Julie Metz for the exquisite cover.

Also to Caitlin Hamilton Summie, Libby Jordan, and Rick Summie, my great thanks for helping me introduce my book, and myself, to the world in a way that feels authentically *me*.

Thanks to Jeffrey Davis for introducing me to the Yoga As Muse practice and for teaching me so many basics of creative writing. Thank you to Linda Bendorf, who helped me find my voice on the page. To Summer Wood, my deepest gratitude for your insightful developmental review. Thanks to Cathy Stocker and Holly Moxley, who in addition to thoughtful feedback on the manuscript, helped me step out into the world as a writer through my website. Holly's fine art, related to *No More Empty Spaces* and other posts, is truly beautiful, and I'm lucky to have it grace my home as well as my website. Thank you to Starry Night Artists Retreat for two residencies where I could immerse myself in the work without the distractions of day-to-day life.

I am fortunate to have many friends and colleagues, readers and writers, workshop leaders and fellow participants—who read bits and pieces, or the full manuscript. You all helped make this book what it is: Nancy Guinn; Carolyn Kinsman; Sara Eisenberg; Serin Bussell; Bambi Sterling; Jennifer Bauer; Sarah Kalika; Duane Kreuger; Andrea Hunter; Nancy Dillingham Waite; David Waite; A. R. Taylor; Kim Casey; James Anderson; Will Mackin; Brenna Gomez; Pat Marsello; Alex Espinosa; Moni Bates; Paula Davis; Laura Brodie; Dory Dutton; Susan Wasson; Elaine Lewis; Marina Daldalian; Barbara Sferra; Sharon Bippus; Gerry Stirewalt; Stephanie Kline-Tissi; Laraine Herring; Anne Grey Frost; Cooper Gallegos; Nancy Wright; Kate Miller; Lilith Ren; Judi Pringle; and the late Jerry Blakely. My thanks to you all, and I ask the forgiveness of anyone I neglected to mention.

Though they are too numerous to name after more than thirty years working in the field, thank you to my geology mentors and colleagues. I would not have aspired to be the GeologistWriter without having been a geologist first. Special thanks to Ed Medley for lending me the "borehole exercise" from one of your Jahns Lectures; I both wrote it into Chapter Thirteen and used it in my own Jahns Lectures. Gratitude and love for my late father, Sidney Green, who inspired my interest in science, and geology in particular.

Gratitude and love, also, for my late mother, Selma Green, who believed I could do whatever I set my mind to, so I did too. And finally, thank you to Eric Hubbard, who never fails to cheer me on, read rough drafts, and brew the many cups of tea that fuel my writing—your support and love mean so much.

ABOUT THE AUTHOR

Photo credit: William Bledsoe

D. J. Green is a writer, geologist, and sailor, as well as a bookseller and partner in Bookworks, a locally-owned independent bookstore in Albuquerque, New Mexico. She lives near the Sandia Mountains in Placitas, New Mexico, and cruises the Salish Sea on her sailboat during the summers. *No More Empty Spaces* is her first novel.